THE
ART
OF DESIRE

THE
ART
OF DESIRE

STACEY ABRAMS

WRITING AS

SELENA MONTGOMERY

BERKLEY
NEW YORK

BERKLEY
An imprint of Penguin Random House LLC
penguinrandomhouse.com

Copyright © 2001 by Stacey Y. Abrams
Foreword copyright © 2023 by Stacey Y. Abrams
Penguin Random House supports copyright. Copyright fuels creativity, encourages diverse voices,
promotes free speech, and creates a vibrant culture. Thank you for buying an authorized edition of
this book and for complying with copyright laws by not reproducing, scanning, or distributing any
part of it in any form without permission. You are supporting writers and allowing
Penguin Random House to continue to publish books for every reader.

BERKLEY and the BERKLEY & B colophon are registered trademarks of
Penguin Random House LLC.

Library of Congress Cataloging-in-Publication Data

Names: Montgomery, Selena, author.
Title: The art of desire / Stacey Abrams writing as Selena Montgomery.
Description: New York: Berkley, [2023]
Identifiers: LCCN 2022060635 (print) | LCCN 2022060636 (ebook) |
ISBN 9780593439425 (hardcover) | ISBN 9780593439449 (ebook)
Subjects: LCGFT: Romance fiction. | Thrillers (Fiction) | Novels.
Classification: LCC PS3601.B746 A88 2023 (print) |
LCC PS3601.B746 (ebook) | DDC 813/.6—dc23/eng/20230113
LC record available at https://lccn.loc.gov/2022060635
LC ebook record available at https://lccn.loc.gov/2022060636

The Art of Desire was first published by Harlequin, an imprint of
HarperCollins, in 2001.

Printed in the United States of America
1st Printing

Book design by Laura K. Corless

To my family, who nurture me.
To my friends, who challenge me.
To my readers, who sustain me (and Selena).

FOREWORD

More than twenty years ago, Raleigh Foster, the brilliant heroine of *Rules of Engagement*, needed a savvy, down-to-earth best friend—and Alex Walton came to the rescue. Of course, Alex had challenges of her own, as she navigated the question of who she wanted to be and how she'd chart her course of discovery. Phillip Turman had a different set of concerns. Left for dead, he had to reclaim his life and determine whether the past was over or simply a prelude to his next phase. His best friend, Adam Grayson, sends him on an errand and changes his life.

At the time, I was a young tax attorney who wrote romantic suspense novels on the side, while pursuing my interests in voting rights and democracy. I identified with Alex's struggle to shape a single identity and Phillip's response to how his love of country would guide his next steps. In fact, my curiosity demanded that they get their own tale. Which wasn't a given. Indeed, when I first penned *Rules of Engagement*, Phillip never made it home and Alex was a cameo. But that's the joy of writing: the characters often chart a course and the author comes along for the ride. Decades later, *The Art of Desire* remains one of the most fun stories I've been permitted to tell. I am still delighted by Alex's wit, her earnest passion for exploration, and her willingness to confront how complicated the heart can be. She found a perfect match in Phillip, a man with every reason to doubt his feelings and to trust no one, but who finds the courage to be vulnerable and true. The opportunity to get to know them anew is a treat, and I am excited to share the journey with you.

THE
ART
OF DESIRE

Zeben lay quietly in his cell, eyes closed, waiting.

The dreams grew stronger, more detailed. The months of captivity rankled, but he did not mind. Allah's plan for his life loomed larger than those of the Jafirian government. God's wishes trumped the petty desires of the ISA. Yaweh would free him from his captivity, if he only believed.

The key to his freedom, to his return to power, had been stolen by the infidels. Taken by one who called him brother and betrayed him. His destiny called to him, its bright truth flickered in his visions. Yes, he now had visions to guide him, since his liberty had been taken.

And in his latest vision, he'd witnessed his truth. Freedom and conquest were his destiny, and he would smite the thieves.

His gaunt body shuddered with the power of his visions. *Show me the infidels, and I will destroy them.* Hands trembling, he clasped them in supplication. *Show me the betrayer, and I will lay him low.* Now, the trembling suffused his body. *Show me the power, and it shall be mine.*

Keva, Zeben's guard, approached the isolated cell, the boy's scattered thoughts on the terrible row he'd had with his girlfriend. She'd been angry about the phone number scrawled in lipstick she'd found in his apartment. His stammered explanation of ignorance didn't satisfy her, so tonight he'd bring flowers and candles. That should make her happy, he decided. Zeben's dinner balanced precariously on a plastic tray, rounded and light. They claimed he was dangerous, would use any weapon at his disposal. But Keva had been assigned to Zeben for weeks now, without incident. Yes, the old man ranted about infidels and possessing a diamond the size of his fist. But he also muttered in his sleep about claiming the throne of Jafir.

Every schoolchild knew the legend of the monarchy.

The last rulers had been drowned in the Mediterranean twenty-five years ago, their bodies crushed against the rocks on the craggy shore. Because Jafir was a constitutional monarchy, the people mourned the loss of the royal family, but did not replace them. Aristocracy was bred in the bone, not assigned.

Zeben was an old, senile fool of little threat, Keva decided. So he no longer hurried into the cell to deliver the meals and administer the prisoner's medication, frightened of his shadow.

"Arm and leg in cuffs," he demanded in a voice not yet settled into manhood, speaking into an intercom. He noted the clicks as the arm and leg were securely attached to the wall, limiting Zeben's range of motion.

Zeben listened as the guard punched in the code that released the metal door to the narrow cell. Dim, milky light trickled into

Zeben's solitary room. To diminish his power, they'd separated him from his followers. But no matter. He was prepared.

"Good afternoon," Zeben offered in a voice raspy from disuse.

Keva ignored him. One didn't talk to the prisoners.

So much fear of an emaciated codger, he sneered. Nevertheless, he kept his distance as he placed the tray on the metal table bolted to the floor. When he left the cell, he'd key in the digits to release Zeben's cuffs, freeing him from the wall.

Would Leondra prefer roses or daffodils? he wondered idly as he prepared the sedative. He tapped the glass of the syringe, the way the prison doctor taught him, and turned to administer the shot. He never felt the bony finger press firmly against his carotid artery, never knew he'd died.

Quickly, Zeben undressed the boy and put on the black uniform. Then he dragged the lifeless body to the hard pallet and cuffed him to the bed. Pulling the black cap low over his eyes, he made his way to the laundry room. There, his source informed him that a door led to the truck bay. With the guard's purloined weapon, he calmly shot the two prisoners toiling inside the cramped, humid room.

Entering the codes he'd been given, he bypassed the security lock and emerged into a black tunnel. He ran then, the sound of the engines drawing him closer. He climbed into the piles of dirty clothes and soiled linen, disappearing in the fabric. Eventually, the truck began to roll forward, halting twice at the checkpoints.

Hours later, Zeben stood on the balcony of his lair, inhaling the sea's cleansing air. The radio carried reports of an unidentified prisoner's escape. The police scanner gave more detail, but none mentioned his name.

President Robertsi would quash all information, to allay the fears of his people, Zeben knew. Zeben knew also that the coward would contact the ISA and request assistance.

Loathing rose to mingle with the salty air. Robertsi was weak, dependent on foreigners to rule. Zeben would enjoy snapping his neck.

He turned and walked inside, his guest waiting patiently in front of his desk. Civelli grinned, the blinding capped-tooth smile ingratiating and reckless.

"Did you bring it?" Zeben demanded, steepling his fingers on the blotter.

Civelli reached into his case and removed a sheaf of papers. "It's everything I could find. Descriptions of the accident, medical reports on the bodies, police reports of the investigation." He leaned into the chair and lit a thin cigar. Smoke swirled around the angular brown face. "I researched the history of the monarchy. If the heir does not claim the throne by midnight on the first, the wealth of the monarchy reverts to the government. Including the Kholari and its mate, the Sahalia ruby."

"'And the heir will be known by the possession of the obelisk. The Rites of Ascension shall be spoken and the rightful heir will take command,'" Zeben recited from memory.

Civelli shifted uneasily in his seat, eager to collect his fee and be on his way. Zeben's fanaticism, though amusing, too often proved to be dangerous. Helping him steal Praxis had landed the old man in jail and sent Civelli on the lam. Four months in Pakistan fencing nuclear reactor parts, and three in India trading for silo specs. He'd been pleasantly surprised to receive Zeben's summons. Research was always preferable to the hazards of war.

"So," he began cheerfully, "I'll take my fee and be on my way.

Everything you requested is here." He slid the sheaf across the desk.

Zeben studied him. Some called Civelli a weasel, others used more pejorative terms. To Zeben, he was merely an instrument, one effortlessly controlled. "I want you to find the obelisk," Zeben announced.

Civelli started in surprise. "Zeben, it's been missing for more than a quarter century. The Tribunal will be disbanded after this sitting."

"There was no accident. The king and queen died at my hand. It was simple enough to capsize the boat, a charge in the motor. But they did not find the boy's body. He is still alive."

Civelli's eyes widened in fascinated horror. A twenty-five-year-old mystery, an urban legend proven true.

"Civelli, I want you to find the obelisk."

"What do I do when I find it?"

"Bring it to me. I have another task for you as well, Civelli."

"Yes?"

"Kill Phillip Turman."

Civelli didn't blink. "Why me, Zeben? Why not one of your minions, I mean, men?"

"The betrayal of Scimitar runs deep, I do not know who to trust," Zeben admitted.

"You trust me?" Civelli gave a short laugh. "Why?"

"Greed rules you, as surely as power is mine to command. I will pay you twenty million dollars if I ascend to the throne. You have one month to comply." With that, Zeben turned away to watch the water. Taking his cue, Civelli stood.

"Where do I start?" Civelli asked.

"Where weak men masquerade as kings. America."

CHAPTER ONE

The panic rises in his throat. He can hear his ragged breathing. The air fills with the acrid stench of sulfur.

In the satellite hut in Jafir, metal screams from the force of being pulled from its moors. A beam falls and midnight comes, shot through with fire.

The cell is cramped and dank. Moaning from prisoners sounds in the twilight that hangs unchanged despite the passing hours. Dawn cannot penetrate the mounds of concrete that shroud his hell. When the guards come to drag him to the room, he pleads for mercy, futile words that only earn him more pain.

Zeben commands his loyalty, and he pretends to believe. Madness gleams in the old man's eyes, quivers in his voice as he foretells his destruction of the world.

Each day, the truth mocks him, but he tries not to believe.

They will not forget him, but they will abandon him. Then the truth is clear, when years pass with no rescue.

He is not Phillip Turman, congressman from Maryland.

He is no longer Sphinx, agent and comrade. He is forsaken.

Phillip shot up, the soft navy cotton falling to his waist. He fumbled for the lamp. The light, dim and unsatisfying, barely illumined the room. As the nightmare receded, he glanced at the digital clock that flashed a blurry red 4:37 a.m. At least he'd gotten three hours of sleep this time, he thought ruefully, staring out the eastern exposure from the window in his bedroom. The sun had yet to take a stab at the morning.

On the bedside table, the phone jangled loudly.

Phillip lifted the receiver. "Hi, Dad," he said, his voice heavy with exhaustion. Right on schedule.

"Hi, yourself. Didn't wake you, did I?" Jake Turman set his fishing pole by the cabinet and cradled the phone to his neck. The weariness troubled him, as did the alertness in Phillip's voice. The nightmares typically left him awake and restless at dawn.

"No, Dad. I was up. How were the fish?"

Steam billowed as Jake poured his morning cup of coffee. The doctor warned him off the caffeine, but he was old enough to make up his own damn mind. And he'd die with Folgers in his bloodstream and a hat brim in his hand. "Not biting. Must be a holiday, the way they're sleeping in."

"They probably need time to regroup. We caught at least a dozen this weekend."

"Yeah, son. That was a good day on the water." He looked out beyond his wood-railed porch to the murky waters of the Chesapeake. Pride swelled in his chest at the memory of the evening it became his. On the drive home from Cambridge, Phillip had driven past the Inner Harbor to a rural highway. Twenty minutes outside of Baltimore, he'd turned into the drive of a ten-acre farm, the blue A-frame farmhouse sporting a jaunty bow. To his father's stunned surprise, Phillip presented the keys to Jake, a graduation present, the boy had said, to the man who'd made it possible.

Phillip had been twenty-five, fresh out of business and law schools, newly wealthy and in love, Jake remembered. As his son had planned, his future was settled, merely awaiting his arrival. Phillip had always plotted the details of each day as though his life depended on it. His mother had been the same way. Like her, he'd always seemed so adult, so mature. Ambition drove him, caution guided him. Now fear edged his son's dreams, waking Phillip in a cold sweat every morning before day broke.

"Maybe you should move back out to the farm, Phillip," Jake said without preamble. "I could use your help in the garden."

"Dad, you won't let me touch your garden. I'll trample the peas, crush the tomatoes, and do heaven knows what to the corn."

Beneath the humor, Jake heard the fatigue and sighed. "I don't understand why you had to move back to DC. The governor offered you a good job, and you could work from here. We've got that DSL line you installed that I'll never use, and the contraption you call a computer just gathering dust in the study."

"We've talked about this, Dad. I've been hiding for long enough. It's time for me to move on. Don't worry. I have a plan."

Always occupied with tactics and strategy, once more Jake wondered about what had happened to Phillip in Jafir. He didn't believe the story of a prison camp any more than he believed

Phillip was simply a politician. Baltimore's City Hall hadn't been a hotbed of political intrigue, but he'd learned to see layers where others saw only the surface. Jake believed his son when he said he worked for the U.S. government, but not necessarily for a branch acknowledged by the powers that be. He also believed that if you pushed Phillip too hard, the stubbornness pushed back even harder. Another trait he'd inherited from his mother. Conceding defeat, for the moment, Jake said, "You still heading to Atlanta today?"

"I fly out this afternoon. I have a few meetings first, so I won't have time to stop by the house."

Phillip didn't add whom he was meeting with, or why.

From habit, Jake didn't ask. Instead, he asked nonchalantly, "Is she going to be there?"

On the other end, Phillip's face tightened, the solemn lines tense. "I imagine so. Lorei and her parents are old friends of the Grayson family. Adam couldn't not invite them."

"Of course he could. He's *your* best friend and you're the best man," Jake grumbled.

"Dad," Phillip soothed, "I'm alright. I'll be okay. It's been seven years. She's moved on with her life and so have I."

"No, you haven't, Phillip. If you had, I'd be bouncing grand-kids on my knees instead of fishing at dawn. You let that girl break your heart. Then you dug yourself a hole of a job and crawled inside. She's the reason those men—" Jake broke off his sentence, but they both knew the ending. Lorei's desertion led to his capture.

Temper threaded through Phillip's body, but he controlled the anger with practice. Years of honing the skill of hiding his feelings, submerging misery from his father and his friends. "Lo-rei didn't break my heart. She wanted a different life than I did. It just didn't work out."

"It took four years of engagement for her to figure that out?" Jake nudged the sore spot, knowing Phillip lied. The calm, sub-dued tones did not disguise the wounds that festered. The boy had a lot of mending to do. Reopening the past was excruciating, but it was often the only way to heal cleanly.

"When she walked away, you threw yourself into your work. I don't think I met another girlfriend, not since you two broke up."

The effort to curb his temper made his next words curt. "Dad, I will not talk about this."

"Shutting me out now too, Phillip?"

"I've got to go, Dad."

Jake relented, hearing hurt join fatigue. He had plenty of time to help his son find his way. With Adam's support, it was just a matter of time. He'd call him in a couple of hours to con-spire. Out loud, Jake said, "Enjoy the wedding, son. Give Adam a hug for me, will you?"

"Of course." Then forgiveness, as easy as a simple phrase. "I love you, Dad."

"Love you too."

Phillip hung up the phone. Shoving the sheet away, he swung long muscled legs over the side of the bed. He tucked battered sneakers under one arm and rummaged through his dresser for a pair of shorts and a T-shirt.

Might as well get started, he decided, as he slid running shorts over lean hips. He certainly wasn't going to get any more sleep.

The streets were shadowed and empty, and Phillip had learned to dread the twilight. Nevertheless, he welcomed the solitude, the freedom of the run. He never thought he'd be happy to be alone again after three years of isolation.

The prison guards had locked him in a lone cell at the end of the block. Fear of his connection to Scimitar and the reputation of his alter ego conspired to condemn him to solitary meals, solitary runs on the yard. The runs saved his sanity and kept his body conditioned for battle.

He knew, of course, that he could have ended his confinement if he'd revealed his identity. But to break cover and seek assistance, he'd have undermined an operation already years in the making. The welfare of other agents and the life of his best friend depended on his silence. So he endured, for two years, relying only on furtive messages sent to the Capitol, with no answer.

Then Cavanaugh appeared, and he reentered Scimitar's world. But the loneliness did not end. As an operative, Phillip was cut off from Zeben's henchmen, in spirit if not body. He had not shared the religious zealotry of the intifada cell, nor did he have the bone-deep greed of the money-hungry. With nothing left to lose, he played his part well. The renegade American who abandoned his country, an interloper with no home.

His skill for siphoning funds from unsuspecting Cayman accounts and re-routing Swiss bank transfers protected him from too much scrutiny. But the loneliness of deep cover, without a confidant or a friend, gradually wore him down.

Until Raleigh and Adam helped destroy Scimitar.

Now, back in America as a hero, Phillip preferred the

desolate sound of rubber slapping against the hard asphalt of Connecticut Avenue to the click-click of the cameras that had trailed him since his return. Reporters hounded him for his story. Publishers begged for rights to the biography.

A robin trilled out a call as the sun pierced the wispy clouds on the horizon. Maybe he would grow to welcome the attention, in a few years. Probably not, he mused. He'd never been very comfortable with his celebrity in the first place. But celebrity won elections, and Phillip Turman enjoyed winning. Spurred by his reminiscence, he picked up speed, the echo of feet against the pavement trailing him. Power was a heady draught, and he'd grown up in a family without power. Instead, they served those who possessed the elixir.

Phillip remembered the nights his father would come home from his position as a janitor at City Hall and empty his pockets. Slivers of paper would reveal a world of deals and machinations, a world Phillip yearned to join.

And, while he served to return power to those who had the least of it, he couldn't ignore the exhilarating rush command brought. From leading the SGA at Morehouse to deal-making at CompuSecure, Phillip reveled in his ability to move effortlessly from thought to action. An ability that Scimitar had stolen from him, he remembered bleakly, one more loss. Desolate, Phillip picked up his pace, crossing the bridge, heading into Dupont Circle. After his third mile, he turned and started the run home.

Later, buffeted by the shower's icy spray, Phillip tried to shake off the last remnants of the dream. Even nine months after his return to the States, the nightmare refused to leave him. He would just have to try harder, he determined as he forced his head under for another dousing. The past was gone. He had to focus on his future, starting in two hours. Wrapping a towel around his taut waist, Phillip moved to the mirror to trim the neat mustache that framed straight white teeth. His dad's insistence on braces had meant two years of peanut butter and jelly for lunch and plenty of school ground fights. Of course, he acknowledged as he checked his reflection, the result made his later teen years well worth the bruises. The orthodontist's magic brought him dates and elections. Lorei loved his smile.

The thought twisted inside him painfully, and Phillip struck the porcelain with a clenched fist. As always, memories of the past reminded him of what he'd lost and would never have again.

Like the Congressional seat he'd won at the tender age of twenty-eight that had been forfeited when the Justice Department declared him dead. And, as he'd discovered six months ago, Congresswoman Celeste Rogers had sailed through her sophomore election with 65 percent of the vote. The seat firmly belonged to her. Not that he was sure he wanted it back anyway. But that was one more question he'd answer later. Much later.

As he dressed, Phillip mentally scrolled through his Friday. First, the meeting with Governor Bundy about trade missions to the African-Arab Alliance. Next, coffee where he would feel out Attorney General Jim Henderson about a return to the Justice Department. Then he had a lunch meeting scheduled with Atlas. At three, though, he would catch a flight to Atlanta, where he would be the best man at his best friend's wedding. And maybe, he thought wistfully, maybe he would finally get some rest.

By noon, Phillip sat at a secluded table in a diner in Columbia Heights, across from the most stubborn man he'd ever known.

In the center of the table, a faux ashtray issued radio waves to scramble their voices and interfere with any detection devices planted nearby. Guerry's was a public and out of the way restaurant, but Atlas took no chances.

The wrangling between Phillip and Atlas had become a ritual since his repatriation. Once a month, Atlas would appeal for him to accept a new assignment for the ISA. The International Security Agency, Phillip's erstwhile employer, desperately wanted him to head off to Israel or Huancavelica. Since his last mission as an operative had broken the back of the terrorist group Scimitar and saved vital technology, he was in high demand. Phillip, however, wasn't prepared to go back.

"Damn it, Phillip! You owe me!" Atlas barked, spearing a piece of steak. Time was running out, especially with the news he'd received from Jafir. He only had a month, and three of his best agents were AWOL.

Phillip sipped from a half-full glass of Merlot. "Atlas, your imagination is unparalleled. How it could be that I owe you for three years of incarceration is beyond me," he returned mildly.

"I got you out, didn't I?"

"After two years in prison and a third as a henchman for a lunatic. And let's not forget that your operative plotted to kill me."

"Chimera wasn't going to kill you. The girl was upset."

"She drugged me, dragged me to a cavern, and held a gun to my head. Seemed damned determined to me."

Raleigh would have killed him, Atlas acknowledged silently, if Phillip hadn't talked quick enough. Aloud, he said, "But she didn't pull the trigger, son. That's all that matters." Atlas gulped down his scotch and soda, then signaled the waiter for another round. He'd been wearing away at Phillip for weeks now, to no avail.

Despite Phillip's weak excuses, Atlas understood he was still haunted and wanted nothing to do with the ISA. Atlas couldn't blame him, but the game wasn't over yet. The reports from the agents still stationed in the region had grown direr lately. And personal. He pasted on his most avuncular expression. "Phillip, we need you. I need you. You are one of my best men."

"Flattery works on Adam, not me. That's how I avoided being full-time for so long. I'm impervious to your charm, Atlas. And I'm not ready to come back yet."

Atlas sighed. True, Phillip had avoided full-time missions until his engagement fell apart. Then he'd thrown himself into the organization, coordinating from his perch on Capitol Hill.

Turning again to flattery, Atlas made another run. "You are one of the best, Phillip. Besides, where's your sense of duty? Loyalty?"

At that, Phillip's deep brown eyes narrowed. His voice, a strong baritone that played with base, steeled. "Never question my loyalty, Atlas. Loyalty cost me my fiancée. It almost cost me my father. Try any tactic you like, but don't question my allegiance." The harsh tone brooked no argument.

As the head of one of the most powerful agencies the world had never known, Atlas understood the value of strategy. Here, logic called for immediate retreat. The threat was imminent, but time was on their side. When Phillip became truly necessary, Atlas would bring him inside. In the meantime, the ISA would continue to collect information and plot. Phillip had not abandoned him yet, as the monthly skirmishes proved. He doubted even Phillip recognized that he wanted to return to active duty. Let him wallow in denial. They had time.

He'd lay the groundwork now, though, he decided.

Atlas asked, "When are you heading for Atlanta?"

Nonplussed but grateful for the capitulation, Phillip answered warily, "As soon as lunch is over. I'm catching the shuttle. Why?"

"I need you to do me a favor."

Phillip cocked his head. Feigning confusion, he said, "I thought I said no. In fact, I am remarkably certain that in the last thirty minutes, over an excellent meal, I told you no. Several times."

Atlas lifted his scotch, leveled his gaze on Phillip. "A personal favor. Not ISA-related." The lie slid out with no difficulty.

Shrugging, Phillip relaxed. "Sure. What do you need?"

The lightning about-face didn't surprise Atlas. He expected it as his due. Phillip was one of his, would always be. Whether he liked it or not. As his boss, it was Atlas's job, no, responsibility, to lead him to water if he didn't realize he was thirsty on his own.

"Liz and Robert Walton are old friends of mine. Raleigh is staying with them until the wedding. Their daughter, Alex, is my godchild." Atlas paused.

"And?" Phillip prompted.

"And I want you to keep an eye on her."

"Is she in danger?"

"Not that I know of, but she's coming home from a trip to South Africa. We know for a fact that some of Zeben's cell escaped there after his capture."

Returned to regroup was more accurate, Phillip thought

sourly. Several of the men to whom Atlas referred were financiers who funded Zeben's campaign. They'd fled Jafir hours after the ISA raid on the warehouse. Although the team had recovered Praxis, the Scimitar spy Darrick Josephs, and even Zeben himself, several of Zeben's henchmen remained at large. Phillip recognized some by sight, others by reputation. The most immoral one, a man known only as Jubalani, trafficked in stolen art and plundered gems. According to rumor, he'd contracted with warlords throughout Africa to mine diamonds and rubies, all to be sold to the highest bidder with no return for the people. His profit-sharing scheme funded border wars in Uganda, civil wars in Sierra Leone.

He and Phillip had met once, during a transfer to finance an aborted insurrection in Zaire. Through the years, Phillip funneled millions of dollars into Jubalani's coffers, at Zeben's command. Shame, as familiar to him now as the fear of twilight, swamped Phillip. With effort, he wrenched his attention back to Atlas.

"Is Alex with the ISA?"

Shaking his head vigorously, Atlas barked, "No! Absolutely not!"

Caught off guard by the vehemence, Phillip stared at Atlas. "Why the need for security? Is she involved with someone from Scimitar?"

"No, nothing like that," Atlas answered, his voice even. "I don't think there's a problem, but I want you to keep your head up. If anything seems suspicious, let me know."

"What am I looking for?"

"I don't know. My instincts are screaming that having you,

Raleigh, and Adam in the same place so soon after Scimitar's demise isn't a good idea. Having Alex there too makes me jumpy. The two of them should have eloped."

When Phillip started to protest, Atlas waved him off. "I know. None of you work for me anymore. Except Raleigh, and I can't very well keep her from her own damned wedding. I know. But I don't like it."

Phillip had no intention of missing the wedding either. To placate Atlas, he responded, "Zeben knows who Adam is, but Adam's too well protected for Zeben to try anything at the wedding. And the only person who knew Raleigh's identity was Cavanaugh. I doubt he told anyone."

Atlas flinched at the mention of his old friend's name. "If he could betray the ISA, I don't put much faith in his protection of Raleigh."

Cavanaugh's treachery hurt them all, but Atlas had known him the longest.

"Until that last minute, Atlas, I think he did try to protect her," Phillip said quietly.

"If Adam hadn't killed him, he'd have taken her out. You and I both know it," Atlas rejoined, dispensing with the guilt that lingered.

Understanding, Phillip looked Atlas squarely in the eyes. "It's done, Atlas. We survived and saved the day. All's right with the world."

Altas's rumble of disbelieving laughter broke the tension. "Be on your guard. I've got a sixth sense about this. Watch Alex for me, okay?"

"Alright. Will you be at the wedding?"

"Can't."

"What, no toast to the happy couple?" Phillip teased. "And how would you introduce me?"

"The pain in Raleigh's pretty ass. The thorn in Adam's Midas side. The boil on my—"

"Smart aleck. I've got a plane to catch."

Atlas signaled the waiter for the check. "Give Raleigh a kiss for me. Tell Adam congratulations."

"Will do." Phillip stood and reached for Atlas' callused palm. "Thanks for lunch."

Shaking his hand, Atlas sneered, "One of these days, you're gonna pick up the tab."

"One of these days." Phillip flashed an impudent grin, the first real smile Atlas had seen in months. "Just not today. See you next week."

"We'll talk about this again, Phillip."

Phillip moved around his chair, bending forward over the high back. "I'll let you know when I'm ready."

Atlas leaned against the railed cane, his hands crossed negligently behind his head. "We may not be able to wait that long."

With a nod of understanding, Phillip replied, "If you need me, I'll be ready."

Walking out of the restaurant, the phone in his jacket pocket rang. He pushed through the heavy plate glass doors with one hand and flipped open the phone with the other.

He'd gotten the phone to deal with press calls, while he'd been living with his dad. Most of the calls had stopped by now, but some persistent reporters badgered him for an exclusive.

He stopped by a bench to answer the incessant ringing.

A young couple exited the restaurant and took the seats

beside him. Out of habit, he checked his surroundings, angled away from the newcomers, and pressed the receive button.

"Phillip Turman," he answered tersely.

"Adam Grayson. Cranky aren't we?"

"Hey," Phillip greeted, his voice degrees warmer. "I'm on my way."

"Raleigh and I are looking forward to it."

"Shouldn't you be convincing Raleigh not to run off with me?"

"She may be certifiable for marrying me, but she's not stupid." Phillip chuckled. "What can I do for you?"

"I need you to pick up the maid of honor at the airport. She's flying in from Johannesburg and her flight arrives a few hours after yours."

"Her name wouldn't be Alex Walton, would it?"

"How'd you know?"

"She's his goddaughter."

Adam quickly recalled the lunch meeting and knew Phillip referred to Atlas. "I'd forgotten. Anyway, Raleigh was planning to drive out to the airport, but Alex's flight was delayed. Raleigh's got a meeting with the caterer and Alex's mom is going with her. Her father is out of town. I've got to meet the minister at the church, and we've decided we'd rather not send a driver. So you're drafted. Come to my house, and you can pick up my car. Do you mind?"

"Of course not. Where do I meet her?"

"We're leaving a message that you'll meet her at her gate. She'll be coming through Customs, and you know what a hassle that can be."

"What does she look like?"

"Tall. Good personality."

"Funny. Seriously, give me a visual clue."

"She'll be the most intriguing woman at the gate."

"That's not much information, Adam."

"Trust me, Phillip. It's all the direction you'll need." Falling back into their familiar banter, Adam said, "Just acquire the package from the airport."

Phillip responded in kind. "Package will be acquired."

Intriguing. Not much to go on, but he'd manage. He was an agent once. How hard a mission could this be?

As he started his car and moved into traffic, he didn't notice the black Lincoln pull in behind him.

Civelli opened a panel on the modified dashboard to retract the antenna. Gadgets amused him, appealed to his sense of humor. The average citizen scoffed at the notion of James Bond, of cloak and dagger. Yet here he sat, in a car leased temporarily from an Interpol contact, filled with listening devices, radar guns, even lasers.

The system replayed Turman's conversation with Grayson. At the sound of the deep, masculine voices, Civelli's smile darkened. Grayson and Turman, known to most as Caine Simons and Stephen Frame, had cheated him more than once. Darrick Josephs had revealed to Zeben their aliases, in a vain attempt to curry favor. To Civelli's mind, the knowledge was better sold than bartered, perhaps to the IRA or Hezbola, two enemies of the ISA. He'd been instructed not to do so, but the information still had proven useful. Civelli followed Frame's trail until he became Turman, the conquering hero, resurrected from the dead, a modern-day Lazarus.

Instinct, aided by well-paid informants, told him Turman was as good a place as any to start his search in America. And he'd been watching for three days. He'd find the obelisk, kill Turman, and collect his fee. Finally, today, he intercepted the phone call between Turman and Grayson. If people only knew the dangers of open-air communication. From the sounds of it, the woman, Alex, returned today from a trip to Durban. In South Africa. His instincts and information had been correct.

Trace Turman and he would find the obelisk and his handsome reward. Next stop, Atlanta.

CHAPTER TWO

Alex sat at her gate at Hartsfield-Jackson Airport and watched the passengers as they headed off to uncertain destinations or greeted friends. People fascinated her. The shapes, the sounds, the stories. And none more than the ones who milled around in airports. Some shuffled along, slowed by time and experience. Others rushed at a breakneck pace, late for a moment that would likely be forgotten in another minute or two. As she watched, an avid voyeur, teenagers held hands and kissed in long, lingering embraces. A wizened man stooped by age led a toddler by the hand.

The people-watching was as much for relaxation as inspiration. In the quiet tumult of the airport, she could see her characters born, her art given life. Had she been at home in DC, she would head out to Reagan National Airport to find her ideas. After a few hours of keen observation, she'd return home and climb the stairs to the art studio on the top floor of her home in Adams Morgan. There she would decide if her newest visions should be captured in clay or stone, by oil or by pen.

It was her greatest fortune to be able to choose her medium, to draw or sculpt. It was also her greatest frustration. Alex knew her talent. Her father had cautioned her long ago that false modesty yielded nothing but mediocrity. She had been blessed with her mother's yen for human contact and her father's ability to transform those encounters into living art. Unfortunately, she'd also been blessed with the attention span of a two-year-old. So a painting rested unfinished on a half-prepared canvas and her novel languished in obscurity between chapters seven and eight.

Today, however, she would not be returning to the redbrick town house to ignore the work that waited for her. In a week, she would stand beside Raleigh as she exchanged vows with Adam Grayson.

The image made her sigh. She understood herself to be a true romantic, a true believer of fairy tales and soulmates, red roses and moonlight picnics. To her, love was a treasure to be savored. For her, romance was an experience to be sought. And seek it she did between the pages of a good novel and in the convoluted plot lines of her favorite soap.

But romantic fantasy paled in comparison to the reality of falling in love. Thus, she made it a point of honor to dive head-first at least once a year.

Unfortunately, she surfaced all too quickly, helpless against the truth. She enjoyed being in love, but had not the faintest idea how to go about staying there. Alex sighed her favorite languishing sigh again and shook her head vigorously to dispel the thought. Her track record with eternal love depressed her, and she made it a rule never to be depressed about men. It caused headaches and accomplished nothing. Better to think of other things, she decided. Like how to convince Raleigh that the midnight-blue concoction she'd selected for her maid of honor was an atrocity and wholly unsuitable for the society wedding of the year. Sage green was a far better color, Alex thought, and it suited her chocolate complexion. Toca said it made her radiant.

Despite herself, her mind drifted back to Durban and to Damon Toca. She'd stood in the center of the crowd gathered for her bon voyage party, too used to being the center of attention to notice anymore. Flamboyant, with a careless charm, men and women vied for her attention, moths to her vibrant flame. With ease, she entertained the knot of guests with exaggerated stories of her misspent youth and her regular causes. Like the quest to save the beleaguered pigeon or the grape boycott resulting in raisin-less bran. Weaving her tales, she'd twirled a wineglass between elegant, artist's fingers sparkling with rings. Behind her, Damon nuzzled her ear. "Alexandra, I must speak with you." He lightly clasped her arm and led her out into the warm evening air. Gulls dived over the dark water, spying prey she could not see. White sand glinted in the moonlight, sea spray perfuming the air. A romantic night. She followed reluctantly.

This was it, Alex thought wistfully, as she covered his hand with her own, her face clouded by the palest grimace. He would tell her he loved her now. It had only been three weeks, but love could come in an instant. And evaporate as quickly.

"Damon." She spoke his name quietly, desperate to prevent his declaration. She knew she'd fail. A moonlit night, an impulsive plea for her to stay with him, absolutely romantic. He'd ask, as her suitors customarily did. Now, as then, she'd be firm, but discouraging. Her career, his gallery, an ocean apart. He'd be hurt, but he'd take it well. There should be mandolins, she imagined. Alex always heard music at these moments.

Damon halted them at the edge of the gallery property, where the beach met the lushly manicured grounds. He clasped her artist's hands in his. Where his touch had only days ago fluttered her pulse, now she felt nothing except the warmth of friend to friend. Blissfully unaware, Damon spoke, his voice clear and mellifluous. Alex loved his voice, a perfect mate to the fallen angel's face and the lover's mouth. She should be so in love with him.

"You have come to mean so much to me."

Flutes joined the mandolin in the background, their notes rising together, as he prepared to declare his love.

Alex heard it all so clearly, knew the next words should be her own. "And you to me. I cannot imagine finding a better friend."

"Friend?" he murmured as he lifted a captive hand to his lips. "We are much more than friends, my love. I will come to America with you, where we can be together."

The music in her head faltered. "Come to America?"

Damon nodded calmly. "When you return to America, I will come with you. I have a visa for travel. We can be married after your friends and move to your DC."

Marriage. Move to DC. Now, the flautist began to bludgeon the mandolin. "Damon, this is sudden."

"Sudden? Do you not feel as I do?"

Alex stammered, unprepared for an argument. Usually, she had a bevy of excellent reasons prepared. But with Damon, there was no obvious flaw. There had been no pressure, no annoying habit, no unsound political beliefs. Alex's mind noted smugly that he was the perfect candidate, but her heart rebelled. A niggling thought pricked her conscience, warning her to stay away. Damon was attractive, compelling, smart. Yet, he worried her, she who eschewed concern as a dangerous habit. The innate knowledge that Damon was not for her swamped her senses, and she jerked her hands from his. To cover, she managed, "It's a romantic offer, but I can't." Alex linked her fingers together. "Damon, three weeks of dinners and dancing and kisses inevitably lead to strong feelings, but this is too sudden."

Damon reached for her hands, but she shoved them behind her with inelegant haste. He noted the motion but did not comment. "Alexandra, you cannot deny what's between us. My darling, we have spent every waking minute together. That is not friendship."

Alex lifted bare shoulders, an unconsciously negligent gesture. "I'm not saying these three weeks haven't been fantastic. You are a wonderful man, Damon. Extraordinary, even. But you are not, you know, my type!"

Damon's hazel eyes snapped with the first sign of temper. "And what exactly is your type? An artist? A businessman? Be specific, Alexandra."

By now, the man had usually turned away in disgust or fled in misery. There was rarely a post-mortem. At a loss, she mumbled, "I'm not sure."

Undeterred, Damon seized her twisting fingers in his hands, the grip rougher than before. "What is it you want?" he demanded.

Thrown, Alex stammered, "I don't know. I mean, I'll know it when I see it. Him, I mean." She halted her faltering speech and tugged a hand free. In mute apology, she touched his cheek, the pale caramel skin smooth. Offhandedly, she wondered why he didn't draw her, as he should. Certainly, he was everything she imagined she wanted, and strangely, he elicited only the faintest of passions, the palest of emotions.

Dragging her mind into the moment, she said with regret, "I didn't mean to lead you on, if I did. I've had a fabulous time during the last three weeks. And you're a remarkable man. The gallery is stunning and you've been an incredible host. But I-I can't marry you, Damon." She waited for the explosion or the pleading.

He did neither. Instead, he embraced her and gently kissed her. "No matter. Come with me," he instructed as he led her inside the gallery. Confused by his abrupt change in tone, she followed him to his office. Once inside, he gestured for her to take a seat. Alex had visited the space a number of times during her stay. The opulence of Corinthian leather and Aubusson rugs complemented the rich paneling and the Hepplewhite desk.

Alex sank weakly into the butter-soft chair, trying to piece together the last few seconds. He proposed. She said no. He said why. She said she didn't know. He said okay.

She didn't know whether to be relieved or insulted.

Scanning the room, she spotted a new painting over his shoulder. Oh, what a wonderful watercolor, she thought. She hadn't noticed it on her earlier trips.

Alex opened her mouth to ask about the painting and noticed Damon studying her. "You're not angry," she stated with bewilderment.

Damon shook his head. "My proposal was sudden. Impromptu. I should not have expected a response so soon. I can be dangerously impulsive." He closed the door and propped himself on the corner of the desk.

Alex slid forward in her seat, prepared to bolt. "Well, what do you expect now?"

Noting her movement, Damon held up his hands in a gesture of peace. "I expect to give you tokens of my affection and to see you to your plane tomorrow. That is all." He turned to a concealed closet and removed a large box and a smaller wrapped package. "For you," he announced.

Warily, Alex accepted the larger package first.

Inside, nestled in tissue paper, was a straw hat with a floppy brim. She'd seen it in a village market but had refused to let Damon buy it for her. The price had been a pittance, but she'd been aware even then of his growing affections.

"Damon, you shouldn't have," she said, handing the package back to him.

"No, please. It is yours. I have no use for it," he countered, pointing at the frilly green ribbon tied to its middle.

Alex set the hat on her head at a jaunty angle. "Thank you," she replied graciously.

"And the other," he said as she moved to stand.

"Really, Damon, this is more than enough."

He placed the smaller package in her hand. "Please?"

Never good at refusing gifts, Alex settled and opened the wrapping. A sculpture, the width of her palm and six inches high, emerged from the box, an engraved obelisk of soapstone.

"Damon, I can't accept this," Alex declared. "Why have me make a replica for you, if you're giving me the original?"

"Always so full of questions, Alexandra. It is by an anonymous artist, and I came upon it by accident. I want you to have it. The inscriptions are Shilha, a language too few speak these days. Please, take it with you to remember me."

"But why make two, Damon? I don't understand."

The indulgent smile hardened for an instant, almost imperceptibly. "Two small tokens. Surely, that is not too much to ask of a new friend."

Torn, Alex wrestled with her conscience. She'd refused his proposal but would accept his gifts? Glancing up at him from beneath her lashes, she considered him.

Damon was a golden boy, in every respect. With burnished copper skin, the regal bearing of a man born to wealth, and an innate charm, he'd rarely been denied anything he wanted.

Their time together had been a welcome respite, and she'd badly sought to feel more than friendship for him. But something about Damon, in the way his smile never reached his eyes or in his careful, well-plotted movements, something disturbed her. Nevertheless, he'd been a good companion, appealing and urbane. She would take his gifts with her to the U.S., as a show of friendship.

"Thank you, Damon. You're too kind."

Damon had pulled her into a hug, and Alex didn't resist. A dark emotion flashed in his eyes. "No, it is you who does me the great favor. We will see each other again, my dear."

————

She'd boarded the plane, the obelisk tucked deep into her satchel, the hat in the overhead compartment. On the eternal flight, time seemed to slow. Like now, Alex thought, why did she have so much of it to spend in consternating contemplation? She glanced up at the traffic scurrying past, then checked the slim gold watch on her wrist. Her flight had been delayed by a few hours, but Adam's message said she'd be retrieved. Alex relaxed with effort, accepting her situation.

A tardy flight or a delayed ride annoyed most people, a sentiment not shared by Alex. To her, time was fluid. A measure to be hurried along or ignored, depending on the situation.

Of course, this philosophy often led to raised eyebrows and clucked tongues and tiresome lectures, but Alex didn't care. These thirty minutes gave her ample time to spy on the unsuspecting thralls in the airport. And she could ignore the fact that her time in Durban had led to yet another failed romance and a new bout of soul-searching.

Alex sighed again at the memory and curled her legs across the metal chairs. She would concentrate on not thinking about Damon. Or Greg. Or Max. Or any of the throng of discarded men. Well, if she didn't think of her debacle of a love life, she could worry about her career. To be honest, art was less of a career than a lifelong hobby. Art fired her father's soul with magnificent results. Alex acknowledged that it only gently flamed her own. Politics interested her, but only as a sideline coach, not as a player. At twenty-seven, she had yet to find her grand passion. Her true calling.

A lukewarm gallery opening and a tepid romantic liaison confirmed it. She led the life of a woman she didn't know, doing her job, falling in love with her men, with less than spectacular results on both fronts.

What she needed was a sabbatical, a time away to decide what she wanted, what she needed. But what better time than the present? Her gravest concern was her steady and inexorable decline into the realm of the dilettante. Soon she'd become one of those bubble-headed socialites lunching at four, soused on doctored cranberry juice.

Priests fasted for clarity, Alex reflected as she considered her problem. When it occurred to her that fasting probably included Coke, she hastily abandoned the idea. Monks, on the other hand, abstained from sexual congress. With a self-deprecating smirk, Alex realized a moratorium on men presented less of a challenge than no Coca-Cola. Unless, she thought meditatively, the suspension extended to emotional congress as well. No romantic dinners or moonlit walks or soul-searing kisses. The last thing she wanted in her life right now was another love affair gone sour. A male moratorium. The alliteration pleased her literary soul, the concept appealed to her errant heart. A male moratorium it is, she decided, starting now.

With a final sigh for all the men she'd just abandoned, she turned to watch a tow-headed cherubim try to escape the clutches of her exasperated older brother. Much more fun than trying to figure out what I'm doing with my life now, she decided. Much better.

———

Phillip stared at the woman who lay draped across the plastic and metal chairs at the airport gate. Impossibly long legs stretched over the conjoined arms of two seats, and narrow sandaled feet propped casually against the opposite arm. The legs displayed so prominently were faultlessly shaped, coffee-toned, and framed by what he assumed were supposed to be shorts. The cut-off denim was frayed around the edges and an electric blue. Could that length be legal? They seemed to stop and start at her navel. As he stared, a sharp punch of desire caught him unprepared.

With effort, he dismissed it as the result of his extended romantic drought. Instead, he continued to note details, remnants of training and natural male curiosity. Thoughtful brown eyes lingered over the point where slim thighs disappeared under the scanty covering of denim.

Amazing.

Then his eyes toured upward, to where she twisted at a flat waist. She'd contorted herself to look behind her at something he could not see. But, from his vantage point, he admired what he did see. The tangerine tank should have clashed with everything around it, but instead seemed perfectly suited, even to the electric blue denim. It didn't hurt that the contrast in colors emphasized the creamy texture of sleekly muscled arms or the gentle swell of cleavage. At that moment, she turned toward him, still unaware of his perusal. His mouth ran dry at the first full glimpse of the gypsy's face. The punch of desire redoubled into an almost physical ache. He let out a breath he'd been oblivious to inhaling. Like the rest of the woman, the face presented a study of too much, working all too well. Long and angular, she sported a strong chin, sharp cheekbones, wide thickly lashed eyes. Waves of rich ebony hair flowed down from a severe widow's peak to caress exquisite shoulders. Her lips, full and painted a deep bronze, were curved into a smile of wry amusement.

Phillip followed her line of sight. Just beyond the plastic chairs, at the tall, broad windows overlooking the runways, two identical imps wrestled on the blue carpet, each one having firm grasp of the other's ear. The cries of the tiny terrors were studiously ignored by who he assumed to be their disinterested older sister. A woman's stern voice commanded a cease and desist, followed by slightly amused male agreement.

The gypsy leaned forward and pulled a large notebook from an oversized leather bag. A bag he could have sworn cost more than her outfit and that of the twins' family's luggage combined. From his vantage point, it looked like it could easily consume the contents of all their bags. With a shake of his head, he circled the bank of chairs. From Adam's cryptic description, it had to be her. He approached her side, noting the first instant of awareness. Almond-shaped eyes focused, then softened. An interesting reaction he'd consider later. Stopping in front of her, he extended a hand. "You must be Alex."

Alex continued her perusal, without responding. The almond eyes were liquid pools of sinful brown, narrowed at the corners. Cataloging him without hurry, they traveled slowly from the crown of his head to the newly polished loafers on his feet. When they hesitated on his mouth briefly during their journey, the urge to pull her out of the chair and into his arms surprised him.

Phillip was not a man ruled by hormones. He had the requisite passions, which he indulged at the appropriate intervals. Yet, the primitive impulse to crush the overripe lips beneath his shook him, and he squashed the image. "Alex?" he repeated with a hint of impatience.

After another eternity, the gypsy spoke. "Given who's asking, I do hope so."

The low, whiskey-soaked voice abruptly wiped every coherent thought from his head. For the second time in as many minutes, he released a breath he hadn't known he was holding. "You certainly are direct."

Alex laughed, the sound as dazzling as the voice. "Oh, did I say that out loud? I have a habit of speaking before I remember to keep my lascivious thoughts to myself. Actually, I have a habit of speaking before I do just about anything, so the qualification of thought isn't exactly relevant. But yes, I am Alex Walton."

"Fascinated." It was no more than the truth. Women, particularly beautiful women, were a luxury he couldn't often afford during his captivity. But those days were past, and lounging before him was proof of the folly of abstinence. From this close and his vantage point of six feet three, Phillip saw the promise of cleavage he'd spied across the room aptly fulfilled. The bronzed mouth was lush and wide, an almost permanent pout. From a distance, she was arresting. Up close, she was stunning.

"I'm Phillip Turman." He reached for her hand and clasped it firmly.

She undraped the bare legs and lithely rose to her feet, noticing that Phillip had yet to return her hand. Alex tugged gently, and slowly he released the overly warmed flesh. She decided it was prudent to ignore the tingle that seemed to arrow up her arm in response.

Alex nodded. "I know. Your face has been plastered on the news for the last few months," she explained when he looked askance at her pronouncement. At five feet eight, she was shorter than Raleigh, but still taller than most women.

So, it was disconcerting to stare up to make eye contact. "I've seen you almost every day."

What the anchors never seemed to mention was the intensity

of gorgeous brown eyes the color of bitter chocolate. Where the cameras captured a tall, solidly built man with broad shoulders, Alex's artist eye saw the physique of a runner with the bearing of a pirate. In loose-fitting khakis and a white button-down that emphasized his frame, she could easily picture him braced on the prow of a massive ship, with billowed sails and a menacing skull and bones snapping on the masthead. The firmly molded mouth that sported a mustache above its sensual peak would shout orders to a bustling crew. With a sword in one hand and a gyroscope in the other, he'd terrorize the sea. And in a darkly lit cabin, he would ravish maidens. When the imagined maiden took on her own form, Alex blinked to clear her vision.

Phillip cocked a brow. "Something wrong?"

"Sorry. I often depart for unscheduled flights of fancy. But I do doubt there is anyone with a television who doesn't know who you are. The brave former congressman held captive by a notorious terrorist group."

"Well, here, I'm just the best man. Or, at least, Adam Grayson's best man. Ready to go?" The pirate's voice was cool and distant, no easy familiarity or warmth.

Still caught up in her fantasy, she responded, "Aye, aye, *mon capitan!*"

Phillip shot her a quizzical look, which Alex pretended not to see. Instead, she turned to gather her belongings. With efficient movements at odds with her carefree appearance, Alex tucked the sketch pad inside the leather bag and slung it over her shoulder. She lifted an oversized garment bag, shifting it for a better grip, then reached for her travel bag. The other four suitcases had been shipped directly to DC. But she needed the other three for her weeklong stay in Atlanta. One day, she decided, she'd learn to pack lighter. Probably the same day she learned to think before she spoke, she thought wryly.

"I'll take that," Phillip said as he transferred the stuffed garment bag to his shoulder. "Is this everything?" Politeness stiffened his tone, hardened the smooth roundness of the voice.

"Yep. I travel with all my bags with me. Less risk of me in Paris and my luggage in Lubbock."

Phillip reached out to take the Pullman. "Efficient, I suppose," he said dubiously.

Their hands grabbed the handle at the same moment.

Again, Alex felt the strange tingling sensation from Phillip's touch. She fought against instant recoil, not wanting to admit the sparks between them. Suddenly, her throat was unbelievably tight. She managed a whisper. "I've got this one. It has wheels."

Phillip maintained his grip on the handle and his connection to her skin. "I insist."

For seconds, neither moved. Then Alex lifted her hand in defeat. "You win," she conceded, oddly bereft.

Phillip gave her a slow smile that did nothing to disguise the threat or promise of his next words. "I like winning. I'm very good at it."

Alex braced herself, as the tingling in her arm gave way to nerves humming beneath her skin. "I can imagine so." Breaking their eye contact with difficulty, Alex lifted her hat from a nearby seat. "A farewell present from a friend," she explained as she led Phillip toward Customs.

With determined strides, more suited to a teenage boy than a coltish young woman, Alex strode up to an agent, a portly man with pale pink skin and a shining pate. And a CLOSED sign displayed prominently in red. Cheerfully ignoring the sign, Alex struck up a conversation with the agent, after setting her hat on the postage-stamp-sized counter. Phillip hung back, waiting for her to be shooed on to the proper line, which stretched for several yards. Instead, Alex waved to him to drag her bags over to the desk.

Phillip watched in admiring disbelief as she convinced the agent to stamp her passport and forgo checking the satchel, the garment bag, and the oversized Pullman he was certain contained contraband. Although, come to think of it, how did she get that monstrosity on the plane in the first place? Phillip wondered. But, as he watched the agent flush a deep red when Alex covered his hand with her own, he guessed that a male attendant had manned her boarding gate.

In record time, Alex sailed through the checkout area and they headed for the terminal. "Nice man," she remarked after a prolonged silence.

Phillip grunted and used his free hand to move Alex past a trio of teenagers eagerly flirting with what he guessed to be a basketball team at baggage claim.

At the feel of his hand on her skin, the tingling sensation transformed itself into a distinct heat. It's only his hand, Alex, she reminded herself. Even so, Alex tugged at her elbow. Phillip did not release her. Rather than engage in an undignified struggle, to distract herself, she did what she did best. Chattered.

"Raleigh must be on the verge of an apoplectic fit. She hates dresses, parties, and flowers, the very essence of weddings. Including the love part, of course. I've proven to be an abysmal maid of honor, which she certainly could have anticipated. She's known me for years and I'm terribly untrustworthy in matters of organization. But I've done as much as I can long-distance, although my show in Durban took longer than expected. I can't imagine how she's managing this without heavy drugs."

Did she breathe? Phillip wondered as his thumb stroked a light line from her forearm to her elbow, of its own accord. The skin there felt like silk. Soft, supple silk. Oh, what did she say about Raleigh? Yes, heavy drugs.

"According to your mother, they sedate her each night."

Alex tried not to jerk away as her arm caught fire from his touch. If he didn't let her go soon, her arm would spontaneously combust. Which would go a long way to solving her concentration issues regarding her art. Her brain in disarray, Alex rushed on breathlessly. "Mom must be having a field day. She loves weddings. Always has. Especially ones she gets to plan. And since she despairs of mine ever occurring, Raleigh must bear the brunt of her enthusiasm."

Phillip glanced at his companion. "Why no wedding for you?" He ignored his own pointed interest in her answer, and his thumb's continuous travels up and down her arm.

The question was merely an attempt to make conversation with the maid of honor. And holding her seemed polite, that's all. "No plans to marry?"

To his surprise, Alex's bright eyes dimmed, as did the full-lipped smile. "No antimarriage plans. It's the male moratorium. Guaranteed to keep me a spinster to the end of my days or at least for the foreseeable future. But I make a great friend." With that pronouncement, she pulled her arm away and scooted through the sliding glass doors and out into the sunlight.

CHAPTER THREE

Phillip started after her, and then stopped. He rubbed a long-fingered hand over the day's growth of beard on his chin. Staring at the astonishing woman bathed in sunlight, he shook his head in bemusement. When Adam described Alex Walton as *intriguing*, Phillip hadn't realized the full import of the term. She was beautiful and witty and unconventional, to say the least. How else could he explain an innocent conversation about the wedding, which had somehow morphed into a declaration of abstinence? A declaration he was tempted to challenge.

Alex stirred him. That dramatic face, the slightly voluptuous form, and a low husky voice that jangled nerve endings. But he had enough on his plate to worry about without acting on a preternatural desire to cover those bee-stung lips with his own.

Like how in the hell she'd bewitched him in less than twenty minutes, his mind countered.

Searching for the cold logic that was as much a part of him as the detailed plans, Phillip forced himself to consider why any interest in Raleigh's odd maid of honor would have to remain here in Atlanta. First of all, he would be on a flight back to DC in a week. Common sense told him no good could come of anything started five hundred miles away.

Besides, he barely knew the woman. Despite the blood-pressure-raising package, Alex Walton was obviously a few crackers shy of a full box.

There was also the uneasy feeling he had of being followed. In DC, he'd checked for tails, and even found himself scanning the highway for too familiar cars here in Atlanta. He'd been trained to worry, to rely on a heightened sense of suspicion. His last conversation with Atlas teased him, as though he should have heard something but didn't.

He would deliver her to the Walton homestead in the Cascades, and then retire to Adam's for the evening. There, he'd run through scenarios with Raleigh and Adam, to ensure the security of their wedding. But first, Alex had some explaining to do. A male moratorium? Phillip hesitated for a moment longer then headed through the doors. "Alex!"

She slowed, waiting for him to catch up. Falling in step beside her, he furrowed his brow. Although she pasted on a wan smile, Phillip noted that it did not reach those exotic brown pools she called eyes. "What were you talking about? What in the world is a male moratorium?"

If anything, her plastered-on smile grew more strained. "Sort of like a romance cease-fire," Alex stated, as though the comparison explained everything.

Now he was confused. As they crossed through the milling traffic, Phillip echoed her latest cryptic comment. "Romance cease-fire?"

Alex set her hat precariously on her mass of hair, ignoring the question. The first balmy breeze rushed past, and she inhaled deeply. Until that moment, she hadn't realized how much she missed Atlanta. She was home. Neither Damon nor any of his predecessors would dim her pleasure at being back with her family.

Phillip negotiated the ramp leading to deck escalators. "Romance cease-fire," he repeated.

The escalator reached the upper level and they left the step in unison. Shaking off her misery, Alex tucked her arm in his and replied, "You know, 'Abandon all hope, ye who enter here.' In this case, it's for all unsuspecting men who dare to flirt. I feel I should warn you as well, not that you've flirted with me. And not to suggest that you might, but I believe in fair warnings to all men of age. Then again, there was the way you were staring at my legs in the airport."

Phillip opened his mouth to speak, but Alex continued unabated. "I, my dear Phillip, have an uncanny ability to break the heart of every attractive man I meet, or at least bludgeon it with mild pet peeves that transform themselves into unconquerable flaws. I lure them in and when no one is looking, certainly not I, I convert previously ideal men into the masses of imperfection. I can transform affection for opera into a character flaw of mammoth proportions. And what I can do with a harmless comment on Sartre versus de Beauvoir has yet to be explained, but it did cause Franklin to drop out of his PhD program. And, if you dare doubt my persnickety prowess, I have statistics."

Dumbfounded, Phillip halted on the walkway and stared at Alex. Statistics? Moratorium? And when did she see him staring at her legs? Not that anyone could blame him.

They were almost as long as her sentences. "Has anyone ever pointed out your tendency to—"

"Run on and on?" The megawatt grin returned with a disarming hint of self-deprecation.

"A bit, yes."

"Ah, but otherwise, I'm a perfect companion. I like ESPN, have an excellent jump shot, and I don't require much in the way of daily maintenance. But with the definite tendency to talk too much."

Definitely a couple of crackers shy, Phillip decided. And still smarting from a recent breakup. He didn't grow up with sisters, but Phillip understood human nature. A bad breakup transformed into a suspension of romantic interest. Sounded familiar, he acknowledged. After Lorei, he'd shut down, refusing any relationships with women beyond the most basic. His partners were aware of the rules—no ties, no commitments. Occasionally, someone would try to develop more and Phillip ended the liaison without hesitation.

One look at Alex told him she didn't want to talk about her aborted love affair, and Phillip understood protecting sore wounds. Besides, how was a man supposed to keep up with that mouth and a serious conversation at the same time? he challenged himself.

Taking her lead, he changed the subject. "I was going to say your ability to pack quite a lot into a single breath. Do you do this often?" Phillip asked as he steered her toward the waiting car.

"Do what?" At his cocked brow, she nodded in understanding. "Oh, the rambling? I'm famous for it. Didn't Adam or Raleigh warn you?"

No, Adam didn't warn him. "Adam said that you were 'intriguing.'"

"Damned by faint praise." Alex laughed in delight, and Phillip felt his stomach tighten. The husky sound slid over his skin and into his bones.

"He didn't mean it that way," Phillip corrected, ignoring the sweet pain of desire.

"Praise, in any form, is greatly appreciated." She mocked both of them with a curtsy. The abbreviated shorts rode dangerously high up her thighs, but she made no move to tug them back down, to Phillip's eternal gratitude.

Man, she was adorable. And a walking contradiction. The gorgeous face and the sex-siren laugh were completely at odds with the scattered conversation and the vulnerability of that last soliloquy. And she still lived in Atlanta, Phillip reminded himself.

Phillip reigned himself in abruptly. Alex was not a candidate for a short romance or a long-distance relationship. He'd known her less than an hour, and what he did know wasn't exactly awe-inspiring. Lust-inducing, maybe. But he had grown beyond the days where he thought only with his hormones. At thirty-five, the idea of settling down appealed to him on several levels, despite his protestations to his father. In his most private dreams, he longed for what Adam and Raleigh had found together. What he'd missed while trapped undercover. A place that felt right, felt special. Someone to miss him and welcome him home. He was mortally tired of being alone. But Alex Walton was not the answer.

Annoyed by his train of thought, Phillip led her across the open-air upper deck. The level was relatively clear on a Thursday afternoon, with no more than a few dozen cars scattered across the steamy concrete. He had parked near the exit ramp, which lay a few yards away. "Before your last verbal marathon, you were telling me about your trip to Durban."

"I was?" Alex tilted her head, trying to remember.

Phillip's profile caught her eye, distracted her. He had remarkable bone structure. Clean, strong lines. A square jaw, slightly softened by the poet's mouth. Despite her resolution about men, she couldn't help but wonder what it would feel like against her own.

"Alex?"

Oops, he'd asked her a question. But it was his fault. That mouth was certainly diverting. "Oh yes, my explanation for missing the tough parts of preparing for the Foster-Grayson nuptials. A prior engagement at a gallery in Durban. Have you ever been? The gallery is on the shore, with clear water and spectacular sunsets."

His one trip to Durban had been to arrange financing for a Jubalani deal. The proceeds paid for weapons sent to guerillas in Bosnia. He didn't remember the sunsets. "No, I've never been."

"You really should go. I was there because I have a tendency to sculpt, and the gallery was showing my work."

Phillip released her elbow to rub at his temples.

Between the incandescent grin and the serpentine speech, he now had a rather good idea of how Alice felt speaking with the Cheshire Cat. "A tendency to sculpt?"

She nodded. "I wouldn't really call it a vocation. Or a calling. But it is more than a hobby." She paused to consider the matter for a moment longer. "Yes, definitely a tendency. No great causal direction, but I do have a bit of a compulsion."

Refusing to engage in what would, without a doubt, lead to another labyrinth in her convoluted brain, Phillip asked instead. "And I understand you paint as well?"

"Not really."

Phillip sighed. He'd been so close. "You don't really paint?"

"Yes, I paint, but not quite as well as I sculpt. Painting is more a hobby than a possible vocation."

"I meant *as well as* sculpting. *In addition to.*"

"Oh. Yes. I do paint as well. On occasion. But I believe I'm giving it up."

"Why?"

"I've been playing at being an artist, but I have the distinct impression the time has come for a change. I'm contemplating historical treatises or perhaps playwriting, maybe even a novel. I haven't decided. Then again, I can always take up photography again."

"I'm confused," Phillip offered in defeat. "What is it you do for a living? Exactly."

"Thanks to my grandparents' generosity, my parents' financial acumen, and a healthy stock market, anything I want. I have an obscene trust fund that pays for my vocational mood swings."

"And what's the connection between writing and sculpting and photography?"

Alex grinned. "A marked inability to make up my mind."

"I can imagine." Realizing he'd spoken aloud, Phillip added, "Not to be critical."

Alex shrugged. "No offense taken. I have a low threshold for sameness."

"Most of us just develop a hobby. Not a new career."

"I'm different that way."

"You certainly are unique, Ms. Walton."

"Why thank you, Mr. Turman. But enough about me. Tell me all about your exploits."

At that moment, Phillip and Alex reached the gray Mercedes. Exploits? Had Raleigh told her about his other life? No, he decided instantly, not Raleigh. She maintained a code as inviolate as his own. Regardless of the personal cost, there'd be no revelation about his role in the ISA. Rather than answer her loaded question, Phillip opened the passenger door. Hopefully, she'd get inside and leave him to marshal thoughts scattered by her presence. He'd regain his detachment, remember he was merely her chauffeur for the day and her guard for the week. Anything else would be foolish.

Alex leaned against the metal frame, warm from the sun. Clouds had drifted into town, shielding Atlanta from the hottest rays. Silently, Phillip began to store her bags in the cavernous trunk.

In the distance, a car engine roared to life.

Overhead, a plane dipped low, making its final descent. On the other side of the lot, an alarm beeped imperiously. Phillip catalogued the sounds, assigning locations to each.

"Phillip?"

"Yes?"

The polite tone had returned, but Alex ignored it. "I'm waiting for an answer." She tilted her head to block the faint trickles of sunlight not deflected by her hat and settled a denim-clad hip on the doorframe. "I did ask to hear about you."

Phillip continued to arrange her bags in the trunk. "Not much to tell," he dismissed, polite sliding into stiff.

Unwilling to accept the distance without an explanation, she prodded, "Come on, I've revealed my deepest secrets to you."

His lips thinned. "I didn't ask."

"That's not the point. Tit for tat." The pout that Phillip now recognized as of her basic expressions pursed the lush, bronzed lips. "Quid pro quo."

He started to refuse more forcefully, when a sudden gust of wind caught the brim of Alex's hat and snatched it from her head. Alex dove for the recalcitrant hat but missed when the wind blew it away from her. She ran after the hat, laughing. At that moment, Phillip caught the sound of squealing tires.

Less than ten yards away, a red sedan bore down on them. Phillip shouted a warning, and Alex's head came up. Her eyes widened in shock. Phillip sprinted toward her. He could feel the heat of the engine, smell the pungent scent of burnt rubber. He spared a few seconds to look into the car. The driver's face was shadowed by a cap, but Phillip could barely discern the lower half of the mouth drawn back into a vicious twist of lips.

In those brief seconds, Phillip identified deliberate intent. This was no accident. Instinctively, he increased his speed. The car was less than five feet away when Phillip tackled Alex. Smoke and exhaust spewed over them and the car slowed its speed. Prepared for a second pass, Phillip gathered Alex to him, but the car accelerated and sped toward the exit.

Beneath him, Alex lay sprawled on the asphalt, Phillip

crushing her to the ground. The ragged sound of their breathing drowned out the fading car engine.

"Are you okay?" Phillip asked harshly, running his hands over her body to check for injury. "Are you hurt?" The car had missed her, hadn't it? But maybe the tackle cracked her ribs or fractured her arm. Why wasn't she answering him? Had he given her a concussion? "Alex, honey, are you alright? Say something," he commanded.

Alex stared up at him, wide brown eyes sparkling with what he assumed to be tears.

"Alex?"

"Phillip," she whispered as she raised her hand and pushed at his shoulder.

Phillip held himself very still. The sight of the car bearing down on her had frightened him, almost as much as the concern he was feeling now. He'd met this woman less than an hour ago, and he couldn't seem to make his heart stop pounding against his ribs. Over and over, his mind played the seconds when the driver took aim. He could hear the echoes of the crunch of straw beneath the tires. She'd nearly been killed. And it was intentional.

Phillip didn't move, trying to figure their next move. A man had nearly run them down. He didn't know if the hit-and-run attempt was for him or her, but he would find out. First, though, he had to decide what to do with her. The last thing he needed right now were questions. And, as adrenaline rushed through him and his body and mind focused on the woman trapped beneath him, he realized all he wanted was Alex. The orange straps fell off one brown shoulder, framing smooth, naked flesh. The overripe lips pursed in an attempt to slow their trembling. He could almost taste her fear, and her relief. Then he knew he must. Inexorably, he lowered his mouth.

With care, he pressed firm lips to trembling, absorbing the feel, the heat of silk. Alex parted her mouth, slowly. The hand that rested on his shoulder slid along his collar to caress the tight muscles cording his neck. Gently, he angled the kiss to taste more of her, lifting her body up to meet his. Softly, the taste of her flowed into him and then flooded his system.

Spurred by adrenaline and a desire more feral because of its newness, he invaded her mouth with his tongue. He swept inside and, pressing against him, she opened, inviting him deeper. Sweet, he thought, so sweet. As her arms wrapped around him, Phillip grew light-headed from her scent as it curled into his senses. She smelled of flowers and cool rain. She felt like that, like spring.

Not so sweet, he thought hazily, as their kiss became a duel of tongues and lips and teeth. He searched for the word, but the wet, velvety haven of her mouth stripped his mind blank. Alex writhed against him, and together, they rolled until Alex covered him. The feel of her against him, her hands stroking eagerly along his face, his chest, stoked flames that threatened to consume them. He streaked greedy hands down sensual curves, skimmed his palms up soft denim. The feel of firm, satiny flesh made him hungry for more. He turned them again, fitting her hips to his own, her mouth to his.

Now there was spicy, a counterpoint to the sweet. Alex slid impatient hands inside the shirt she'd tugged free of his belt. Phillip cupped rounded, full breasts, molding them to the shape of his hands. He needed more. He needed her beneath him, with him. Mindlessly, he turned them again.

The crunch of straw beneath his back snapped the spell. Quickly, he rolled them over one last time and broke their kiss.

Inches from their bodies, Alex's hat lay mangled by the speeding car. As Alex contemplated the crumpled straw, Phillip stared down at her. Drawing in a labored breath, Alex finally spoke. "Damn it! He crushed my hat!"

With a deadly softness, he asked, "You're nearly mown down by a maniac and your first concern is that silly hat?"

Despite the quiet tone, Alex heard the underlying fury, but not the fear. She shrugged, as much as one could when stretched out on asphalt, having nearly been kissed senseless by a relative stranger. So much for her moratorium. Grasping vainly at calm, she retorted, "I have a peculiarly shaped head. A good hat is hard to find." Particularly when the top of your head is about to blow off.

The taste of her lingering on his lips, Phillip struggled with a boiling rage. They'd nearly been killed, and had more nearly made love on the top level of the parking deck, and all she could think of was her damned hat. "Of course. I should have known. You have an oddly shaped head. Which would explain why you chased a cheap five-dollar hat into the path of an oncoming car. Makes perfect sense."

If anything, Phillip's voice grew even quieter, ominous. Alex recognized the method, if not the intensity. From her mom, the quiet implacable tone signaled a precursor to wrath. Phillip's anger strained his tone, and Alex decided to humor him. "My gorgeous hat cost more than five dollars, thank you very much, but it was a gift. And I didn't chase it in front of the car. I was chasing it and the car came at me." She would process the near-fatal hit-and-run in a moment.

If her hands were beginning to shake, she'd deal with that later as well. For now, she would focus on the enraged man above her. No, she had definitely not seen this look before. Primal, irate, he pressed against her, suspended between control and abandon. Alex shifted delicately beneath him, and stopped abruptly as heat pooled where their bodies met. Hot, angry eyes bored into hers.

As though taming a wild animal, she tried a calming smile. "But I suppose I can find another one. Eventually."

The midnight stare did not waver, nor did his voice warm. "That's important. Finding a new hat."

"Absolutely." Alex tilted her head back to study the man still lying across her. As the shaking spread across her frame, she began to notice the body that pinned hers to the ground. Phillip seemed to be made entirely of muscle, without a spare ounce of flesh. She'd been too busy to notice that before. During. Wanting to distract herself and Phillip, she commented, "You have excellent reflexes. You saved my life!" She tried a second smile, slightly more ingratiating. "Thank you?"

"Don't you dare thank me, you shallow, addled idiot! No wonder you can't pick a job. You have absolutely no sense! You go flying in front of a speeding car to save a two-dollar hat, risking my life and yours."

Alex made a note to be impressed by the incensed yet hushed delivery. A good technique. One she would likely give to the hero of her novel. Seconds later, though, his words began to register. "I told you, the hat cost more than two dollars. And did you call me an idiot?"

"No. I called you a shallow, addled idiot. One with no respect for anyone's life, including her own."

"Excuse me—"

"You risked your life and mine."

She'd tried to diffuse the tension, but now he was simply being mean. "Don't you dare blame this on me! The wind blew my hat off my head, and like anyone would, I tried to get it back. And I didn't see the car. Obviously neither did you."

"That's not the point—"

Infuriated, Alex pulled one arm free and awkwardly poked at his chest. "And no one asked for your help." Working the other arm out from between their bodies, she shoved futilely at a chest made of granite. "If you're going to yell at me, please get off of me."

Phillip didn't budge. "I am not yelling."

He had a point. But it felt like yelling. "Fine. If you are going to quietly shout at me, get off!" With that, she tried to move him again. Certainly, he couldn't be that solid.

Apparently he was, she decided as he settled himself more firmly above her. Somehow, every curve of her body seemed to fit into a hollow of his. And the shaking she had finally managed to control now threatened to spread again. "I said off. Now."

She lifted an uncertain hand to his shoulder, perhaps to push him away. She wasn't sure. All she knew was that he was going to kiss her again. And she didn't know if she could resist.

If he didn't move right now, he was going to kiss her again, Phillip thought. And they were still in the open, making out on the asphalt like two overgrown teenagers.

More importantly, if he didn't kiss her again, he was going to throttle her. Silently, Phillip stood, then lifted Alex from the ground.

"Put me down," she demanded. "I can walk."

"Shut up, Alex," Phillip said calmly.

Held high against his chest, Alex decided discretion might be the better part of valor. Phillip carried her the short distance to the car and gently handed her inside. He efficiently secured her seat belt, without touching her, and closed the door. As he rounded the hood, Alex fought against the urge to touch lips still warm from their kiss.

"I'm sorry," Phillip began in his deep, quiet voice, as he slid behind the wheel. "I shouldn't have yelled at you."

"You don't yell," Alex reminded him as her anger dissipated. "But you do insult rather well."

Phillip did not say anything as he made his way through the tollgate. After she gave him directions to her house, he merged onto the freeway. Who the devil was Alex Walton? The woman is nearly killed by a crazy driver, then he attacks her in the parking lot. He called her an idiot and worse, *and she wasn't mad*.

With every second spent in her company, Phillip understood that *intriguing* described her perfectly. As a man trained to uncover mystery, Alex Walton could prove too enticing to solve. Better to apologize now and put distance between him and his hormones.

"You didn't deserve that either. I was mad at the driver, and I took it out on you."

Now he's apologizing for kissing me. "Don't worry about it," Alex mumbled. Step one, she thought. Phillip glanced at her, his brown eyes troubled. "Are you really alright?"

Alex didn't dare answer that question honestly. The trembling had stopped, and no bones were broken. But she certainly was not "alright." She could feel it starting again, the vicious cycle. Already, she could hear desire strumming between them.

In a few days, after close quarters and unadulterated romance, they'd kiss again.

Maybe more. She'd begin that fateful slide into love and she'd suddenly decide she preferred obsidian black eyes to sexy brown or fallen angel looks to severely handsome.

"What are you talking about?"

Embarrassment swept over her, and she closed her eyes in dismay. "I was talking out loud, wasn't I?" she muttered.

"You can 'hear desire strumming between' us?"

"Oh, God." No longer satisfied with the closed eyes, Alex dropped her mortified face into her hands. "Can you drop me off here? My house is only ten or fifteen miles from the interstate. Or I could simply die of embarrassment right now. We could have a funeral and a wedding all in the same week."

The soft chuckle made her lift her head. Eyes narrowed, Alex glared at him. "Are you laughing at me?"

"I don't think so," Phillip said hastily, in mock fear. Another chuckle escaped.

"It is a dangerous idea to laugh at a woman who was nearly mown down, ravished, and humiliated, all in the last fifteen minutes." She deliberately tapped the steering wheel. "Especially one who just left an international flight and lost her head. I mean hat."

Losing the battle, Phillip laughed, a full-throated sound that widened Alex's eyes and tightened her belly. The sound was hoarse, surprised, as though he hadn't laughed in a while. Of course, he hadn't, Alex reminded herself. He'd been held in a prison camp for years. She doubted there would be many chances to laugh inside hell.

She watched him as the laughter faded away, replaced in measured increments by stiff and distant. He drove the Mercedes with masterful restraint, skimming just below the speed limit but pushing the vehicle to its limits as he wove between cars. In profile, the rugged good looks resembled a relief she'd once seen of a tribal god in Mozambique. Strong, powerful, capable of both cruelty and compassion.

Her hands itched to capture him in clay or perhaps a hardwood.

"You should pose for me," she announced, twisting in her seat to retrieve her sketch pad.

"No," Phillip answered coldly.

Undeterred, Alex rummaged in the oversized bag for a pencil. "Why not? I am quite good."

"I don't doubt your talent. No, thank you." The response was brisk, not inviting conversation.

He wouldn't shut her out so easily, she decided.

Running a hand through her fall of hair, she scooped it into a ponytail and secured it with a band from her wrist. She turned in her seat to face him, and propped her leg on the gearbox. With efficient movements, she flipped the pad to a clean page and began to sketch.

"What are you doing?" Phillip demanded, taking his eyes off the road to glare at her.

"Watch the road," Alex rebuked him mildly. "Given our recent encounter, I'd rather we be very careful with this car."

Phillip returned his eyes to the road. "Alex, what are you doing?" he repeated.

Alex was not fooled by the calm tone. She had always been a quick study. "You said you didn't have time to sit for me, therefore, this will have to do," she placated.

Briskly, she outlined the contours of his profile on the parchment, light strokes that barely registered on the page.

"I'd rather you not," he began, fighting the urge to squirm.

Why, he's embarrassed, she surmised. To toy with him, she said, "You have a remarkable face, Phillip. Planes and hollows. The strong patrician nose and the cleft chin." Not to mention, a gorgeous mouth with a sexy mustache teasing his upper lip. "You would make an excellent model."

Phillip cleared his throat. "I am not a model, Alex."

"What is it you do for a living?"

He'd never met a woman who would not be ignored. Relenting, he answered vaguely, "At the moment, I'm a consultant."

"Ah, the great non-job. I think it ranks a notch below entrepreneur."

Phillip stifled a smile. "Has anyone ever pointed out that you are incredibly nosy and intrusive?"

"All the time. Usually before exasperating." Alex swept her pencil over the arch of his eyebrow. On Phillip, it was cocked in perpetual suspicion.

"Are you going to stop?"

"Are you going to tell me what you do for a living?"

"No."

Alex shifted in her seat, bringing her legs up to form a makeshift desk. "Then nope." She tossed him a saucy grin as the cocked brow rose higher and the mustache lowered threateningly. "Before you begin your tirade, you're about to miss the exit."

With a grunt, Phillip steered the car onto the exit ramp, and Alex's grin widened.

"It'll be good to be home. It's been a while."

"You were only in Durban for three weeks. When's the last time you were here?"

"I flew in for my mother's birthday party in July."

Phillip's stomach sank as he asked, "You don't live here in Atlanta?"

Alex shook her head. "Nope. I live in DC. What about you?"

The sinking feeling masked a wave of pleasure at the information. "Washington."

Smiling, Alex pronounced, "So, we're neighbors."

Neighbors, Phillip thought fatalistically. Wasn't it a bad idea to become involved with your neighbor? While he pondered the issue, Alex directed him to the Walton homestead. A wide, sweeping driveway led up to white stucco with a profusion of flowers in the front yard. Phillip pulled up to the front door and parked. Alex jumped from the barely stopped vehicle and ran up the steps. The door opened and she was embraced by an older woman with gray dreadlocks and identical planes and angles to the younger woman she embraced. Phillip had met her mother earlier, but seeing Alex standing next to the tinier Liz Walton, he saw the resemblance clearly. The nose and the eyes must be her father's contribution, he decided, because the chin and the cheekbones were definitely from her mother.

Alex held her mother tightly, and Liz squeezed hard in return. "Oh, Mom. It's so good to be home."

CHAPTER FOUR

Raleigh, how could you do this to me?" Alex tugged on the midnight-blue satin, trying vainly to improve the drape. Unlike the horrid picture Raleigh mailed to her, the actual dress was much, much worse. The monstrosity cinched in like a medieval corset at the waist, or, at least, where the near-sighted dressmaker thought a woman's waist should be. Layers of scratchy tulle and poorly woven satin exploded at the skirt into a cowboy's fantasy. "The color makes me look sallow. And the neckline." Moving beyond the theory of high-necked, the hideous gown threatened to swallow her whole, with lace tickling her ears.

Trying not to grin, Raleigh rocked in the antique oak chair, updating her to-do list. She crossed off "select flower arrangement" and placed a star beside "pick up wedding broom." The latter item was Adam's responsibility, but she'd ask him about it at dinner. Without looking up, she countered, "The dress is perfect. It emphasizes your slender neck."

Pouting, Alex twisted in the full-length mirror to examine the side view. "Sure. I look like a blue giraffe."

"Well, we can remove the lace if you'd like."

"I look like Great Aunt Agnes on her way to chaperone a cotillion," Alex whined.

"You don't have a Great Aunt Agnes," Raleigh contradicted.

"Well, if I did, she'd wear this dress to your wedding." Alex looked down at the flounces that edged the skirt. Even with tailoring, the eyesore reminded her of something from a hackneyed musical.

"Adam's mother picked it out."

Immediately, Alex grimaced as guilt rose. "Oh. Carolyn chose this? I always thought she had such wonderful taste," she muttered. Defeated, Alex examined her reflection. "Alright, I suppose it's not that bad. It does frame my face. Yes, and tulle gives it that old-fashioned elegance."

Raleigh sniggered, and Alex turned from the mirror, eyes narrowed. "Raleigh? Mrs. Grayson didn't do this, did she?"

Unable to stop herself, Raleigh burst into giggles. "I wanted to see if you could do it. Wear something horrible just for me."

Looking around futilely for something to throw, Alex exclaimed, "You are so mean!" As a nearby pillow sailed past Raleigh's head, she reached behind her to unzip the offending garment. "Where on earth did you get this?"

"A.J. and Rachel found it at a garage sale," Raleigh explained.

"You shopped garage sales for your bridesmaids?" a horrified Alex asked.

"Breathe. The Graysons were donating items to a charity sale."

"So where is my maid of honor dress?" Alex demanded, as she wriggled out of the blue fabric.

Raleigh rose and opened the closet door. "Here you are," she said as she handed Alex a garment bag from a couturier Alex loved.

Trying not to salivate, Alex unzipped the bag with reverence. At the first glimpse of sage green, she grabbed Raleigh and spun her into an off-balanced jig. "How'd you know?"

Catching her breath, Raleigh sneered. "Maybe it was the forty-three emails or perhaps the sketch you sent."

"I'm nothing if not subtle."

While Alex shimmied into the dress, Raleigh glanced around the bedroom. It was quintessential Alex, with the wrought-iron bed and the delicate Queen Anne's desk.

"Oh, Raleigh, it's perfect!" Alex exhaled.

Raleigh turned back and had to agree. The narrow tube of material fell from slender straps anchored at the neck by a diamond brooch. The color added vibrancy to the wide eyes, texture to the bronzed flesh. Where Raleigh rounded at the hips, Alex's more compact body hinted at curves. A delicate slit in the side allowed the dress to tease and demur at the same time. Raleigh wasn't certain her best friend knew it, but the dress was consummate Alex. "You look fantastic," Raleigh sighed. "You'd better not upstage me at my own wedding," she added with a smile.

With reverence, Alex removed the dress and replaced it on the hanger. She glanced at the bedroom clock. "Uh-oh. If we don't leave soon, you'll miss your appointment with the wedding coordinator."

"Alex," Raleigh began, with a hint of desperation. "You're the maid of honor, can't you go?"

"After what you just did?" With a shake of her head, Alex gently patted her cheek. "Wish I could help. But I've still got jet lag." She yawned for effect. "But you enjoy it."

"Come on, you're the maid of honor. You could fill in for me and the dragon lady would be grateful for the reprieve. I don't think she likes me very much."

Alex pushed Raleigh toward the door. "Adam is meeting you there. We'll all catch up tomorrow."

"But she scares me. She carries a color palette with her everywhere. And she wants me to love pink. I can't love pink," Raleigh whimpered as she left the room.

"You're a strong woman, Raleigh. You'll survive." Alex gave her one final shove and closed the door smartly.

Dressed in her own clothes, she plopped onto her childhood bed, covered with handmade quilts. Home. Absurd as it seemed, she missed the familiarity of this space, even after ten years away. She'd built a life in Washington, one that she relished. Yet, it wasn't the same, she thought. In this space, she had been free to dream, to fantasize, to plan. Here, she had been able to indulge her every whim and call it experimentation, be it art or boys. She had only to ask her parents, and instantly, the lessons or the easel or the palette would appear. No trail of broken relationships or unfinished projects.

The evidence surrounded her, contradicting her recollection. On the wall above her bed, a signed Bearden, which inspired her short-lived collage phase. Shelves constructed haphazardly called to mind her wood-working stage. Even the quilts beneath her had been a chapter in her artistic wanderings.

Washington, too, was littered with discarded imaginings, failed romances, and unfinished projects.

The result, she knew, of childhood as well. She was aware that for all of her freedom, Alex had never really found direction.

Her parents had provided structure, in their own way, but neither quite understood their mercurial daughter.

Robert Walton always knew himself to be a painter, one whose oils and watercolors graced museums and galleries from New York to New Delhi. From childhood, he'd been focused and driven, achieving critical acclaim before he was thirty.

Liz was an artist in her own right. With charisma and cleverness, she'd built a place in politics that few women had ever dared imagine. From a stint on Capitol Hill during the Civil Rights era, she moved to Atlanta's City Hall. She led the City Council for years and would likely be mayor soon, when she decided to run. Brilliant and focused, she and Robert pursued vastly different careers, with the same discipline and drive.

Then there was Alex. To those who questioned her changeable nature, she had practiced retorts. She considered discipline a confinement. It was designed to drain the creative energy, to stunt the passions. Though, were she to be honest with herself, lately, she'd managed to do that quite well on her own, in love and in art.

Yes, she was stuck in a rut, she decided, but she had choices. What she needed now was focus. A project to hold her attention while she weaned herself off the notion of love.

Climbing off the bed, she began to pace. Quick energy shot

through her, as an idea caught hold. The new project needed to be time-consuming. She didn't want to do another show, since the painting or sculpting would leave her too much room to think and procrastinate. She wanted a project that would hold her attention and keep her occupied. If she found an audience for it was irrelevant. All that mattered to her was finding a focus.

She stopped in front of the mirror. Oh, be honest, Alex, she chided herself. *If you're going to soul search, be honest.* Whether it was one fan or a bevy of critics, she found an audience as essential as a subject. Art relied upon consumption to make it relevant. People didn't have to like it, but they needed to know it was there.

Now, what medium? Sculpture had its finer points, namely the chance to capture beauty in clay. Painting took more concentration and skill than she'd prefer to invest. The only talent she had that could survive her attention deficiencies and her peripatetic lifestyle was her writing.

She frowned, remembering the stack of unfinished novels and plays lining her desk at home. Maybe not even writing would work. Defeated, Alex sighed and sank into the rocking chair. If only she could find a subject that would challenge her, compel her to tell the story. What she needed was a muse. A topic that drew her, enthralled her.

Like Phillip Turman. The idea popped into her head and waited. A complex man, Alex thought, as she rocked back and forth. A hero. A man who didn't lose his temper easily, but when he did, the power was a velvet-gloved fist rather than a steel hammer. And just as devastating.

Her reaction to him seemed equally complex. As with her art, she knew she flitted from relationship to relationship. Yet, despite her penchant for falling in love, Alex didn't often experience the kind of instant attraction Phillip sparked. He tugged at her.

She obviously hadn't had the same effect on him, she thought ruefully. After those first torrid seconds, when he'd nearly consumed her on the concrete, Phillip had found it easy enough to break off their kiss, while she'd still been spellbound.

Let's not forget his flattering description, she reminded herself. "Shallow and addled" he'd called her without compunction.

That alone should keep her moratorium safe, Alex told herself, as she curled her legs up and wrapped her arms around her knees. She had her art.

And now she had her muse.

A knock at the door broke her reverie. She uncurled her legs and called out, "Come in."

"Finally made it home, huh?"

At the sound of the gruff voice, Alex bounded from the chair and leapt into her father's arms. "Dad! When did you get here?"

Hugging her tight, Robert answered, "My meeting with my agent ended early. I couldn't wait to see my girl." He stepped away from her, holding her hands in his. "Where are the rest of your clothes?"

Too used to him to respond, she pinched his cheek. It was still taut, not yet showing his age. At fifty-three, Robert Walton still possessed the striking male beauty that made him nearly as famous as his work. Steel gray threaded through black hair, lightening the temples and peppering the top. Alex knew her eyes had come from him, the wide shape, the thick lashes. He ran daily, in deference to his penchant for Krispy Kreme donuts. She'd missed him so much. "The show is on Thursday, Mom said."

"At the Alexander gallery."

"That's such a lovely space. Light and airy. You're showing watercolors, of course."

Robert tweaked his daughter's ponytail. "Of course. I thought we'd stop by tomorrow, after church."

"Sounds good." Alex leaned her head on her father's shoulder. "Oh, Dad, I've missed you."

"You don't come home enough. We see more of Raleigh than we do you."

"I've been busy. With the showing in Durban and the one in San Francisco before that," Alex explained.

"You know that every flight in America stops in Atlanta for at least an hour," Robert admonished. "Your mother misses you."

"Mom isn't the worrywart, Daddy. You are." She kissed his cheek. "Let's go find dinner."

Downstairs, her mother placated their housekeeper, Mrs. Downey. "The caterer will be here at two to check out our kitchen again. She wants to show her staff."

Mrs. Downey bristled. "My kitchen is impeccable. I don't know why they need to be here before the reception. I told that snotty young woman that we had everything she'd asked for." Her soft Southern drawl grew more pronounced. "I know what an industrial oven is, for goodness sake, and I told her we have one. Young whelp coming to check up on me. I'll be dead in my apron before she touches another tool in my kitchen. And you, letting her waltz in here like she owns the place."

With a look of apology, Liz took Mrs. Downey's arm and began to lead her to the kitchen, while the older woman's rant continued.

Alex turned to her father. "Sounds like the start of a tantrum. An eight on the Downey scale. I suppose this means we'll have to fend for ourselves."

"Actually, honey, your mom and I are going out. I'm kidnapping her tonight to help her wind down." He squeezed her to him apologetically. "She's trying to pass a referendum on homeless shelters. I thought you would want to hang out with your friends tonight, but, honey, you're welcome to join us."

Alex missed her family, but she'd seen the look of exasperation in her mother's eyes. Between Raleigh's wedding and her Council battle, she more than needed the respite. "I'll be fine." She kissed him again and headed into the living room. "I'll leave a message at Adam's for Raleigh."

Alex dialed the number and waited for a connection. "Grayson residence."

At Phillip's voice, Alex's heart tripped and her smile faded. "Phillip. I was looking for Adam."

"Alex." Phillip felt the surge of heat that was fast becoming a habit. "Adam's not here. They're meeting with the wedding coordinator."

"I know. I wanted to see what y'all were doing for dinner. My parents are abandoning me on my second night home."

"Adam's siblings are out for the night. Rachel has court in the morning, Jonah is on call, and A.J. has a crisis at the office. I think Raleigh and Adam are dining with the minister."

"Oh. Well, I guess I'll order in," Alex said.

Disappointment flared, stronger than she'd have expected. She wanted to see him, to watch those distant eyes warm with laughter. She wanted to ease the strain that etched his mouth, to tease the subtle curves into a smile. It was better for them both if she didn't.

Sitting in the Grayson living room, Phillip offered, "Why don't we have dinner out?" Where did that come from? He'd been planning a quiet evening, with a long conversation with Atlas about the man that tried to kill them yesterday.

Alex agreed eagerly. She hadn't forgotten her resolution, she assured herself. But if she went to dinner, she'd raise the question of writing about him. Dinner was a simple meal, one she could handle. And Phillip was only a man. She'd be fine. "I'll change clothes and be there in half an hour."

"Alright. I'll see you in thirty minutes." Phillip hung up the phone. He had thirty minutes to call Atlas and get a few answers. As he reached for the receiver, the phone rang.

"Grayson residence."

Laughing, Alex spoke quickly. "I lied. It will take me at least forty minutes. Make it forty-five and I'll be on time."

On the other end, Phillip grinned. "Sure. I'll see you when you get here." He replaced the receiver, and then reached up to rub his face. He was smiling, an unfamiliar action lately. Tension seemed to drain away in Alex's presence, even over a phone line. He wasn't sure he liked it. Tension was an essential ingredient to vigilance, and if his instincts were right, his past had followed him to Atlanta. Alex could prove to be a dangerous distraction, one he couldn't afford.

He dialed the numbers, in special sequence, and was finally connected. "Atlas. We have a problem."

———

The Thai restaurant Alex chose was hushed and friendly, with mellow jazz playing through hidden speakers. Phillip watched her as she flirted with the teenaged waiter, almost causing him to drop their drinks into her lap. When she helped him steady the tray with a hand under his undoubtedly sweaty one, the boy nearly swallowed his tongue. And he wasn't her first casualty of the night.

She'd greeted the maitre d' with a charm that made the man flush and stammer.

At first glance, an observer would assume the reaction was to her appearance. She'd traded the cut-offs and tank top for a purple swathe of material that masqueraded as a dress. On a hanger, he supposed, it probably looked demure. No daring dips or scandalous slits. Instead, it flowed easily over her rangy body, promising more with discretion than revelation. She was sex poured into silk and no man could not want. Unable to help himself, Phillip watched Alex. In the candlelight, the sharp cheekbones and gorgeous eyes demanded attention. She probably knew how stunning she was, but it didn't matter. How had she put it? Yes, he hummed with desire for her, despite himself. Perhaps it was the fragrance of tropical flowers and rainwater that teased him when he helped her from the car. Or the dark eyes, so innocent and earthy, a heady combination. The spy in him yearned to unravel the mystery, the conflict of confidence and insecurity, of talent and caprice.

When her mouth curved into a slick red tease of lips, he wondered hotly what she'd do if he slid closer in the secluded booth, sheltered from prying eyes, and covered her mouth with his.

Which he had no intention of doing, he warned himself.

His brief conference with Atlas raised significant questions about the wisdom of his presence in Atlanta and anywhere near a civilian. If he had any sense at all, he'd have canceled dinner and holed up in the Grayson residence until Adam and Raleigh returned.

But it wasn't simply the alluring dress or goddess face. There was something about her that made him exchange his jeans for khakis and a tie, even after Atlas's warning. Maybe it was the way she tilted her head when she spoke or her unaffected conversation with flashes of sharp, dry wit. On the drive, she'd regaled him with stories of growing up in a home with parents who encouraged her mind to wander.

How, during a rainy afternoon, she had painted a mural in the foyer because it had the best light. She spoke as freely about her calamities as she did her triumphs. He didn't know what it was about her, but whatever it was, he was compelled to learn more.

"How did you and Raleigh meet?" Phillip took a sip of wine and studied her over his glass.

"Raleigh's boss is my godfather. He suggested we become roommates when I moved to DC. We clicked."

"Raleigh's boss?" Had Raleigh told Alex about the ISA?

"Yes, James Russell. She's a chemist in a government lab he heads up. That's how she met Adam, you know. GCI did a joint project with the government, and Raleigh and Adam fell in love."

Good, Phillip thought. She'd recited the cover story Adam had given him. "What brought you to Washington? I'd think an artist would head to New York or San Francisco."

"Oh, it seemed like a good idea at the time." Alex lifted her menu until it all but covered her face. Phillip reached over and pushed it back down. He knew her by now. "What was his name?"

Alex took a sip of her drink before she confessed. "Milton Donald. He was a political activist. Wanted to save the world, one union at a time. I was at Spelman, and we met in a political science class. He was handsome, in a scruffy, antisocial way. We talked about truth and justice and overthrowing the establishment. Of course, it bothered him a bit that my mother was the establishment, but we worked through that."

"What happened?"

"He got into Georgetown for law school and I got into their arts program. By the end of the first semester, I decided that my bourgeoisie upbringing disturbed him too much. We could be friends, but he needed a partner in the struggle."

Phillip's eyes dripped with amusement. "How noble."

"Absolutely. And I was right. Two weeks later, he met a political refugee from Eritrea, and they lived happily ever after. I even made them a ceremonial bowl for the wedding."

"You went to his wedding?" Phillip asked incredulously. "After you dumped him?"

"Had to. I introduced them. I was a bridesmaid." Alex arched a brow. "And I have never dumped a man. Men have been exasperated, irritated, and rendered romantically impotent toward me, but they have never been dumped."

Phillip chuckled and poured more wine for them both. The waiter came to the table and took their order. When Alex's latest conquest left the table, Phillip asked, "So, you're in DC. What did you do next?"

"Got my Master of Fine Arts. For a while, I thought I'd become a glassmaker. Glassblowing is fantastic, really, very sensual. You collect molten glass, called a gather, at the end of a blowpipe. You brace it, then shape your lips around this instrument. Because the gather is so hot, your only connection to the art is your mouth. For hours, you work, shaping the thickness and form of the glass by marvering it. You can flash it for color or use a mold for a particular shape." While she spoke, Alex dipped a finger in her glass. She circled the rim, then lifted her finger to her mouth.

As she licked the last of the wine away, Phillip felt his blood pressure spike. He remembered dimly what else that agile tongue could do. Their embrace at the airport came back in a heated rush, and he shifted uncomfortably as his body recalled it too. Alex lifted her glass to study its form. The flute had a long, slender stem. She gently caressed the glass. "My favorite part was necking."

Phillip only stared. "Necking?" Unbidden, he could clearly imagine the two of them in the back seat of the toy car she drove. The little MG would barely accommodate much, but certainly a little necking would be possible.

Seemingly unaware of the direction of his thoughts or her double entendre, she explained. "It's the process they use to create the stem of a glass or the neck of a vase. Using tongs called pucellas to determine the form."

How could she make the creation of glass erotic? His system flooded with an unfamiliar sensation. Desire mixed potently with something softer, something more dangerous.

"Phillip? Are you okay? You look peaked." Alex scooted over toward him. She braced one hand on his thigh as she leaned forward to lay a palm on his forehead.

Beneath her hand, corded muscles shifted and tensed. "I'm fine," he said hoarsely. Then, on impulse, he slid closer, closing the distance between them. Phillip took her chin in his hand and toyed with her lower lip. Her breath escaped on a note of surprise. "You are fascinating, Alex Walton."

With effort, Alex found her voice. "You've said that before. I think it was right before you called me an idiot."

Phillip moved his thumb up to sweep her cheekbone, then slid his hand into the midnight fall of hair. "I apologized for that." He angled her head, trailing his fingers down her slim neck. At its base, her pulse beat madly.

Alex closed her hand around his wrist. "Phillip. Don't do this."

Phillip lifted his other hand to cup her face. "For the life of me, I can't remember why I shouldn't." He lowered his mouth to hers, the pressure of lip to lip light and easy. "Remind me."

Helpless to recall her excellent rationale, Alex increased the pressure. "I'm sure I have a reason," she murmured.

"I'm certain you do," Phillip agreed, feathering his lips across her mouth. She tasted faintly of wine, rich and potent. Her scent rose between them, and his eyes slid shut.

Tenderly, he parted her mouth, invading her by strategic forays. First, his tongue traced the seam of her lips, where they trembled in anticipation. Next, he tested the corners of her mouth. When she moaned, almost inaudibly, he slipped inside. Too aware of their surroundings, he maintained a tight grip on his control. One small taste, he thought, then he'd let her go. But one became two, then the kisses blurred into an endless stream.

Alex pressed a hand against his chest, to stop herself, as much as him. "No. I can't," she whispered.

Instantly, Phillip released her. He cursed himself silently for holding her in the first place. To give them both space, he moved back across the bench. Alex simply watched him.

"I'm sorry," he began in a subdued voice.

"Don't apologize again, Phillip. If you do, I'll strangle you."

Alex shook her head. "I like you. And I'm attracted to you. Maybe too much."

Her honesty forced him to ask the next question. "Then why did you stop me?"

"Because I want you. I don't know why this has happened so quickly, but it has."

"I don't see the problem."

"We're going to be friends, Phillip. With Raleigh as my best friend and Adam as yours, we're bound to see each other often. Now that you've returned to DC, it's even more likely. You wouldn't be an easy man to turn away from, but I'd do it. I always do it. And then there'd be this tension at their anniversary parties or, heaven forbid, the first christening."

"Alex—" he interrupted. "Don't be ridiculous."

"I may joke about it, Phillip, but I'm serious. No more men for me. Not for a while. I can't do it again."

"Do what?"

"Not fall in love."

Phillip started to reply when the waiter arrived with their food. Alex lifted her chopsticks and said, "Don't worry, Phillip. I make an excellent friend."

"You probably do."

Hurt at his simple acceptance of her edict pinched her heart, but she'd be grateful for it later. A man like Phillip didn't leave when dismissed, and she'd by no means ask him to stay. Pasting on a cajoling smile, she said, "In the spirit of our newfound friendship, I have a favor to ask."

"Yes?"

Alex saw the aloofness, heard the detachment. She'd not known how much she'd miss the warmth. "I want you to let me write about you," she declared. When Phillip opened his mouth to respond, she rushed on. "It wouldn't be a biography. More like a novel inspired by actual events. I'd want to interview you, find out about how you became a congressman so early. About your mission."

"My mission?"

"The fact-finding junket that led to your capture by the terrorist group."

"Alex, I don't talk about that. To anyone."

"I'm not anyone. I'm your friend. We just decided that, didn't we?"

"Alex—"

"I'd fictionalize everything. Phillip, I need a muse. Since I've abandoned my hobby of not falling in love, I need something to occupy my mind. Don't you consider it serendipitous that despite living in the same city for nearly a decade, we happen to meet at the wedding of our mutual best friends in a different city? Obviously, the fates or gods are trying to tell us something. Your story should be told and I'm the one to tell it. Without a single reference to Phillip Turman, the man." She finally stopped talking and smiled up at him. "So, what do you say?"

"Absolutely not."

———

Hours later, Phillip met with Adam and Raleigh in the Graysons' living room, to tell them about the car in the parking lot and his conversation with Atlas.

"You're certain it wasn't an accident?"

"I saw his face. And Atlas is concerned too. They have a man in the prison with Zeben, Jack Minnear. He said that three days before his prison break, Zeben was ranting about the kingdom of Jafir. The royal family has been dead for almost twenty-five years." Phillip stood by the fireplace and fiddled with the candelabra on the mantle.

Adam and Raleigh sat on the sofa, grim and uneasy. "He also mentioned Jubalani."

Raleigh spoke again. "Jubalani. Has he been sighted?"

Phillip shrugged. "No one knows. The only description we have is that he's young, attractive, and charismatic."

Adam joined the conversation. "Phillip, if Zeben is free, he's definitely coming after you."

"I thought I could escape," he replied softly.

"We never escape, Phillip," Adam commented as he rose from his seat to stand next to his old friend. "We change names and addresses and identities, but we don't escape." He paused beside Phillip but turned to look at Raleigh.

Love pulsed through him, catching him unawares, as it always did. His escape nearly cost him the love of his life. Only returning had saved him, and he spent every day thankful for it.

"Zeben blames you for his defeat. The African-Arab Alliance is strong and Israel has agreed to talks. You helped to destroy his empire. He won't forget that easily."

"I won't forget it either. I don't regret betraying him. What I do regret is that he lived to tell about it." His voice was brisk and determined. Phillip clasped Adam's shoulder and shifted to make eye contact with Raleigh. "Atlas's information confirms that I'm the target, not the two of you. I'm heading back to DC in the morning. It's the only way to protect everyone."

"Phillip, no." Raleigh crossed over to the two men.

Without thinking, her fingers twined with Adam's. She rested her free hand on Phillip's arm. The tight circle they formed spoke volumes. Here were the men who helped bring her peace, after her mentor betrayed her. "There wouldn't be a wedding without you."

Adam added, "You're my best man. I'm not doing this without you."

"As long as I'm here, you're in danger," Phillip argued.

"We can take care of ourselves. I can put a plastique bomb in the bridal bouquet just in case." Raleigh squeezed his arm. "We need you here. If Zeben is after you, you need our help too."

Phillip felt himself weaken, and he thought of Alex.

He didn't repeat Atlas's request that he protect her. Raleigh had enough to worry about without fretting over an invisible danger to her maid of honor. "I don't want to put you or your guests in danger. Dammit, Alex could have been hurt. I wasn't paying attention."

"So you'll be more alert," Adam responded.

"Alex can be distracting." At dinner, after their impromptu kiss, Phillip found himself forgetting to worry about Atlas's report. Candlelight and conversation. For the first time in years, Phillip had felt relaxed and at ease. After refusing her request for an interview, they'd enjoyed a wonderful evening. They debated politics and art, sports and music. He'd only known her for a few days, and already, she'd broken through barriers few others had.

Acquaintances described Phillip as affable and quiet, with a dry wit. Opponents called him honest and dogged, possessing an incisive humor that disarmed. With Alex, he'd found himself compelled to charm, to tease out the sultry laugh.

And with her, he forgot how treacherous her kind of woman could be. Lorei had taught him a fine lesson, one he'd do well not to forget. With irritation, he scowled. "She's disturbing."

Raleigh exchanged a knowing glance with Adam. "Alex is unique. And curious. If you leave now, she'll keep asking questions."

"I'll tell her I have an emergency assignment."

Raleigh shook her head. "She might ask the wrong questions, to the wrong people. Zeben doesn't know that you know it was a murder attempt."

"A car tried to run me down. What else would I think?"

Raleigh moved away to pace. "That a bad driver nearly hit you. Phillip, think. If Zeben wants you dead, why not shoot you? A hit-and-run is a bit sloppy."

"Zeben's style is more direct," Adam agreed. "Something else is going on here. We need to find out what he's planning. Atlas can use Minnear to spread a rumor. The ISA tried to warn you of Zeben's plans, but you didn't believe them. You refused their protection."

Phillip clenched his fists in frustration. "I'm not putting your lives at risk to save my neck."

"This is what we do. Phillip, look at me," Raleigh commanded quietly and waited until Phillip's eyes met hers. "Adam left the business, but I haven't. So, I'll do my job. I'll check in with Atlas tomorrow and get more information. We'll rendezvous at the Walton's tomorrow for church." She moved to the sofa and picked up her purse.

Adam walked over to her and spun her into his arms. "I love it when you talk spy," he murmured as he captured her mouth in a devastating kiss. Raleigh's arms encircled his neck, and she pressed herself against him.

"Ahem." Phillip cleared his throat loudly, his lips curved. "Save it for the honeymoon."

Setting Raleigh on her feet, Adam left an arm around her. "I'll run Raleigh to the house. You try to get some rest. Sphinx, we're a team. Chimera and Merlin won't let you down."

Adam grabbed his keys and led Raleigh to the door.

Phillip watched and envied. He'd once thought he'd found a love like theirs. For him, it had been Lorei. Beautiful, wealthy, and enchanting. Like Alex, she'd played at careers, all the while waiting for him to take a corporate law job to keep them in the style to which she was accustomed. Despite agreeing to an engagement, Lorei put him off again and again. In the first year, it was that his Justice Department salary wouldn't support the two of them. When the congressional seat opened, she wanted to wait until after the election. Finally, when she realized he had no plans of achieving the level of wealth that Adam and her father had, she'd dumped him.

Her desertion left him free to do more for the ISA, to move deeper and deeper into the organization. To lick his wounds, he'd agreed to help Adam with Scimitar and with Praxis. The decision that cost him his freedom.

Now, he had his freedom, but he'd lost his life. For the first time in years, he didn't know who he was or what he wanted. Part of him yearned for the adventure of life as a secret agent. Part of him wished for another shot at politics. A more secret part of him craved the simple honesty of a love like the one Raleigh and Adam shared.

An image of Alex took shape, and he tried vainly to clear it. Regardless of what life he eventually chose, for now he was Sphinx. Alex was a complication and, if connected to him, a target for a ruthless maniac.

Suddenly, a thought occurred to him. The driver of the car had seen her, could identify her. Even now, Alex could be in danger.

Phillip pounded a fist into the mantle. They never considered that Alex could become a pawn. He had no choice. He would stay for the wedding and protect her.

Once they returned to DC, he'd remain with her until the threat was over. He walked to the sofa and slowly lowered himself onto the cushions. In order to shadow Alex for the next few weeks, he'd require a solid cover. Phillip Turman was about to become Alex Walton's muse.

CHAPTER FIVE

Days later, Alex's new plan to change her life was precisely on schedule. As she pulled her hair into a simple twist, she smiled at her reflection. Phillip had capitulated and agreed to a series of interviews about his life as a politician and a political prisoner. To her lesser satisfaction, she'd nearly convinced herself that the way her stomach wobbled whenever they spoke was probably a nasty bug she'd picked up in Durban.

Better she identified the tugs and pulls as a virus rather than attraction, than admit the truth. Phillip worried her. Well, she thought, to be precise, her attraction to him petrified her. He wasn't a man to be transformed into a buddy when love settled comfortably into affection. His calm demeanor masked complicated passions she wasn't positive she could control. He hadn't survived Jafir or, for that matter, Washington, she thought frankly, with that air of unflappability.

She didn't know why, but instinctively she realized he was dangerous. Dangerous to her peace of mind and her body. Dangerous to her heart. At the mere thought of him, the steady pulse trebled, threatening to leap from her skin. In her mind's eye, she saw his dark pirate looks, lean and sharp, with the mouth of a dreamer. Penetrating brown eyes and a sexy mustache to feather against willing lips. Then there was the body. Beneath his clothes, the hard body belonged to a street fighter, not an overindulged politician. Where there should be paunch, Phillip was spare, trim.

More treacherous was his manner, Alex decided with suspicion. Unlike many of his ilk, he kept his own counsel, which completely threw her off. Having grown up with her mom and assorted cronies, Alex had an antenna for the type. Brash, good-looking, without two thoughts to rub together. Usually, she knew, Phillip's type talked early and often, rarely pausing to pay attention. Yet, from the minute he picked her up at the airport, Phillip had done little but listen.

What frightened and intrigued her most, though, was his control. A car nearly kills them both, and he doesn't yell. Although he was rather mean, Alex reminded herself. He called her names. Shaking the memory off before she began to pout, it occurred to her that the two times she'd seen the iron discipline fail, she'd been in his arms. The searing kiss in the parking deck and the impromptu embrace at the restaurant. Both times, she sensed that he was struggling against wanting her as much as she was trying to resist him. The difference, she realized with a start, lay in what each was resisting. In the end, Alex pulled away from Phillip. Phillip, on the other hand, seemed to be fighting himself. Broodingly, Alex tucked this last bit of information away.

She heard the chime of the doorbell downstairs. Her parents

had gone out for morning meetings, and Phillip had agreed to join her for breakfast. Since his surrender to her begging, she'd mapped out her strategy between visiting old friends and cataloguing wedding presents. For their morning session, he'd agreed to tell her about his campaign for Congress.

She would focus on the topic of elections this morning, to ease them both into the graver subjects after he'd grown comfortable with her. Today, she'd ask him for more than the logistics of a campaign. Those she knew by heart. She wanted to know about the feelings. Emotions were the soul of art. To mine a good story from Phillip meant plumbing the depths of his emotional well. She only hoped she didn't drown.

Later, after they'd eaten the omelet Mrs. Downey prepared before heading to her yoga class, Alex explained her goal to him.

Phillip snorted. "I don't have an emotional well, Alex." He drank coffee at the marble island in the center of the Waltons' kitchen. Alex perched on the stool next to his. "I don't have depths to be plumbed. What you see is what you get."

"What I see is a smart, quiet man who spends more time observing than speaking. Anger is ruthlessly controlled, channeled. And I am intimately aware of the fact that you're domineering. I also know that you have a sense of humor." Smugly, she picked up her tea to take a sip.

"How do you know that?" Phillip watched her over the rim of the coffee cup, the cool voice revealing nothing.

He had the most incredible eyes, Alex noticed for the millionth time. A pure, luminous brown, they seemed to absorb everything and say nothing. Much like the man himself. But he had just asked her a question. What was it? Oh, how she knew he was funny.

"Adam showed me your caricature of him. An intellectual dollar bill. Cute." Alex took another sip from her tea. "I never mastered the art of cartooning. All my characters look like Charlie Brown. Even the animals. I'd love to see more of your work."

"I don't draw much anymore." There had been little to make light of during the last three years.

Though he didn't say the words, Alex understood instantly what he was thinking. On impulse, she reached out to cover his hand with her own. The warmth of his skin against her own felt familiar and real. Too real.

Pretending a nonchalance she didn't feel, she drew her hand away. "Do you miss it?"

"Drawing? Not really. It helped to pass the time in school, made me popular. A good cartoon of the principal is an invaluable tool against bullies."

"I can't imagine you being bullied."

"My growth spurt hit late. For a ghastly stretch of my youth, I was short, gangly, and wore braces."

"You certainly made up for lost time, then. Girls must have loved to sit for you," Alex teased. "What a chore."

"I took my art seriously," he deadpanned. "No sacrifice too great. No woman too beautiful."

"I'm sure." She scanned her list of questions. "You grew up in Baltimore, right?"

"In the shadow of Camden Yards. We could hear the crowds on Game Day. Kids and their dads, cheering and booing. Great big yells when a player knocked one over the fence. Death threats to Mets fans."

"Did you want to play baseball?" Alex twisted on her stool to lean against the island, her knees bumping Phillip's. She'd never gotten this much out of him before.

"I was more interested in becoming manager than third baseman. Frank Robinson was my hero, and when he came back to the Orioles in 1989, I nearly dropped out of law school to beg for a job. I'd have been happy to be the bat boy."

Laughing, Alex considered him. "I bet your parents are happy you decided otherwise."

"It's just me and my dad. Mom died of cancer when I was a baby. Dad raised me by himself." It was a debt he could never repay. Life in Baltimore on a janitor's salary taught Phillip resourcefulness. Some might say he'd learned the lesson too well. For the ISA, theft was his stock in trade. Of course, he mused, his dad had also trained him to use his talents. A skill with untraceable wire transfers and illusory accounts had served him in good stead. Phillip corrected himself. Despite the little his father knew of Phillip's life, he knew his dad was proud.

"What are you thinking about?"

"My dad," he answered without thinking. "He made the best of our situation. We always had what we needed."

Pleased by the unexpected opening, Alex probed further. "What did you need?"

"Stability. Faith. A ten-speed."

"A ten-speed?"

Phillip propped an elbow on the counter and rested his chin on his fisted hand. "Yeah. When I was eleven, I desperately wanted a new bike. A ten-speed Schwinn in black and gold. My middle school nemesis, Emmanuel Langford, had one. He would whiz past me on the way to school every morning, smirking. I had to have that bike."

"I take it your father didn't agree."

"Since I'd gotten a BMX for my birthday the year before, Dad didn't see the sense in buying a new bike." Phillip could hear himself pleading for the new wheels, convinced his life would end if he didn't get it. "Dad told me I could have the bike if I bought it myself."

"Ouch."

"Exactly. I got an allowance, but it was a pittance. I'd been saving up for—Well, what I was saving up for isn't important."

Alex playfully tapped his knee. "Come on, what was it? What were you saving for?"

"Mind you, it was 1977 and I coveted what every American boy did."

"A Millennium Falcon."

Surprised, Phillip nodded. "Absolutely. You like Star Wars?"

"I was too young for the premiere, but I did see *Return of the Jedi* six times. Technically, I think I stalked Billy Dee Williams. My mother eventually pointed out the fine line between fan mail and obsession."

Disconcerted, Phillip couldn't restrain his laughter. "You're crazy, Walton."

"Enthusiastic," she asserted. "When he finally wrote me, I cried. Of course, I cried harder when Kristen Indermark got a letter too. The exact same one. I was crushed. Two timed by Billy Dee, after my faithful devotion. But I digress. Or I digress you. Although I don't think that's grammatically correct either."

By now, Phillip recognized the beginning of a verbal avalanche. He took Alex's hand and kissed her palm. "Crazy."

Without noticing, she linked her fingers with his where they rested on his thigh. "The ten-speed," she prompted.

"Ah, yes. To make a long story short, Dad's edict gave me a choice between a Millennium Falcon or a bike. The Falcon was cheaper, of course, but incomplete without the entire action figure collection. If I bought those instead of the bike, the bike would take me twice as long."

"I hear a con coming on," Alex guessed.

Lost in reverie, Phillip toyed with her captive hand, lacing and unlacing the slender fingers with his. "I convinced Emmanuel to trade me his bike for mine twice a week."

Alex could hear the male pride swell in his voice. "In exchange for?"

"Weekend custody of the Falcon and her crew on alternate Saturdays, holidays excluded."

Approving of the deal, Alex beamed up at him. "And your father said?"

"He asked to see if I had the contract in writing."

"Which you did, of course."

"Of course. I never trusted Emmanuel Langford. The contract included a penalty clause for a delay in returning the Falcon or for irreparable damage to the figures."

Alex focused with effort, trying to ignore the slide of skin as he meshed their hands. "Financial?"

Phillip noted with interest that the question emerged with husky undertones. "Yes, financial. I let him pay on credit, which eventually resulted in him forfeiting his bike to me. I loaned it back to him, with a reasonable return."

Despite his relaxed story, Phillip wasn't unmoved by the feel of their skin intertwined. The soft elegant hand caught in his bore calluses along the pads and at the base where joints met palm. Years of manipulating clay, hammer and chisel, paintbrush, had taken their tool. The result was astonishingly erotic.

"I've never been so turned on by a hand before," he announced thoughtfully. He lifted it to his lips and began to nibble on her fingertips.

Alex remained motionless for an instant, shocked and delighted by the warm, wet slide of his mouth over her flesh. "Phillip," she whispered warningly.

"Mmm-hmm?" Phillip mumbled absently, tracing the webbing of her hand with his agile tongue.

Struggling to recall her vanished thought, Alex tugged at her hand. At once, Phillip let it drop. Pleased and vexed by his abrupt surrender, Alex opened her mouth to speak. When Phillip repeated his actions on her other hand, she lingered in silence for precious seconds. She'd protest soon, she thought hazily.

Finally, she managed an unimpressive, "Phillip, you shouldn't do this."

Phillip took no note of her faint protest, intent on sampling each available inch of skin. Nimbly, he stroked a thin, moist line across her palm and along a tracery of vein running up to her elbow.

Alex swallowed with difficulty but didn't protest.

One more second, she thought rashly, and I'll remember all the reasons why this should stop.

Completely occupied with his task, Phillip dotted openmouthed kisses up her bare forearm and past her elbow, halting only when he met the barrier of her sleeve.

Undeterred, he nudged the fabric higher. "You taste like

spring. Like your scent. Flowers and rainwater. Cool and exhilarating. In my dreams, I can smell you, taste you."

With great effort, Alex tried to recall their conversation before his sensual assault on her hand. Frantic to pick up the thread, she breathlessly yelped, "Your dad!"

"My dad?" Phillip glanced up. "What about my father?"

Quickly, Alex tugged her arm away and linked her fingers together behind her back. Leveling her breathing, she asked with a tenuous measure of calm, "What did your dad say about your arrangement with Emmanuel?" Since she refused to make eye contact, in case he entranced her again, Alex focused her gaze on a point beyond his shoulder.

Irritation warred with amusement at her discomfort. "Dad applauded me on my ingenuity and double-checked my interest rate. I pegged it at two points over prime, well within acceptable standards."

"So you were bright and practical. Very inventive for an eleven-year-old. I bet you'd been helping to run the household for years by then." Caught up by her musings, she continued. "The sharing of responsibility between you and your dad would have been comfortable. Enough to give you ownership, but not so much that it became a burden.

"You'd be in charge of dinner once a week, probably kitchen duty every other night. He would have to work nights on occasion, but he wasn't afraid to leave you alone when you were older. Silence and solitude were natural companions, and you enjoyed the time to think. Love for your father is palpable, and so is your pride. You respect the men he made of himself and you. Probably talk to him once a week." She fixed him with a sly, self-congratulatory look. "How'd I do?"

Amazed by her quick, accurate reading of him and his father, Phillip locked eyes with her. Her perception was unnerving, and not completely welcome. He said quietly, "You see too much." Unable to resist, he stroked a slightly roughened finger down her cheek. "Beneath that chatter, you're not at all what you appear." He tucked a stray hair behind her ear. "Not at all."

Alex worked hard not to shift beneath his touch, uncertain whether she'd move toward him or away. "I'm exactly what I seem. A dilettante in search of direction. You're to be my grand experiment."

Phillip felt an unexpected anger rise at her self-deprecation. His hand dropped to her neck to tilt her face up to his. "You know you're not a dilettante."

"I'm a textbook case. I flit from project to project, from man to man. What is it they say, a jack of all trades, master of none? That's me," she finished with feigned insouciance.

"Shut up, Alex," he snapped. "Adam's father owns a painting that hangs in his study. Two children panhandling on the street corner. There's such fury at the passersby, made all the more real by the artist's admiration for the children. Only a woman of substance could have seen their bravery. You."

"I painted what I saw," she demurred.

"Like I said. You see too much." The hand cupping her neck sank into the thick, soft hair at her nape, pulling the loose twist free. Hair tumbled around her shoulders, framing the exotic face. His eyes darkened with desire as he looked down at her. "Against my better judgment, I want to see more."

Phillip watched her intently as Alex's eyes fluttered close, then reopened. "We talked about this. I'm not interested."

"Yes, you are," Phillip contradicted simply. "Moratorium or not, you are very interested."

"I said I'm not," Alex argued frostily. "I may be shallow and addled, but I do know my own mind."

Smiling now, Phillip set his coffee cup down and leaned closer. "I never doubted that you did. I won't underestimate you, Alex."

Alex raised a brow. "I don't underestimate myself. I'm good and I know it."

"You don't lack confidence, I'll give you that. However, confidence doesn't mean you appreciate your full potential." Suddenly serious, he stood and loomed over her. "I'm sure you know you're beautiful, but I doubt you know why. This habit you have of changing subjects and projects and forms proves me right."

Against her will, she asked, "Proves what?"

"Art takes skill and insight. I think you flit from medium to medium at that moment when you might see something important. I'd guess the same about the men you cast off. At the moment when you might learn more about yourself, about life, you turn tail and run. Of course, you part as friends, because anything less would have meaning."

Pushing his hand aside, Alex retorted, "What rubbish!" She slid from the stool and snatched up their empty coffee cups. As she stalked over to the sink, she told him, "An interesting theory, but pure garbage. I paint and sculpt and try different forms because I can." She spun around, eyes flashing, her hair cascading down her back. "I start and end relationships because I can. Fear has nothing to do with it. It's a matter of choice, and I choose not to have one with you."

"I don't recall asking," Phillip returned mildly, reclining against the island. Alex thoroughly angered was a glorious sight. Even the outfit was appropriate. The crimson top and black skirt were both dramatic. The top ended abruptly above the skirt, which itself had no communication with her knees. Both were made of a silky fabric that clung to every curve, dipped at every valley, shimmered in the light. His fingers itched to trace those sinuous lines. Deliberately, suddenly, he moved to crowd her against the sink. "You'll know when I do."

"I won't hold my breath. Move," Alex demanded, pushing at his chest.

Lifting a hand to the tousled waves, he gathered the heavy mass of midnight. Phillip leaned in and pressed a light kiss to her mutinous mouth. He only wanted to taste, to see if the anger darkened the sweet, enhanced the spicy. "Open your mouth, Alex."

"No," she muttered between tightly closed lips.

"Please," he whispered softly. "I have to know why."

Baffled, her eyes met his. "Why what?"

"Why I want you so badly. Why I can't stay away." He nipped softly at her bottom lip. "Please," he repeated.

Alex felt the ridges of muscle beneath her hand. Her skin heated from the warmth of his mouth just above her own. Logic told her to push him away. Common sense reminded her of her resolve. Desire overrode them both, and her hand slid up to the nape of his neck. In a few seconds, she decided vaguely. She'd be angry again shortly. "Since you ask so nicely."

Without waiting for her to change her mind, his tongue slipped between her lips, expertly finding and teasing her own into an erotic dance. Quickly, irrevocably, he spun them into a maelstrom of sensation, one shot through with deeper, unmentionable needs. Spring surrounded him, engulfed him. Clean, sweet, ripe. Flavors exploded on his tongue and he dove deeper to sample more.

Her mouth moved eagerly beneath his, meeting him step for step. He tasted faintly of coffee, completely of male. Drowning, she strained to remember her decision. Instead, a single word pounded in her head, throbbed through her body. More. More. More. Never had a man pulled at her like this. Calling to her, commanding her. Dangerous emotions beckoned to her. To ignore them and their meaning, she surrendered to his kiss.

Hard arms pulled her away from the sink and banded her to him, tipping her hips into his. The point of contact tore a groan of pleasure from him, echoed by her soft moan. Of their own volition, her hands explored the breadth of his back, the width of his shoulders. Flesh sought flesh, as she tugged his shirt from the waistband of his slacks.

She slanted her mouth against his, stealing kisses. Scattered kisses, sharp kisses, greedy kisses. It didn't matter, as long as there were more.

Hungrily, Phillip used his tongue, his lips, his teeth to ravage every part of her mouth, dragging startled moans from her. Licks of fire streaked down her neck, to torment and soothe. Needing to feel her, to hold her, he found the exposed skin at her waist and eased her onto the edge of the counter. Lost in the storm, she pulled him to her, settling her legs around him. At every point of contact, heat flared and flamed.

Desire raged through him and in answer, Phillip reached between them to cup her breasts. Through the dark red fabric, he could easily discern that she was bare beneath its thin covering.

By touch, by sight, he knew the perfectly rounded globes required no additional support.

Through the cloth, she burned him, drew him closer. Molding and plucking, he tormented them both, refusing to push the barrier aside. He angled her body and closed his teeth around the captured flesh. With his free hand, he plucked at her other breast, and then kneaded the taut peak.

Alex gasped, a strangled sound of pleasure. Her head fell back, exposing fresh skin for his ministrations.

Blindly, she unfastened the buttons of his shirt, craving the feel of him under her hands. The palms he'd feasted on earlier swept over dark, defined muscles. Tiny calluses feathered across flat male nipples, urging them to life.

Ravenous, she pressed her open mouth to the uniquely male flesh. When Phillip dragged her impossibly closer, she smiled in triumph. The wild hunger consumed them both, would take them both.

"Come upstairs with me, Alex." Phillip fused her mouth to his, as he gave into temptation and slipped his hands beneath the crimson top. Her nipples budded against his palms and low sounds of longing erupted from his chest. "I want you. Now."

Alex froze, abruptly realizing where she was. In her parents' kitchen, making love on the counter. Mortified, she wriggled back along the tile, stopping only when her head bumped the cabinets. "Phillip, no." With shaking hands, she tried to push him away and scramble off the counter.

Phillip stopped her escape with an arm around her waist. "Why not?" he demanded, nipping at her throat. "You want me. You want this."

Her head fell back, in desire, in despair. "I told you, I can't," she breathed. Breath shuddering in her lungs, Alex pushed him again, and this time he stepped away. "I can't."

"You won't," he corrected, his breathing still harsh. His shirt hung open, the tails freed from his waistband by her hands. Alex awkwardly tugged her clothes into place, but Phillip ignored his own dishabille. "You want me," he stated imperiously.

Refusing to meet his gaze, Alex muttered, "How I feel is beside the point."

"It's exactly the point. You want me and I want you. We're adults, Alex."

Sliding off the counter, Alex moved past him and behind the protection of the island. She wanted desperately to run upstairs and hide. More, she wanted to leap into his arms and finish what they'd begun. With effort, she controlled the shivers skating along every inch of skin he'd touched. As much to herself as to Phillip, she explained, "I won't do this again. I'm no good at relationships, Phillip. Nothing good can come of it. My priority right now is my project."

"I'm your project," Phillip reminded her curtly. "Remember?"

"Your story is. Not you." Holding her hands up in a plea, she said, "Phillip, please stay away from me. I'm begging you. Please."

"Not unless you can give me a better reason. This femme fatale argument isn't very convincing."

Angrily, Alex retorted, "I have no obligation to explain anything to you."

"You will if you want me to back off. Every time, Alex, you've been with me. Until you pull away. Tell me why." Phillip advanced, and Alex automatically retreated.

Hastily, Alex decided that bitter honesty would be her best weapon. "I forget to be alone when I'm with you. I need to focus on deciding what I want, and I can't do that if I start falling for you. I have to find something to hold on to. It can't be you."

Within Phillip, fury battled with compassion. The seductive siren who had him hot and ready only moments ago had been transformed into a frightened young woman. He'd seen a glimpse of this creature at the airport, a woman riddled with self-doubt. He wanted to cross to her and take her in his arms, to soothe away the worry. Knowing that if he did, he'd probably wind up kissing her, Phillip remained on his side of the kitchen. Alex thought she needed space.

Phillip knew he needed time to find out if she was in jeopardy because of him. When he'd reported in on Sunday, Atlas told him of an intercepted communiqué, one that mentioned a sculptor and an obelisk. Whether it referred to Alex or not was unknown, and there was no casual way to inquire. With a few more interviews, he'd ask about her work and find out if she was the sculptor. If so, they might both be Zeben's targets. And if he scared her or made her too angry, she'd never let him anywhere near her.

He intended to be near her and inside her before this was over. He had time for both, if he was willing to be patient. Phillip and his alter ego, Sphinx, were renowned for their patience. It helped him survive a prison camp and being cut off from his family and friends. And it would help him seduce Alex Walton, when the time came.

Phillip raised his own hands in a sign of truce. "I won't kiss you again, Alex, unless you ask me."

Alex exhaled, relieved and contrarily disappointed. "That won't happen."

Amused, Phillip smiled. Adversaries would recognize it as a

challenge. "Of course it will," he corrected. "When it does, I promise not to gloat."

Incensed, Alex strode over to where he stood. "Before I ask you to touch me, Phillip, demons will skate in hell."

Phillip shrugged and dropped a companionable arm around her shoulder, and together, they headed out of the kitchen. "I understand ice hockey is catching on down there."

Unable to stifle a laugh, Alex elbowed him in the ribs. "You are an arrogant man."

"Confident."

"Whatever. The point is, I know men. Sooner or later, you'll see someone else who interests you. In fact, I know a number of nice women here and in DC. I'll find one for you. Oh, this will be fun. If you and I had given in, I'd have ended it eventually. This way, we can start off as friends."

Suddenly, Phillip stopped. He caught her arm and turned her to face him. "No matchmaking, Alex." He speared her with a molten glance, and Alex felt a quiver of fear mingled with a resurgence of desire. His dark, sexy voice washed over her, weakening her will, drawing her close. "I promised not to kiss you, but listen to me carefully. I won't kiss you until you ask, but I will seduce you. I'm not like any man you've ever known. And when I finally take you, you won't want me to let you go."

CHAPTER SIX

Plotting wars had to be less taxing than the planning of a society wedding. There were tuxedos to fit, guests to coordinate, egos to soothe. For the thousands of tasks accomplished, a million sprouted anew, a Hydra's head of responsibilities. The duty of the maid of honor, Alex knew, was to alleviate the stress of the bride and inoculate her from the travails of planning her wondrous day. Alex had shirked her responsibility for nearly a month, a marvelous escape she'd scarcely appreciated until now.

As the Grayson-Foster nuptials headed into the home stretch, only the rehearsal dinner, the bachelorette party, and the wedding itself remained as obstacles to pulling off a successful mission. Although an army of coordinators, caterers, and gofers had been hired, it was her obligation—no, pleasure, she corrected—to personally retrieve the gown and the flowers and the ring.

Maid of honor also meant, she'd realized, she-who-bears-all-insults.

To make matters worse, sleep provided no respite.

Rather than slipping beneath the sheets to slumber for four or five hours, the night tormented her with dreams of Phillip. Of hungry kisses and sizzling caresses.

Pleasured sighs as hands held, fondled, kneaded slick flesh. In her fantasies, when Phillip invited her to join him upstairs, in her bed, she agreed. He swept her high against his chest, his touch hard, almost bruising. Naked, eager, they tumbled over sheets, flowing over, around, into one another. Full, ready, he rose above her, his expression a tight mask of sensual need. She arched her back in impatient invitation and—

"Time to wake up!"

Alex lifted her head groggily from beneath the covers, pleas for ten more minutes of sleep ignored by a termagant bride-to-be. Trembles from the aftermath of her dreams left her disoriented and uncomfortably aroused.

"Alex," Raleigh repeated. "Get up."

"Go away," she pleaded, futilely hoping she could return to her dream lover.

Raleigh stripped the covers from the bed, exposing Alex's scantily clad skin to the air conditioner's blast.

Defeated, Alex opened one sleepy eye and squinted at her tormentor, dragging the nearest sheet around her body. "The sacrifices I make for friendship," she mumbled irascibly. "What decent human being schedules an appointment at dawn?"

"Dawn occurs earlier in the morning," Raleigh returned mildly from the foot of the bed. Already dressed in black slacks and a navy top, she input the day's to-do list into her electronic organizer. The day before her wedding, there seemed to be more to do than less, but Alex had been a godsend. Gratitude for the grumpy maid of honor softened her retort. "Dawn is when the sun rises, a sight I'm sure you confuse with bedtime."

After an exaggerated moan, Alex wriggled out of the bed. She stumbled into the sunny yellow bathroom, brushing wild black tendrils of hair from her face. The mirror filled with her image. Winged brows and thick lashes framed sleepy eyes. A pointed chin made a habit of rising in confrontation. Full, sulky lips curved in exasperation. A mélange of angles and curves and planes, Alex appreciated her face. As an artist, she welcomed the unusual composition that challenged convention. As a woman, she enjoyed the attention, the admiration. Unlike her best friend, Alex never questioned her femininity or her beauty. The first was a blessing, the second a gift.

Raleigh joined her in the bathroom. She, too, noted the arch of brow models would kill for, the doe brown eyes that truly reflected Alex's soul. What she saw that Alex did not were the dusky shadows beneath the eyes. More than a lack of sleep, Raleigh easily identified worry and confusion.

"What's wrong, Alex?"

Deliberately ignoring the concern, Alex grumbled, "Daylight. A pox on humankind." Alex twisted a pearl knob and tepid water gushed from the taps. While it warmed, she secured the slippery mass of black hair in a haphazard braid and splashed her face.

"Alex. I'm serious. You haven't been nearly as talkative as usual. In fact, you've been downright sedate." Raleigh shifted so brown eyes met amber in the mirror. "There's no Coke in the refrigerator and your secret stash is running perilously low.

Something's wrong. Talk to me," she demanded, an echo of Alex's favorite phrase.

"What could be wrong, Raleigh? It's the day before your wedding. A clear, bright day and all is right with the world," she quipped.

"It's overcast and cloudy. And you're lying," Raleigh corrected. "You've been noticeably less sarcastic and whiny, Alex. What gives?"

With practiced motions, Alex slathered on cleansing cream. She'd successfully avoided unburdening her troubles onto Raleigh this long; she wouldn't cave in now, no matter how welcome the thought. To distract her, she demanded, "Have you been using the facial products I bought you?"

Raleigh looked away guiltily. "I haven't had time." Then, recognizing the ploy, she said in mild rebuke, "And don't change the subject."

Water splashed against her skin and Alex grabbed a towel to blot the extra moisture. When she reached for her toothbrush, Raleigh snatched the instrument from her fingers. "No more diversions."

Alex grabbed at the brush, but Raleigh's extra inches gave her the advantage. "Give that back! I will not be responsible for morning breath."

Pinching her nose with her free hand, Raleigh replied, "A bit late for that now. Come on, Alex. What's wrong?"

"This is your week, Raleigh. I'm not going to ruin it by whining about my silly problems," Alex said.

"A week I wouldn't be having if not for you. We're best friends, Alex. As you so brutally reminded me not too long ago, we can't be very close if you won't share your problems with me." Raleigh bumped her hip into Alex's. "You're my sister, Alex. If you're unhappy, I'm unhappy. Which would make Adam very unhappy. We might have to call off the wedding until we recover from our collective malaise. You don't want to be responsible for that, do you?"

Alex smiled in surrender. Collecting her thoughts, she brushed past Raleigh to walk into the bedroom. Raleigh followed and handed Alex the purloined toothbrush as she joined her on the bed.

"Damon Toca proposed to me," she announced breathily.

"The gallery owner?" Raleigh raised a brow. "Three weeks? That's a record, even for you. Hmmm, pretty impressive." She studied her friend for a moment. "So, why did you say no? Too erudite? Too combative? Too wealthy?"

"Too attentive," Alex muttered.

"*Too attentive.* Now, that's a new one. I guess it would be too much to hope that by attentive you mean obsessive. Knowing you, though, I bet he plied you with gifts, treated you to fabulous dinners, hung on your every word."

"Exactly." Alex held up her hands in confusion. "He thought I was the center of the universe, and I felt nothing. Not even a smidgen of love. I usually feel a smidgen. What's wrong with me?" she cried.

Raleigh took one of the raised hands. She held it gently between her own and rested her free hand on Alex's shoulder. "Nothing new is wrong with you."

Alex glared at her, and Raleigh continued. "Honey, you always do this. Remember Carlos? You broke the poor man's heart after two months because he preferred the Cubists to the Impressionists. And Victor? He criticized romance novels as trash. You wrote a thesis on the legitimacy of the form and concluded the paper by dumping him."

The hand Raleigh held clenched in frustration. "So you see what I mean? I discard wonderful man after wonderful man. Why?"

"Because you enjoy everything up to the point where he really needs you. You leave when you become necessary."

"But why would I do that?"

"You're afraid," Raleigh said simply. "And because you expect too much. You're looking for Prince Charming, Einstein, and Paul Robeson wrapped into one guy. You enter each relationship as much for fun as for the challenge of figuring out why it won't work."

"I'm too judgmental."

"Alex, you're the least judgmental and the most critical person I know. It's never the man you don't want, it's who you are with him. I can't tell if it's because you're a hopeless romantic or an unbearable cynic."

"How can I be nonjudgmental and hypercritical at the same time?" Alex argued, deliberately ignoring the rest of the analysis.

Raleigh recognized the avoidance tactic and played along. "You don't begrudge the differences between you and the men you date. In fact, you knowingly seek out those differences. Which is why you have the uncanny ability to maintain a bevy of male friends most women would envy."

"I am good, aren't I?" Alex preened. Quickly though, she sobered. "After Damon, I declared a male moratorium."

"Yeah, right," Raleigh scoffed. "I suppose this will be like the time you gave up oils in favor of watercolors. Or the antikiln phase. Alex, your life really does imitate your art. You have this fantastic passion for everything you see, and the remarkable ability to have it. There's nothing you can't do and no man you can't have."

"So why am I unhappy?"

Raleigh tugged on Alex's makeshift braid. "Because you seek perfection in a flawed world, Alex. And you refuse to admit the flaws are the best part."

In for a penny, in for a pound, Alex decided. She took a deep breath. "Tell me about Phillip," she demanded as she scooted off the bed.

Raleigh propped her elbows on her denim-clad knees. Thoughtfully, she said, "He's strong. Noble, really. In that ancient hero way. He survived three years as a prisoner of terrorists, when revealing one state secret would have freed him." Raleigh repeated the story ISA had fed to the world after Phillip's return. Although her job wasn't a secret to Alex, and she had probably guessed Adam's connection, it wasn't Raleigh's place to reveal the truth about Phillip.

From the bathroom, Alex said, "I can't quite put my finger on his type. He's full of power and energy. You can hear it thrumming just beneath the surface. Then he speaks, there's that deep, resonant voice, yet so detached. Well, not detached so much as self-contained. He can sit in absolute silence and find nothing uncomfortable about it in any way."

Raleigh heard the tinge of interest and grinned.

Phillip and Alex? Wait until she told Adam. Alex was the perfect antidote to Phillip's cold calm. And Phillip was just what Alex needed. Phillip wouldn't be hypnotized and dismissed by her friend. Schooling her voice to disguise her amusement, she said, "He's a good guy. Why the questions?"

"I've decided to be a writer this month. Remember my character Allegra? Phillip will be the model for her partner, Nelson. He's agreed to be my muse."

Raleigh smothered another smirk. Phillip told them he'd found a way to stick close to her until the threat was identified, but he didn't mention playing a male Calliope to Alex's epic tale. Surely, he realized the wedding offered an adequate cover without the pretense of sharing his life story. His sacrifice went beyond the call of duty, and beyond the week. She'd definitely have to ask Adam about Phillip's intentions.

For a second, she considered warning Alex about Phillip, to caution her not to underestimate him. She opened her mouth, but thought better of it. The possibility of Alex finally getting her emotional comeuppance, of being forced to follow through, this was the stuff dreams were made of. Alex had no idea whom she was involved with, and Raleigh considered it for the best. Alex's complacency when it came to charming and dumping men was likely over. Whether she knew it or not, her best friend had finally met her match.

Out of friendship, she said, "Phillip is wonderfully solid, but don't let the calm veneer fool you."

Alex laughed from the bathroom, the sound not quite steady. "I can handle him, don't worry."

The routine for the wedding week included running errands and transporting guests. More often than not, logic dictated Alex and Phillip do the tasks together. Although Phillip knew the city from his college days, Alex traversed the city's streets like a general leading a guerrilla attack.

During the stretches of time they spent alone, Alex peppered him with questions, driven to learn as much as she could. She told herself it was for the story, but she knew better.

He'd told her more stories of his childhood, some comical, others heart-wrenching. For those, he didn't seek her pity, and respect demanded she not offer. In fact, she mused, his comfort with both his rags and his riches added yet another facet to admire and explore.

College exploits and his friendship with Adam were favorite sources of information. Surprisingly, Phillip was a good storyteller, clear and funny, with excellent timing. Natural reticence aside, he possessed an uncanny method of captivating an audience, even of one.

"You did not!" Alex gasped in disbelief. "You and Adam hacked into the school's computer system and programmed a virus?"

"Nothing fatal. It simply converted all outgoing emails into poetry by Mari Evans and Paul Laurence Dunbar. In honor of Black History Month."

Alex doubled over in laughter as they walked through the West End, ostensibly to select Atlanta souvenirs as party favors for the rehearsal dinner.

One of the most venerable sections of the city, the West End served as home to several of Atlanta's colleges, including their alma maters. In the neighborhoods surrounding the colleges, pretty little houses sat neatly side by side, dotting a landscape with renovated housing developments. Signs of new construction were evident, but the character of the neighborhoods shone through. During her visits to Atlanta, Alex rarely took the time to visit her old haunts. It was a shame, really, she thought, as a group of camera-wielding out-of-towners jostled past.

Tourists enjoyed what natives too often took for granted.

Phillip seemed to take nothing for granted. For hours, they'd wandered down cobblestone walkways, poked their heads into tiny shops. In Phillip, she sensed a desire to recapture a time when life had been simpler, less demanding.

She said as much, and Phillip launched into another tale of his misspent youth. Alex chuckled in response, deciding not to press the issue.

Instead, she wondered plaintively why, in six hours, Phillip only touched her to help her out of the car or across the street. Gone were the searing glances and the heart-stopping looks. She'd gotten exactly what she'd asked for. And she was miserable.

He'd been the perfect companion, solicitous, and when a street vendor offered a clutch of roses for sale, Phillip purchased the bunch and presented them to her.

Struggling not to be charmed by the gesture or the extra twenty she saw him slip between the dollar bills, Alex accepted the flowers. "Phillip, you're incorrigible."

"I haven't done a thing."

Alex lifted the roses for the faint fragrance of late summer. "I noticed," she grumbled.

Hearing the note of irritation, Phillip asked, "Now you're angry because I haven't broken my promise not to touch you?"

In her mind, the torrid images of her dream flashed in arousing sequence. As background to the graphic picture show, Raleigh's assessment of her dating habits played. Phillip was attentive, but not possessive. Interested, but not in pursuit. "No. I'm not angry," Alex muttered. She tried to recall why she was upset though.

"I want you," Phillip said softly as he traced a line of fire along her jawline. "But now isn't the time or the place."

"Right," Alex agreed, her pulse fluttering madly. The simple touch of skin to skin weakened her resolve.

"There will be a time and a place," Phillip continued, pressing his lips to the tender pulse inside her wrist.

Helplessly, Alex absorbed the silky brush of mustache, the penetrating heat of firm lips. She told herself conceding was not an option. "No, there won't," she stammered. The lie didn't convince her or Phillip.

Phillip watched with curiosity as confusion and longing flitted across her expression. In a charitable mood, he wrapped a friendly arm around her waist. "Shall we visit our old stomping grounds?" he offered.

Grateful for the diversion from her muddled feelings, Alex confessed, "I'm not sure I'm permitted to return to Spelman yet."

"That makes two of us," Phillip commiserated. Alex sent him an inquiring look, and he explained. "A midnight encounter with the Spelman police department outside of the Abby dorm remains on my permanent record. I believe I was barred from ever crossing the campus or speaking to Spelman women. They refused to believe that I was delivering a term paper to save a student from imminent failure of a physics class."

A giggle escaped as Alex imagined a younger Phillip trying to justify his transgression to the guards at Spelman. Their legend as surrogate fathers to the students was well-earned. Alex smiled. "Well, my crime was a bit less heinous, at least to the guards. I did manage to offend several alumnae. I led a demonstration against our dress code."

"I'm shocked and amazed," was his dry response, as he took in today's outfit. More demure than most, the flirty skirt skimmed her knees, paired with a floral halter.

Still, he acknowledged the tremor of need, now a permanent condition that had a known cure. But he'd given his word. "I imagine you were quite a rabble-rouser during your time," he told her.

"Although I didn't lead the student government like some overachievers"—she shot him a mocking grin—"I did manage to do my part for social justice. I once staged a sit-in in the president's office on behalf of the maintenance workers. And there was the day I chained myself to the gates."

Intrigued, Phillip asked, "The cause?"

With a sheepish grin, she replied, "Anticurfew. A dedicated nonconformist, that's me." She leaned her head against his shoulder as they passed the library. "My mother confined me to two protests per semester and one suspension a year. Dad's job was bail."

"You were arrested?" Phillip had difficulty picturing her behind bars. She certainly wouldn't go quietly.

The memories brought a warm smile to her face. "Apartheid rallies, environmental justice marches, and a campaign to end homelessness. My parents decided it was best if Dad handled the times I railed against the city's injustices. The better to avoid the mere appearance of impropriety. Especially since Mom may have been the one to call the police."

She amazed him, Phillip thought in bewilderment, as she laughed at her past. Alex wasn't a woman easily categorized. Like her scent, she was fresh and vibrant. Like her eyes, open and

guileless. Deceptively insubstantial, she championed the under-
dog and the pursuit of justice and the freedom to dress half-
naked with a deep core of conviction. Don Quixote in a miniskirt,
he thought with an absent smile.

Casually, Phillip drew her closer as they squeezed past students rushing into the weekend. Supple, taut, she fit into him
as though made for his body, his arms. He remembered the feel
of that lissome body under his hands, under his mouth. Desire
thundered heavy through his blood. He ached and blamed her
for the frustration. Soon, he thought darkly, soon she would ac-
knowledge the want that bound them inextricably. Inexplicably.

As a man, he expected to want her, the tall, gorgeous body, the
endless, dancer legs. The face that hypnotized with its startling
looks.

What he didn't expect was to like her, to welcome her company as they shopped for wedding gifts and planned parties. He
admired the quick mind, the faster tongue. It showed in her wry
commentary on life as the only child of dynamic parents. Artists
with whom he was acquainted only by reputation were happily
dissected and exposed. She spared no one, not even her mother,
in biting observations of city politics. Her remarks about Washington demonstrated a keen understanding of political subtleties.
Comments on the players he'd worked with showed an intuition
present in the best of pundits. Alex would move effortlessly between her parents' worlds, comfortable in both, belonging in
neither.

Phillip led them to the Oval, and they leaned into one another, relaxed by nostalgia. Unable to resist, he shifted to pull her
into him. Alex tensed for a moment, and gentle breath sighed
out. He knew the instant she gave in to the moment, her head

fitting itself in the hollow of his shoulder. Her soft hair grazed his cheek, and he savored the feel, winding strands around his fingers. Waves of desire flooded him, and he wondered that they both did not drown. How could she not feel what stretched between them, tight and fine, ready to snap?

To succumb would complicate their lives, he understood, his more than hers. Pursued by an invisible enemy, he had no right to crave the generous curves.

Demons haunted him, denying him the provocative satisfaction of her kiss. Protecting her was his first priority, and clouding their relationship with emotion was a recipe for disaster.

He didn't care.

The hand threaded in her hair smoothed the thick skeins, slanting her head back along his arm. Alex watched him, eyes shuttered by a thick fringe of lash. Phillip lowered his head, determined to assuage the craving.

Triumphantly, he saw her eyes flutter closed, her mouth part in welcome. She was his to take, no resistance.

It wasn't enough.

Phillip had vowed not to kiss her again until she asked, not to protect her but himself. The pounding of his heart warned him that he wanted, no, needed more from her. Caught between desire and a more fragile yearning, he needed her to want him enough to ask. To take.

Alex started when his lips brushed her forehead in a chaste peck. A breath she'd been unaware of holding sighed out between lips longing for the hard, deep invasion of his mouth. Her eyes met his in question.

"It will be your move, Alex. It has to be," Phillip answered with a solemn look. "Anytime you want."

She nodded her understanding, and moving away, she hooked her arm in his. They headed for the car they'd parked in the college lot. "I won't give in, Phillip. I have too much to lose."

Phillip smiled, an arrogant curve to his masculine lips. "I'm not the one you're fighting, sweetheart."

Alex stiffened at the comment. She looked up at the face that crept into her sleeping hours, sometimes serious, sometimes sensual, always compelling.

"Maybe you're right, Phillip. Perhaps I am fighting myself. But I know I'm right. You're a complication I can't afford. There is something dangerous about you." She unlocked her mother's Lincoln and they climbed into the car.

"Dangerous? How? I'm an ex-politician." Phillip reclined in his seat. "What is there to be afraid of?"

"Beneath that sober, polite exterior lurks a man of mystery. I'm better off not having the answer, I think."

Phillip made an impatient gesture, dismissing her analysis. "You do have an active imagination." He refrained from probing what she thought she saw. Alex was smart and intuitive. To divert her attention, he asked about her trip to South Africa.

"What led to the gallery exhibition in Durban?"

"The Tocas are old family friends. My father went to school with Mr. Toca, and my mother assisted a resistance cell led by Mrs. Toca. The parallels amused them. After apartheid fell, Dad had his first showing in South Africa in their gallery. Tucker and Bill have retired, and their son Damon runs the gallery and his brother, Nelson, is an art dealer. I'd met them once, when we were very young. Damon saw an exhibition I held in New York and invited me to show."

Atlas needed to run a check on the Tocas. He'd transmit the

information once Alex dropped him off at the Grayson house. "Did something happen between you two?" he asked.

Alex hesitated.

Phillip watched the expressions cross her face—chagrin, embarrassment, resolve. "I assume he has something to do with the moratorium."

"Yes, I made my decision after I left the gallery, but it was my decision." Alex stared at the traffic as it sped past. "Damon had nothing to do with it."

From her vehement denial, Phillip knew Damon had everything to do with it. But a love affair gone bad normally didn't lead to intercepted communiqués and murder attempts. Feigning ignorance, he said, "At a showing, you just bring your pieces, set them up, and wait for buyers, I guess."

Alex laughed, grateful for the new subject. "Essentially, yes. However, I produced additional pieces particularly for the gallery. Damon requested one additional sculpture."

"Is that unusual?"

"A bit. He requested a specific piece, with dimensions and markings." Alex wrinkled her nose in thought. "In fact, he had me replicate a piece he already owned. I assumed it was commissioned for his personal collection because neither the original nor my piece were included in the show."

Tension prickled along Phillip's neck when he asked his next question. "What were the pieces, Alex?"

"An obelisk. I thought it was for a mythology exhibition, but the inscriptions were Shilha, not Egyptian or even hieroglyphics."

Phillip reeled from her descriptions of the statues. A statue inscribed in Shilha. He'd used the language to communicate secretly with Raleigh and Adam during their tournament. Fewer than three million spoke the language, and Alex was asked to replicate a sculpture bearing a message in the language. Damon Toca and Zeben. The connections eluded him, as did the point behind the sculptures. A warning to them all? A message to Zeben? He'd notify Raleigh and Adam at the rehearsal and send word to Atlas. Time was running out.

———————

In a small room, heavy with the pungent aroma of incense, Zeben issued orders. "You said they are together."

Civelli sat ramrod straight in a chair half a world away and felt the malevolence as surely as if Zeben held a knife to his throat. "Yes, sir. When I followed Phillip to the airport, he met the girl. She's the one my contact told us about."

"Does she have the obelisk?"

"He believes so."

"I must have it. And the Sahalia. Do we have word of it?"

"No, sir. But Jubalani is searching for it."

"I will have it now!"

Civelli heard the madness, borne of fanaticism.

Obsession confused him, muddied the waters of profit. But Zeben wanted his assistance and was willing to pay handsomely for the help. Though he typically limited his services to trade, he was not above murder. He preferred to avoid the messiness of taking human lives, but money cured squeamishness.

"I will find it, sir."

Zeben controlled himself with effort. "Time grows short. The day of Ascension is near." Zeben's eyes glowed with anticipation. "I will have my revenge," he said in a voice that crackled with lunacy. "With the Kholari and the Sahalia, I shall rule at last."

"I will deliver the obelisk and the ruby as promised, Zeben. When Turman has led me to it, I will finish him."

He tossed in the last because they soothed the despot's erratic mind.

"See that you do not disappoint me this time. Your failure in your last task helped the traitors capture me."

When the line went dead, Civelli finally relaxed. If he succeeded this time, he'd never have to see Zeben again. With the money he'd saved and stolen over the years, he'd retire with a tidy sum that would last him a lifetime.

The beautiful woman Turman met at the airport had been at the arrival gate for Johannesburg. She had photographed nicely, and he'd faxed copies to his contacts in South Africa. At last, he'd heard from one of his favorite thieves, Jubalani. He wired a message identifying the lady as Alex Walton. When he put it together with his other information, either Ms. Walton or Turman had to have the damned statue.

He had another job tomorrow, or he'd grab them then.

Instead, he'd wait until they returned to DC. In a matter of days, he'd be a millionaire several times over and on a flight to paradise. And all he needed was a statue.

CHAPTER SEVEN

Saturday dawned clear and bright. Storm clouds had hovered ominously over Atlanta only a few days before, spitting rain and shouting thunder. Frantic caterers had checked and double-checked the tarpaulins and canopies to be used if the offending weather did not dissipate.

Anxious guests had rescheduled flights halted by the precipitate weather.

By Saturday, however, the sun shone with a gentle ferocity, daring the rain to return. It was, Alex announced as she slid into the limousine beside an unusually pensive Raleigh, a perfect day for a wedding.

Liz sat on the opposite bench, clutching a lace handkerchief in one hand and what Alex proclaimed to be a duffel bag in the other.

"What could you possibly be carrying, Mom?"

"Only one of us has ever been married, my dear," Liz retorted serenely. "Each item in this bag has a special and distinct purpose."

"In case Raleigh and Adam elope?" Alex reached across the seat to take Raleigh's icy hand. "It's not too late, you know. Mom and I can call the other car, whisk you to the airport, and we can catch the next flight to Las Vegas. I've always thought a moonlight wedding, illumined by billboards announcing *all nude girls all the time*, had a certain panache all its own."

Raleigh chuckled weakly. "After all the dresses I tried on and flowers I've sniffed and dry chicken I've eaten, I think we'll skip Vegas."

Not reassured by the tepid laugh, Alex cradled Raleigh's other hand. It was as cold and tremulous as its mate. "Raleigh, honey, are you okay?"

Snatching her hands away, Raleigh twisted the engagement ring on her finger. "Okay? I'm marrying a man I swore I hated, a year after I tried to kill his best friend," she finished on a choked sob.

Alex cast a wary glance at the partition separating the driver from the rear of the car. "Raleigh, you tried to kill Phillip?"

"He's one of them," Liz assured her.

Distraught, Raleigh nodded and clutched the beringed hand to her stomach. "Oh God, Alex. What am I doing? What do I know about marriage? Or family? You're my best friend and I hurt you. What if I break his heart? I love him so much, I couldn't stand it if I hurt him."

Alex cupped Raleigh's chin and waited until tear-soaked amber eyes met her own. "Of course you'll hurt him, and he'll hurt you too. Then the hurting is over, and what's left is all that matters. You love him, Raleigh. And he loves you. There's nothing more important that you need to know."

When Raleigh opened her mouth to speak, Alex shook her head. "Anything else that might come in handy, you learned from my parents."

Extending a hand to her mother, she continued. "Marriage is about partnership and sacrifice. It's about loving Adam enough to trust him to let you be yourself, tortured tirades of angst and all. He knows you and loves you anyway. You know him and love him. It's simple, but that's the whole lot. Raleigh, you said it yourself. I've never met anyone who knew me, who understood me the way Adam gets you. Once you've found something that miraculous, you don't have a choice. Right, Mom?"

Liz squeezed her daughter's hand and reached past Alex to dab at Raleigh's tears. "I have one daughter by birth and a second by choice. I would never let an unworthy man take her as his bride. You two belong to each other. Forever."

With a watery smile, Raleigh said, "I feel like such an idiot."

Alex hugged her. "Brides are duty-bound to be jittery on their wedding day. Far be it from you to not follow the rules."

When Raleigh stuck her tongue out, Alex knew the crisis had passed.

Imagine Raleigh, afraid of marrying the man she loves.

She'd been frightened of her feelings before, but eventually, it had been Raleigh who flew to find Adam and tell him how she felt. Then, as now, Alex envied her courage, the same way she envied Raleigh this day. To find the man she loved, that had always been Alex's dream. She didn't begrudge Raleigh her happiness, but she couldn't help the miserly lump of jealousy lodged near her heart.

The fact was, she longed for a soulmate, for a true love. She searched for him like other women shopped for shoes. Alex couldn't remember the last time she thought she'd been close, though. Damon had been entertainment, not a serious candidate. Damon, the paramour in San Francisco, made her laugh, but didn't stir her. A dozen names swirled in her head, but the one man who had reached her in the last few years waited at the church with the groom.

Phillip moved her, a fact she was loath to admit.

Instant attraction aside, he wasn't her type at all. Rugged and somber, with a hard face unused to joviality. Her tastes typically ran to the devil-may-care artist or the dashing entrepreneur. Kevin, of the hot-air balloon for Valentine's Day. Or Carlton, with his Lear and impromptu trips to Antigua.

Yet, the longer she spent with Phillip, the more she grew to care for calm and dependable. Phillip watched Alex as though no one else existed, whether they stood in a checkout line buying party favors or sat in an airport bar, awaiting a passenger.

Yes, he was reliable and steady. And edgy and exciting. When they talked, he would brush her hair from her forehead with feather-light caresses, claiming the bangs distracted him. In the middle of a diatribe about campaign finance, he'd trace idle, electric lines along her skin, until she fairly vibrated with want. Standing in a crowded shop or strolling down a sidewalk, invariably, he'd find another way to touch, to stroke, to feel.

She had the distinct impression he hunted her as a lion stalked prey. As he'd promised, he never kissed her or moved beyond contact that couldn't be easily explained away. He was breaking her down, stripping her resolve away, layer by layer, Alex realized. And like prey mesmerized by the hunter, she didn't know if she wanted to resist.

———

Miles away, Adam shifted restlessly in his seat at the church. "I'm getting married. Today."

Phillip raised his eyes from the book he'd been reading. "So you've said, at least twelve times now. And, no, before you peek out the door, she's not here yet."

As eager as a little boy on the last day of school, Adam leapt from his chair. "This is real, right? I'm not dreaming, am I?"

Phillip gave up on his book, after reading the same sentence for the umpteenth time. "No, you're not dreaming, although I wouldn't place odds that you're not high," he answered with a touch of resentment.

He was happy for Adam, happy he and Raleigh had found their way back together. But appreciating his friends' good fortune couldn't appease the ache seeing them together brought. Adam and Raleigh deserved bliss. He'd done his level best to help them recapture love and hold it with both hands.

As he watched, Adam measured off the room, whistling beneath his breath. Unlike Mr. Sunshine, he'd been spending day in and day out with Alex, which definitely didn't help matters. The wanting he could stand, but it was need that wound its way through him.

The nosiest woman he'd ever met, she'd poked into every

crevice in his past, rooting out stories he'd forgotten, memories he'd stored away. He told himself she would eventually get tired, or better yet, grow bored.

Instead, she delved deeper, and he found that with her, he couldn't stay silent.

Those who knew him best would not describe him as taciturn, simply private. Phillip could hold his own in conversation, but his companions left feeling they'd shared more than they learned.

With Alex, though, he never managed to keep his head about him. When the strong, sweet scent of spring filled his head, caution was forgotten. How could a man be expected to remain aloof when big brown eyes widened with excitement or narrowed in censure? The woman possessed this mysterious ability to seem completely absorbed, regardless of the topic. It bewitched him. He'd missed talking to a woman when he had her undivided attention.

With a grunt, Phillip flipped open his book. After reading the same passage again, he closed the cover with a frustrated snap. He wasn't bewitched, he corrected. Sure, he and Alex had been inseparable this week, but it was a good thing that she stuck so close to him. Reconnaissance from Atlas had confirmed that Phillip was indeed the target of a vengeful Zeben and Alex might be as well. He'd kept Alex close out of concern for her safety, not because he felt incomplete without her. The twinge of loneliness was surely not because leaving her at her doorstep grew harder each time.

And while he fully intended to make love to Alex Walton, it would not be because of a desire unlike any he'd ever known. It had nothing to do with the way barriers crumbled away whenever he was near her. The way the silk of her skin or the scent of her hair tangled inside him until his dreams were made of her.

Phillip gritted his teeth and lifted the discarded book once more, until Adam's whistle made him toss it away. He folded his arms and glared at Adam's back. When he made love to Alex, he'd merely scratch an itch. There was no future for him with the complicated woman who made light of herself in a vain attempt to divert attention from her depth. Any need to learn more about her was born of his own natural curiosity.

It had nothing to do with falling in love.

———

Violins serenaded Adam and Raleigh as they made their way to the dais after cutting the cake. Tuxedo-clad waiters whisked away the last remnants of dinner. A second legion presented slices of decadent chocolate to the salivating guests. Alex embraced the glowing couple, wiping away a bit of cake from Adam's nose. After congratulating Raleigh with a generous kiss, Phillip raised his glass in a final toast, and motioned for quiet.

"To proof of love's infinite patience and sublime wisdom! To Raleigh and Adam." The guests clapped madly, and Adam gallantly spun his new bride into his arms. With his arms wrapped firmly around her, Adam leaned into the microphone. "Shall we dance?"

The quartet struck up a jazzy tune to entice the crowd onto the parquet floor laid beneath a canopy dotted with fairy lights. Seeing only each other, Adam and Raleigh swayed to the songstress as she crooned a Platters ballad. A misty Alex looked on and tried not to sigh. So beautiful, she thought wistfully, they are so beautiful together. She sipped the champagne and tried not to look at Phillip.

Throughout the ceremony, she'd fought not to imagine herself in Raleigh's place, exchanging rings and vows with the cursed man. For heaven's sake, she barely knew him.

Oh, yes, he loved his father and was devoted to his friends. Sure, he was a bona fide patriot and hero. But smart and sexy and funny weren't reason enough to change her mind about her decision. With her keen sense of self-destruction, she'd found those traits in other men and fell for each and every one of them. And the instant she thought he could be the one, she ran. So, she wouldn't think Phillip was the one. He was simply the best man. At the wedding, she added quickly. The best man at the wedding with whom she was just friends.

"You're mumbling again, Alex," Phillip said quietly.

"I said 'nice wedding,'" she muttered inanely.

He fixed her with that dark, soulful gaze that weakened her knees and her resolve. "Beautiful," he replied. Eyes locked, he lifted his fork and speared a bit of cake. "And, might I add, you look spectacular." When she raised her head, he fed her the morsel, wiping an errant crumb from her suddenly sensitive lips. "Much better than the typical bridesmaid attire. I nearly swallowed my tongue watching you walk down the aisle." He replaced the fork, then ran an absent finger along the back of her hand.

Alex shifted under his touch and wondered if it would be inappropriate to tackle and kiss the best man. To quell the impulse, she took a small sip of champagne and leaned away from him, moving her hand out of reach.

Good manners dictated that she return Phillip's compliment, she reminded herself. "You don't look half bad yourself," she murmured.

"Such high praise."

Alex shot him a sarcastic look. "Phillip, you know you're gorgeous."

Eyes dancing with mischief, Phillip replied, "Sometimes a man just needs to hear it."

While Alex gurgled with laughter, Phillip rested a hand on her shoulder. "Alex, we need to talk," he began.

"Phillip?" A languid Southern drawl forestalled Alex's response.

Simultaneously, Phillip and Alex turned to see who had approached the table. The honey-soaked voice perfectly complemented the pixie face. Alex thought she looked familiar, but she couldn't place the interloper. Instead, she returned her attention to Phillip. He seemed poleaxed. Haltingly, he rose from his chair. As Alex watched in disbelief, he took the young woman's hand between his own.

"Lorei," Phillip finally said.

The Southern belle in the blush pink evening gown was none other than Lorei Alexander, Phillip's ex-fiancée.

Alex had been years behind her in school, but Lorei had been a legend. Head cheerleader, salutatorian, president of the National Honor Society. Her mother owned the gallery that showed much of Robert Walton's work. Lorei's dad ran one of the city's oldest banks.

Without sparing a glance for Alex, Lorei clasped Phillip's other hand. "I wanted to speak to you at the wedding, but I didn't think it would be appropriate."

"Why not?" To Alex, Phillip's voice sounded different, unsteady and unsure.

"I have so much to say to you, Phillip." Lorei still had yet to look at Alex. Instead, she lifted limpid gray eyes to Phillip's.

The artist in Alex acknowledged that the shade was natural and ideal for the café au lait complexion, framed as it was by cascades of dark brown curls. Of course, a woman who looked like Lorei Alexander had tresses and not something as mundane as hair. Alex fought not to smooth down her own windswept locks as her chest contracted with apprehension. This couldn't be good, she thought fatalistically. The fact that she couldn't have Phillip for several excellent reasons aside, the thought of him with Lorei made her livid and scared.

Lorei held Phillip's shell-shocked gaze for an infinite moment. The honeyed drawl whispered, "Will you dance with me?"

Phillip didn't answer for several tense seconds. When he unexpectedly dropped Lorei's hands, Alex felt the unfamiliar tightness in her chest ease until Phillip circled the table to join Lorei. Although he muttered, "Excuse me," Lorei said nothing to Alex, which was just fine by her. If he wanted that Southern barracuda to break his heart again, who was she to stop him?

She'd heard most of the story from her mother. How Lorei had broken off their engagement after three years of stringing Phillip along. According to local gossip, first, she'd refused to set a date because he accepted a post with the Justice Department. After the two-year position ended, Lorei had been incensed when Phillip accepted a permanent post, rather than the lucrative offer from an Atlanta firm. The proverbial straw had come, however, when he ran for Congress. It seemed Lorei had always planned on returning to Atlanta, and Phillip's political career effectively ended any chance of that happening. The story had it that Lorei packed her bags the night of the election and announced that she was going home. A devastated Phillip stayed in DC, gracefully serving nearly two terms before his plane crashed in Jafir. All the while, pining for Lorei.

Alex took a bite of Phillip's cake and tried not to sulk. It didn't matter a whit to her that Lorei was batting her eyes so furiously, Alex was shocked she and Phillip didn't take flight. Phillip was a grown man, if not a smart one. He made his own decisions. And wasn't she the one who insisted they were only friends? Whatever was between Lorei and Phillip was between them. Better that she hadn't given in to temptation. Obviously, his heart belonged to another. Yes, it was better that she'd resisted, she thought wanly as Phillip gathered Lorei closer.

On the dance floor, Lorei whispered, "How are you, Phillip?" From his height, he'd have to bend to hear her. With that in mind, Lorei tilted her head to meet his eyes, well aware that the angle offered a clear view of the shimmering bodice. She'd spent weeks selecting the delicate dress. It reminded her of candy-coated sensuality, shell pink and innocent, with a plunging neckline and open back.

Phillip replied, his hand resting on the sleek skin laid bare by the gown's drape, "I'm doing well. And yourself?"

Lorei batted her eyes, to blink away false tears. "I've been so worried about you. After the news reported you'd been found, I was overcome. I never stopped thinking about you, Phillip."

"Thank you." He stared down at the woman he danced with, amazed by his response to having her in his arms again after so long. He'd spent years being in love with her. When she left him, he'd thrown himself into his work. He agreed to more ISA assignments, to political junkets to war-torn countries. Anything to fill the hole she'd torn in his soul.

Adam had warned him that she'd be at the wedding, and he'd thought he was ready. But seeing her after years of silence caught him by surprise. The love of his life stood before him, and he felt nothing. Not anger, not sadness, not want. Nothing. Except regret.

He looked into eyes the color of storm clouds and longed for chocolate brown. Alex's eyes. Soft, dulcet tones made him long for Alex's sultry sarcasm. He stared down at Lorei, and all he could see, all he could want, was Alex.

Stunned, he'd blindly accepted her offer to dance. He had to be sure that he was free of her. Yet, even the diminutive feel of her in his arms brought to mind the strong, agile feel of Alex's body.

"Are you listening to me, Phillip?" Lorei was asking impatiently, the dulcet tones giving way to waspish.

Phillip dragged his mind back to the woman in his arms. "I'm sorry. What did you say?"

She wriggled closer to him and flirted her pretty eyes. "I said I missed you, Phillip." The drawl carried a hint of annoyance, so she dutifully softened it. "Even before the plane crash, I thought about calling you."

"I thought you'd said everything when you broke our engagement." Over her head, he could see Alex doing her best not to watch them. Good, he thought mischievously.

"I was upset. I thought we'd made the decision to come to Atlanta, then you agreed to take that government job." She pouted a bit because the memory still rankled.

"You made the decision, Lorei," Phillip answered. "I told you I was applying for the position at Justice."

"I thought you were being idealistic. We were going to move home, raise a family." She swayed seductively, in time to the music. "We had a dream, Phillip."

Phillip withdrew a space but continued to dance. "Your dream, Lorei. Your home."

Lorei closed the gap between them and caressed the nape of his neck. "It was our dream, Phillip. I know we disagreed about Atlanta, but it was our dream."

Unmoved, Phillip gripped her wrist and pulled the hand playing at his neck down to their side. "Come on, Lorei. We charted different courses for our lives. And we forgot to tell each other. Our breakup was as much my fault as it was yours."

Lorei smiled in agreement and reached up to twine her slender arms around his neck. "And we can fix it," she drawled. "Now that you've left Congress, Daddy can find you a place in a firm here in town. Any one of them would love to have you."

Laughing shortly, Phillip unwound her arms and steered them to the edge of the dance floor and out beyond the canopy. The evening air was balmy and rich with the last scents of summer. Magnolia and azalea mixed with exotic flowers, the scent heady and romantic. The night smelled like Alex. It seemed every thought led to Alex, but Phillip returned his attention to the current problem.

Leading Lorei to a seat on a garden bench, Phillip propped a long leg on the arm.

"We've always been fantasies for each other, Lorei, each of us ignoring reality. You never wanted to stay in DC, and I refused to accept that. And I didn't leave Congress, Lorei. I lost my seat because I was held captive in a foreign prison." Phillip rested a gentle hand on her shoulder and said, not unkindly, "And, while

I thank you for the kind offer, no thanks. Whatever I plan, whatever I do next, it will be my decision. You did us both a favor when you left me. Let's leave it at that." He released her. "Thank you for the dance," he said as he turned to walk away.

Lorei clutched his elbow to stop him. "Phillip, don't do this!" Suddenly petulant, Lorei's voice lost its silky tone. "You have an opportunity here. This celebrity you've enjoyed for this year won't last forever. We can build something here. Together. But we need to do it now."

He spun on his heel to face her, the woman he'd once thought would be his world. For the first time, he noticed the hardness around her full mouth, the glint of steel in her beautiful eyes. The waterfall of brown ringlets promised an innocence he couldn't see anymore.

Thoughtfully, he said, "You're not a bad woman, Lorei. But we don't belong together. I don't regret that Adam introduced us, but for once, he made a mistake. Don't make another one and make a scene at his wedding. Enjoy your night, and give your parents my best." With a short nod, he strode farther into the gardens. He stood in the shadows, letting go of his dreams.

When someone touched his arm, he whirled around, prepared to be agonizingly direct. "Lorei, I told you—"

"I'm not sure what you told her, but she's dancing with Adam's brother now." Alex carried an open bottle of champagne and two glasses. "I imagine you could use this."

Phillip ignored the proffered glass, watching Alex instead. The scene with Lorei had been more difficult than he realized. "I'm fine," he grated.

"Then take the glass anyway, so I don't look like a lush."

Phillip chuckled, the tension evaporating. "Thanks." He gave her a contemplative look. "Were you eavesdropping, Alex?"

"Didn't need to. Body language speaks volumes." Alex led him to the gazebo. Inside, she settled herself on a garden bench and patted the cloth seat beside her. "Lorei seemed agitated and annoyed. I've got to figure that she tried her hand at reconciliation, and you rebuffed her advances."

At Phillip's arched brow, she continued, "And you stayed out here. Since she approached you and did the bulk of the heavy flirting, it seemed logical you'd be out here, feeling bad about telling her no. Naturally, you'd give her time to compose herself."

"Naturally." Low sounds of a piano filtered into the night air. Soon, a drum picked up the tempo. Phillip noted how his pulse thudded in time to the drummer's rhythms. A pulse that had been steady only seconds before. Before Alex. Temptation sat across from him, bathed in moonlight, sipping wine, smirking. Desire beat in his veins, a primitive sound, urging him to take her in his arms. But he'd promised.

Promised not to kiss her. However, he'd made no such agreement about dancing. Phillip stood and reached down to tug her up and into his arms. The beat of the drums punctuated the night, setting a primeval rhythm he couldn't ignore. Driven by the need to wipe away even the memory of another woman in his arms, he wrapped her against him, hip to hip, thigh to thigh. Warm, sweet breath seared his skin where he tucked her head into his shoulder. Neither spoke as the piano swept them into the dance.

He wanted her. Desperately. Definitely. The low thrum of the bass echoed his longing. He molded her to him. Her long, slim length fit him as though she'd been made for his arms, for his body. Quietly, he whispered dark, seductive words into willing ears. Silently, he rejoiced in the trembling response.

Languorously, Phillip slid craven hands down green silk, smoothing the fabric over a delicately muscled back, bunching it in his fists where a flat waist flared into rounded flesh. Trumpets rose on a note that commanded he gather her nearer, impossibly closer.

Alex arched against him, gasping. Music played in her head, sang in her veins. There, where heat pooled and spread like wildfire, she wanted him there. Now. Instead, she taunted him, circling as the pulsating jazz quickened. Lost in the night's spell, she trailed reckless fingers across his hard chest, fluttered them over firm, masculine lips.

She was aroused, hungry, wanton. The cadence of desire surrounded them, pressed them together. Maddened, gloriously sane, she put her mouth over his. She exalted as he hesitated, then hungrily thrust his tongue inside, lifting her against him, into him. With sinuous, sensual strokes, he explored the moist cavern. Alex could feel him, hard and ready, and she strained to take more of him.

Every moment before, every man before, meant nothing. Could mean nothing. She'd never been alive until his arms, never felt desire until his touch. Alex pulled away to tell him so, but he refused to allow her the space.

Murmuring, threatening, cajoling, he swept her deeper into his embrace.

Alex felt herself falling, then he landed on the bench, tumbled her into his arms, and settled her across his chest. His kiss mellowed, teased her tongue into a softer ballet of advance and retreat. Where her body lay along his, he stroked with slow, deliberate movements. Fires ignited along her skin, eased by the waves of pleasure drowning her.

"Phillip," she moaned, the word a blessing.

"Let me have you," he groaned in plea.

"Oh, Phillip," Alex sighed.

"Alex Walton?"

A voice, which definitely did not belong to Phillip, broke the moment. Alex heard her name, the sound hesitant, alien, and embarrassingly familiar.

Mortified, Alex rolled off Phillip's chest to land in a jumbled heap by his side. Phillip rose lithely to his feet, frustrated and angry.

Brusquely, he helped Alex to her feet. Shifting to shield her from the stranger, Phillip spoke first. "Can we help you?"

The intruder seemed vaguely amused by the situation, which did nothing to ease Phillip's temper. Who the devil was he? In the shadows, he couldn't make out his face.

After a slight pause, the man inclined his head imperiously. "No, thank you, sir. I am searching for Ms. Walton. I believe I have found her." The light, accented voice carried a trace of a clipped English accent, rounded by the tempo of a different native tongue. The careful enunciation and manor-born delivery reminded Phillip of a character from a Gilbert and Sullivan opera. Surely, Alex would dismiss the stranger as unwanted and send him on his way. Phillip shifted to let Alex send him packing.

When Alex eagerly advanced to greet him, hands outstretched, Phillip scowled.

"Damon!" she said in welcome. "How wonderful to see you. You should have told me you were coming."

Phillip watched with narrowed eyes when the man's pampered hands brushed her bare shoulders. The dandy ignored her hands and instead drew Alex in for a courtly kiss. Phillip stifled a snarl and the urge to rip the man's hands off. He satisfied himself by stepping between them to shake Damon's hand. The firmness of the handshake may have been more than polite, but it brought him a small modicum of satisfaction.

"I am Damon Toca, of the Toca Galleries," he announced as though that explained everything.

Damon Toca. The man who wanted the obelisk. A memory hovered, not quite real, but vital and important. "Oh," Phillip said dismissively, "the hat guy."

"The hat guy?" Damon repeated.

"My sombrero, senor," Alex teased. "It was unfortunately crushed by a speeding car on my first day home."

Only Phillip noticed the odd gleam in Toca's eyes, a look he thought he recognized as satisfaction. Disturbed by the implications, he placed a protective hand on Alex's arm and drew her beside him.

Alex fixed him with a quizzical glance, which Phillip proceeded to ignore. He focused his attention on their guest. "So, what brings you to Atlanta, Mr. Toca?"

"I lost something very precious last week, and I believe Alex can help me locate it."

"I can?" Alex wrinkled her forehead in concentration. "I have something of yours?"

Damon smiled, a smirk of lips and white teeth Phillip was fast growing to detest. "Yes, my dear. My heart."

"Oh, brother," Phillip exclaimed in disgust.

Alex elbowed Phillip in the stomach. She didn't look at him, amused and more than a little warmed by his displeasure.

"Damon, we've talked about this." She glanced at Phillip. "I'm flattered, but no."

Damon followed her gaze. "Ah, beautiful Alexandra, I had to try."

"Let's go inside and say hello to my parents. They haven't seen you since we were both in diapers." Alex smiled apologetically at Phillip. She hooked her arm in Damon's and guided him inside.

As they strolled through the garden, Damon glanced back at the gazebo and said, "Turman. He is the reason you will not have me?"

"No. I adore you, Damon, but we are friends. Nothing more."

"And him?"

Alex faltered. "We're finding our way."

She steered them through the dancers on the parquet and found her parents in conversation with the Graysons.

"Mom, Dad, look who I found," she began. "Damon Toca, you remember my parents, Liz and Robert Walton. And the parents of the groom, Carolyn and M.G. Grayson."

Damon bussed Liz's cheek, had his hand enveloped in Robert's hearty grasp. "My parents send their best." To the Graysons, he said, "Congratulations to your family. I apologize for intruding, but I could not miss a chance to bring greetings from my family."

M.G. waved away his apology. "The more the merrier, Damon."

"Dad, here's your drink," A.J. said as she approached the

group. Alex watched with fascination as Damon's eyes slid over the newcomer. The bridesmaids wore green as well, with simple spaghetti straps rather than the halter Alex sported. On A.J.'s trim, neat little body, the dress trained the eye on the flare of hip, the curve of waist.

Damon crossed to her and extended his hand. "Damon Toca."

"A.J. Grayson."

Alex observed the lingering touch, how A.J.'s normally husky voice dropped a note. Interesting. Almost as interesting as the fact that Damon continued to hold her hand long after the greeting ended.

"Would you care to dance, Ms. Grayson?" Damon murmured.

"I'd be delighted," A.J. answered. Without another word, the two headed to the floor.

"Who is that man?" M.G. demanded the moment they were out of earshot.

Alex placated him with a consoling hand. "He's a friend, M.G. Your niece is quite safe."

She chatted for a while, searching the crowd for Phillip. Once, she spotted him dancing with Rachel and twirling Lorei across the floor. Later, he led a final toast to the happy couple. Each time she approached him, though, he moved away, into a knot of guests or onto the dance floor. As the guests trickled out, she finally trapped him at the dais.

"Have you been avoiding me, Phillip?"

Phillip barely reacted to her presence. "It's a wedding, Alex. I've been mingling."

"Damon is a friend. I had to speak with him."

"You don't owe me an explanation."

"Could have fooled me," she muttered. "Will you at least look at me?"

Phillip lifted cold dark eyes to her harried ones. He remembered angrily the way she lit up with pleasure at Damon's arrival. One smarmy declaration and she'd instantly forgotten how close the two of them had come to breaking the tension that stretched between them moments before. Unfortunately, with Toca's untimely interruption, tight bands of need snapped into place with a vengeance.

He didn't like the feeling. "Yes?"

"What happened. Before Damon. I meant it."

"Meant which part? The quick tussle with me on the grass? Or leaving with another man?"

"Phillip! Be fair. I didn't leave with another man. I brought him to see my parents and I introduced him to some guests."

"I see he hit it off with A.J. Replaced so soon?" he sniped.

"Are you jealous?"

"Of course not." What a ridiculous idea! Jealous of a rich boy who had to fly around the world to pursue women? Not likely.

"Yes, you are," Alex concluded. "Of Damon? That's ridiculous," she said, echoing his silent thoughts.

"I didn't appreciate your desertion, but I managed."

"For the last time, I did not desert you. Unlike your dance with your ex. But if you insist on acting righteously indignant because I showed courtesy to a guest, then by all means, go ahead. I'll see if I can find Damon or some other total stranger and have him drive me home." Alex lifted her skirts and turned to stalk away.

"Toca left thirty minutes ago. I don't think he was alone." He had been, but Phillip didn't want to tell her that. Just as he didn't want to admit he was jealous.

Bitter with it, in fact. She'd walked away, leaving him churned and needy. And nothing would cure him except her touch.

But he'd have to hold off until he contacted Atlas in the morning. He had a sinking suspicion that he did know Toca. The hazel eyes, the fallen angel looks. Phillip was afraid Toca was known by another name: Jubalani.

Until he'd conferred with Atlas, his personal feelings would have to remain on hold. And he'd have to keep Alex away from Toca. In the final hours of wedding preparations, he'd been unable to finagle a viewing of the obelisk. Perhaps on the plane ride home, she'd show it to him.

"I'll drive you to the airport tomorrow," he announced.

"No." Alex folded her arms across her chest defiantly.

"Don't be obstinate."

"Obstinate. If that isn't the horse's ass calling the mule stubborn."

"Alex. Be reasonable."

"I will arrange my own transportation, thank you very much. And I will bid you goodnight, sir!"

"You sound like a Victorian novel. And you are no virginal maid."

"Well, you've just lost your chance to find out," she shot back and strode off the dais.

CHAPTER EIGHT

Where on earth was the woman? Phillip had spent the past forty-eight hours calling every person he knew in Atlanta. He hated that she'd gotten the last word at the reception. At the Sunday brunch, she'd flirted shamelessly with Toca, studiously ignoring him.

He liked even less that he missed her. With Adam and Raleigh safely away on their honeymoon, he had no reason to see her. To talk to her. Yet, again and again, he forced himself not to lift the phone to call. Two days without seeing her, without hearing her low, sexy voice, was trying his patience. No wonder she never finished anything, he decided irritably. She convinces him to let her have access to his life, then she does nothing.

Leaving her behind in Atlanta happened because, in true Alex fashion, she'd elected to stay an extra couple of days with her parents. Phillip had a meeting he couldn't reschedule, but he still had his reservations about Toca.

At his urging, Atlas had assigned an agent to escort her to DC. But she could still be with Toca.

Damn, he didn't want to picture that lush mouth touching anyone else. Those husky tones whispering another man's name. Phillip clenched his fists in impotent rage.

She had no right to stir him up and lead him on and leave him behind. He'd never reacted to a woman this way before in his life, and he hated the sensation. It felt as though he'd lost something. He couldn't name it, couldn't describe it. But he knew whatever it was was his and it was gone. Wanting Alex, needing her, was fast becoming an obsession.

It was his fault, though. He knew better. Alex Walton and Lorei Alexander were two of a kind. Rich, spoiled, and easily distracted by a brighter, shinier trinket. If he'd followed his initial instincts, to steer clear of the flighty gypsy, he wouldn't be thinking of her every other second of every day.

"Mr. Turman? Is everything alright?" the plump, pleasant secretary queried. At his quizzical look, she explained. "You were frowning. Do you need something?"

Phillip waited in the vestibule of Governor Bundy's office suite. He was a few minutes early for their ten o'clock appointment, but that was his habit. With an effort, Phillip pasted on an agreeable expression. "No, I'm fine," he replied.

"I'm sure the governor will be with you shortly," she offered with a placating smile.

"I'm fine," he repeated. Governor Bundy, a friend from childhood, had called the morning before to request a meeting. The meeting's purpose hadn't been revealed, but Phillip had an inkling of its cause. Jafir. His suspicions were confirmed minutes later.

Governor Bundy explained, "During his press junket to Washington, President Robertsi of Jafir announced the results of the first quarter's use of Praxis. The environmental technology has been an unadulterated success. In turn, the African-Arab Alliance has decided to pursue long-term trade agreements with the U.S., Europe, and South America."

Bundy remained silent, and Phillip allowed the quiet to fill the room. Bundy wanted something, and he'd have to ask. A novice would have spoken, uncomfortable with the silence. Phillip was no novice.

"You've always been better at this than me, Phillip," Bundy chuckled. When Phillip didn't respond, he continued good-naturedly. "I want Maryland to be in on the ground floor. Virginia has Fairfax County and DC is, well, DC. Maryland should be as big a player in this game as Virginia will be. I need you to broker a trade agreement with Jafir and the Alliance."

"What can you offer them?" Phillip asked.

"Baltimore has the Columbus Center, a leader in biotechnology. We've also made great strides in aquaculture. Praxis can make the Mediterranean more than a shipping place. Maryland can help." Governor Bundy's excitement was palpable.

"What do you want me to do?"

"I'd like for you to head up a trade mission to Jafir. The Alliance will be meeting there in two weeks. Present our trade package and negotiate a deal."

Phillip had no need to ask why Bundy had chosen him. He only questioned if he could go back. Was he ready to return? Restless dreams plagued his nights, colored his days with sepia tones of nonreality. A thousand polite refusals formed in his mind. *No thanks, Tom. I'm not ready to leave my father again so soon.* Or, maybe, he would claim another job offer, explain this visit away as an exercise of courtesy and friendship. He could even offer to draft the proposal, to train the trade mission staff.

Treachery, betrayal, and death remained his clearest memories of Jafir. When he struck a deal to assist the devil, all to save his own life. The litany of illicit deals, of minor wars funded by his deeds, played through his head with the staccato report of gunfire.

Quickly, Phillip rose from his chair, desperate to escape. "Tom, thanks for the offer. But I can't accept."

Puzzled, Bundy stood as well. "You look ill, Phillip. Are you all right? Gladys," he called out.

Gladys appeared at the door instantly. "Yes, sir?"

"Please, get Mr. Turman a glass of water," he barked out.

"Certainly. I told him he wasn't looking well," she muttered as she hurried off to fetch the water.

Embarrassed by the attention, Phillip forced a wan smile. In his chest, his heart began to thud. "I'm okay, Tom. Just tired." I need to get out of here, he thought to himself. Before I crumble. He lifted his briefcase with one hand. Shaking the governor's hand, he repeated, "I'm just tired. I'll let you know."

"Phillip, I think you should sit down for a second," Bundy instructed with concern.

"I need the fresh air," Phillip replied. Neither commented on the graying sky, pregnant with the promise of rain. He moved to the door, nearly colliding with Gladys.

"Here's your water, sir," she said, pressing the cup into his hand.

Phillip drank it down in a furious gulp and set it on a nearby table. "I really must go now, Tom. I'll call you."

He quickly moved past Gladys and out to the elevators. Unable to remain inside, he headed for the stairwell. When he finally emerged outside the building, Phillip loosened his tie. With impatient motions, he freed two buttons and dragged air into his starving lungs. Relying on the stone façade for support, he forced himself to methodically inhale and exhale. Slowly, his pulse regained its normal rhythm and the memories receded.

Cautiously, Phillip pushed away from the rough wall.

Panic attack, he thought. It had been a while since one had found him in the daylight. Tom Bundy must think he's crazy, he realized. Drawing in a final calming breath, Phillip readjusted his shirt and tie. Jafir. So tiny an island to wield such influence over his world. No matter where he turned, it crouched in hidden corners, waiting to spring out at him. To disturb his hard-won equilibrium and yank him once more into despair.

Petitions for relief from his torment had gone unanswered for nine long months. But no matter what Jafir and its treacherous inhabitants attempted, he would not let them win. He would have his life, without the haze of fear and guilt. Fear of losing himself, guilt over saving his own life. He'd waited long enough for peace to find him.

No, by God, he decided, he would not let them win.

Not the prison guards or Zeben or Cavanaugh. With a short, determined laugh, he began the walk to his car. Atlas was in for a surprise. He'd return to Jafir, as trade representative for Bundy. And as Sphinx.

The '67 Corvette Roadster gleamed a glossy black in defiance of the stormy sky. He'd restored it himself, during college summers, between jobs. The pleasure of letting the top down and welcoming the rush of wind had been stolen by those years, but he was slowly regaining his time. Rather than the surge of pain the recall of Jafir normally brought, behind the wheel, all Phillip felt was composure. Where turbulence had weighed him down, serenity now reigned.

With quick, efficient motions, he twisted the key in the ignition and headed toward Washington. Daring the rain to start, he drove home with the top down, the gloomy skies threatening. He dismissed the rain as impossible.

He'd already made his plans, and a fractious storm wouldn't deter him. The rest of his day would be spent restoring the brick row house he'd closed on last month. The grand old house brought up the rear on a block that dead-ended into Kalorama. Oatmeal shutters hung at odd angles from the second story windows, their slats cluttered with cobwebs. An awning the realtor swore used to be blue now sported an oxidized pasty hue. Renewed by his choice, he felt like tackling the projects for the first time since moving in. Heck, he might even go next door to say hello. Despite his three-week occupation and their close quarters, he had yet to meet his neighbor.

Phillip maneuvered the car into the alley beside his house. Outside, the sounds from the annual Adams Morgan Day festival filtered over from 18th Street. Voices jumbled together in a concert of languages and accents. Caribbean flowed into Spanish, accented by Eastern European.

Deciding to move into the neighborhood had been natural. Before, he'd had an apartment on Capitol Hill, straddling the wealth and poverty of the area. Adams Morgan appealed to him during this second life, with its diversity and constant motion.

His new house would require a great deal of hard labor, yet he'd known intuitively it was supposed to be his. With his investment portfolio, Dupont Circle or Woodley Park were easily in his range. But it was Adams Morgan that caught his imagination. Phillip raised the top on the Roadster and circled behind it to head to his front door.

And stopped. Beneath the scaffolding he'd erected to help with repairs, Alex perched on his stoop.

She stretched out her hand for assistance, and Phillip automatically pulled her to her feet, absorbing every detail. Today's outfit consisted of black shorts and an ivory T-shirt stretched thin over those distracting curves. The woman seemed to own nothing acquainted with her knees.

Blood poured out of his head to pool in other regions. How could he have imagined she was anything like Lorei? he wondered dimly. More than night and day, the two were as different as a summer breeze and a gale-force wind. Where Lorei may have quickened his pulse, the sight of Alex's coolly sculpted features thundered his heart.

Just as automatically as he'd helped her stand, Phillip jerked her up and into his arms. Before she could open that damnable mouth to protest or remind him of his folly, he covered full, pouty lips with a hungry kiss. For endless seconds, he held them together, sating himself after days, a lifetime of abstinence.

Alex hung in his strong, corded arms, mesmerized.

Every clear, coherent thought slid neatly from her head. Around her, inside her, there was only Phillip. As she shifted to free her arms to touch him, he halted the sensual assault and set her on her unsteady legs.

"Well, hello," she managed as her nerves struggled to settle.

Reams of sensation flooded her system, but she swore to herself she wouldn't melt into a puddle on his front porch. She'd be more dignified and wait until she crawled home. To gather her dignity, she bent to lift her satchel.

Phillip watched her through opaque eyes, their expression revealing no hint of welcome. "Hello," he responded tersely.

He's still upset, Alex surmised. It was to be expected, given her behavior at the wedding reception. She only prayed he would give her a chance to explain before he ordered her off his property. "I guess you're wondering what happened to me after the brunch," she started lightly.

"Not really," he answered as he opened his front door.

Nonplussed by the casual dismissal after his devastating kiss, Alex blurted out, "You don't care?"

"No." Phillip flicked on the light switch and dropped his briefcase on the marble pedestal in the foyer.

Uninvited, Alex marched inside. Phillip glanced over his shoulder and saw her framed in the doorway. He lifted a brow. "Is there something else you wanted?"

"I want to know why you kissed me like that if you don't care about me," she demanded hotly. No one liquefies her bones and then claims it doesn't matter, damn him!

Phillip didn't respond immediately. Instead, he removed the charcoal gray jacket, draping the Italian wool over the staircase rail. Alex found herself staring helplessly as he shed the day's suit. Matching pants emphasized a flat stomach, lean hips, powerful thighs.

Today, he reminded her of a twenty-first-century pirate, she realized, danger cloaked in urbane dress. Where she had once imagined the billowy white of the ship captain, a white button-down shirt closely covered broad, capable shoulders.

"Why I kissed you? Hmm," he mused, breaking her reverie. Long, adroit fingers unknotted his tie, and soon the colored strip of fabric joined the discarded jacket on the railing. "It seemed appropriate. Anything else?" he asked, not turning around.

Incensed, Alex repeated, "Appropriate? Ravishing me on your porch seems *appropriate?*"

Phillip ignored the note of outrage and headed into the living room. With a negligent gesture, he offered her a seat on the sofa. He perched on the arm, the length of a sofa cushion separating them.

Flouncing down onto her seat, Alex dropped her bag on the sofa and prepared to sulk. Beneath her, textured cotton in soft taupe yielded luxuriously. Knowing he watched her, she unhurriedly crossed her legs. Phillip's bedroom eyes darkened in response and his mouth tightened into a thin, flat line.

Alex checked the urge to smile. Appropriate, my butt, she thought triumphantly. He couldn't help himself. With a leisurely motion, she traced idle lines along one shapely thigh. "Appropriate, Phillip?" she purred. "Why?"

"Don't be coy, Alex. It doesn't suit you." Phillip swallowed tightly. He couldn't be in a room with her without wanting, without wishing. She had to leave. His babysitting days were over, as was his infatuation with Ms. Walton. Conquering Jafir was his new mission and she had no place in that life. When he returned to the ISA, there would be no room for distraction. Yes, Alex definitely had to go. Before he gave in to the compulsion to lift her into his arms and carry her upstairs, where no one and nothing would disturb them for hours. Days. Unbidden, torrid images of tangled limbs flashed in his mind. "Is there anything else you wanted, Alex?" he grated out.

"I need to explain about Damon," she began.

Phillip cut her off. "There's no need to apologize."

"I wasn't going to," Alex retorted. "I said explain." Alex slipped off red leather sandals and tucked her legs beneath her on the sofa. "Damon finding us, um, together in the garden was discomfiting. We needed to speak privately, so I took him aside."

"And left me standing there," Phillip reminded her.

Alex nodded. "Yes, and left you standing there. On the dais, in front of a crowd of two hundred guests, to go and dance with my former fiancée. Whoops, that was you, not me. As for Damon, I couldn't very well invite you to join us because that would have defeated the purpose. And he wasn't really in love with me. We talked it all out at the brunch."

"When you took him up to your bedroom," Phillip reminded her.

Alex nodded. "Yes, to my bedroom. Which has a perfectly lovely sitting room. Guests occupied every free space on the ground floor and why am I justifying myself to you?" She frowned at him, her eyes flashing. "What I do in my bedroom is my business. If I wanted to have an orgy with the groomsmen and the wait staff, you have nothing to say about it." In magnificent, outraged flight, Alex railed, "Damon Toca is my friend and I can do with him what I please. In any manner I please. However, out of courtesy—a concept with which you obviously have only a passing familiarity—I came to offer an explanation, but not an apology."

"So you've said," Phillip murmured with quiet amusement.

He wondered idly if she even required an audience for her rants. She seemed entirely capable of venting with or without him.

As she continued, he noted how passion flushed her cheeks, and the arrogant tilt of her head. And he wondered what she'd do if he did sweep her into his arms and carry her upstairs. Now, more than ever, he needed the touch of those clever artist's hands, the heat of those moist, angry lips. When righteous indignation set fire to her liquid chocolate eyes and glowed beneath her flawless skin, he desired her more than he imagined possible.

"So?" Alex huffed.

"So what?" Phillip replied, confused.

Alex spoke slowly, as though explaining herself to a dimwitted child. "Do you want to hear my voluntary explanation?"

"Yes. What's your explanation?" Phillip asked patiently.

Satisfied, Alex plunged ahead. "Well, he's the one who led to my moratorium. Against men. Or, I suppose, on men. I'm not sure what the right adverb would be."

"Alex."

"Right. Anyway, Damon's a perfectly wonderful man. But, as always, when he fell in love, I fell in deep like. Which definitely isn't the same emotion," she proclaimed.

Hiding a grin at her didactic tone, Phillip agreed, "No, it's not."

Alex scooted off the sofa to roam. Books lined every free surface of the room. Randomly, she lifted the bound pages, examining the titles. As she moved, she went on, "On my last night in Durban, he told me he loved me and wanted to marry me. I explained that I had to return to the States for the wedding the next day." Delighted by a dog-eared copy of *The Lord of the Rings*, Alex paused to thumb through its pages. When Phillip cleared his throat to prompt her, she shrugged. "So, he plied me with gifts and promised to pursue me."

Objectively, Phillip considered the cold fury surging through him. The emotion had sharp edges that clawed at already raw nerve endings. It felt suspiciously like jealousy. "He proposed?" he clarified, his fists clenched.

Oblivious to the undertones, Alex said, "Yes, on the beach in the moonlight. It was quite romantic. The light sparkling on the water. The waves lapping at the shore." On the mantle, she spied a framed photo. Lifting the picture, Alex saw a younger Phillip and an older man, as beautifully male as his son. "This must be your father," she declared.

With deliberate care, Phillip rose from the sofa, closing the space between them. "Yes, that's my father. Alex, are you engaged to Toca?"

"Heaven's no! If I was, why would I need a moratorium? An engaged woman has a moral obligation not to date other men."

"Not to mention kissing them," Phillip murmured, his eyes narrowed to focus on her mouth.

Alex inhaled sharply, amused and embarrassed. "You started it," she sniffed with a touch of humor. Her pulse tripped unsteadily, reminding her of the potency of his kiss. How he filled every sense and every thought with him.

Thoughtfully, Phillip grazed a finger across unpainted lips. They parted at his touch, unconsciously welcoming further exploration. He whispered, "I didn't notice any great resistance on your part, darling."

Alex lifted her shoulders and acknowledged tremulously, "You're very good at what you do." Perhaps skill drew her back to him, in spite of her resolution. He seemed to know exactly where to caress, where to stroke.

"You're no slouch yourself, Alex," he responded at length. Waves of thick black were bound at her neck by a vibrant scarf. Phillip played with the gossamer ends and finally pulled it free.

As the dark wave fell around her shoulders, Phillip murmured, "Each time I see you, I have no intention to touch you. You've declared your moratorium, and I have problems of my own. Common sense is screaming that nothing should happen between us. Our best friends are married, we live in the same town, we're bound to find ourselves in the same circles." Silk strands wrapped around his fingers, their feel cool and welcoming. When Alex tried to remove his hand by sidling away, his grip tightened, holding her still.

Phillip continued, his voice mild and patient. "First, I resisted you because you reminded me of Lorei. Wealthy, beautiful, fickle. Add to that your marked inability to not say anything that comes to your mind."

"I haven't said what I think of you," she muttered with annoyance.

"Another problem," Phillip suggested with a half-smile. "I'm a very private man and you want to write about me. What would you say if something did happen between us and went sour?"

Irritation snapped into her eyes and she jerked her chin. "How dare you suggest I would be less than fair! I may be wealthy and fickle, but I do have integrity." She circled his wrist and tried to untangle his fingers, without success. "Leave me the hell alone, and we won't have to worry about any of this!" she demanded angrily.

Curling a finger under her chin, Phillip succumbed to impulse. "Beautiful," he murmured as his breath fluttered across her mouth. "Wealthy, fickle, and beautiful. Smart, funny, and loyal," he breathed.

Alex attempted to ignore the tendrils of fire along her mouth. "Don't try to flatter me, Phillip." With effort, she maintained the breath of space between them.

"Flamboyant, thoughtful, stubborn," he added as his hands slid through the thick mass of hair to cradle her head.

From the tips of his skillful fingers, fire shot out, suffusing her in heat. She'd never known desire could come in an instant. Love, yes. But love was ephemeral, with as much substance as a dream. Desire was heavy, filled with cascades of sensation, refusing to be ignored. With every man before Phillip, desire had come, but not at the sight, at the sound of him. Phillip stunned her senses, aroused her to a fever pitch, before he said a word. And love?

Would loving Phillip overwhelm her as wanting him did? If she let herself fall, would it be real this time? Could she recover?

Panic quickly quenched desire, and Alex tugged Phillip's marauding hand away. "I've got to go," she stammered. "I can't stay." Swiftly, she gathered her purse from the couch and all but sprinted for the front door.

Heavy oak swung inside and bounced against the interior wall. Alex stepped onto the porch, anxious to make it home. The sounds of the festival filled the air, the chatter of excited children, the patter of keen salespeople plying their trades. Yet, underneath the hum of the festival, Alex heard a creaking noise.

Phillip, who followed close on her heels, heard it too. Wood splintered painfully and he glanced up. In the space of a heartbeat, he saw the beams of the scaffold buckle, with Alex directly below.

"Alex, watch out," he yelled as he rushed to grab her.

As the structure collapsed, Phillip leapt off the porch onto the lawn. He tucked Alex against his chest and twisted to absorb the impact of falling. They landed in a jumbled heap, Phillip on his back, his arms banded tight across Alex's breasts. On the porch, lumber, paint cans, and brushes dropped to the shallow steps and bounced onto the grass. The cacophony continued for a while, an echo of their thudding heartbeats. Winded by the fall, Phillip remained motionless, never loosening his grip on Alex.

For her part, Alex lay still, stunned. In as many weeks, she'd nearly died twice. Both times, she'd been with Phillip. Suddenly, her mind clicked into action, pieces falling into place. How had she never considered it before? Adam and Raleigh, secret agents for a shadowy extra-governmental organization. Phillip Turman, a congressman who supposedly dies in a mysterious accident, only to miraculously reappear days after Raleigh returned from a mission. Phillip, like his best friends, was a spy. And someone was trying to kill him. A someone who might still be nearby.

Gingerly, Alex rolled off Phillip and levered herself into a sitting position. He had yet to speak or move. "Phillip," she hissed quietly.

"What?" he returned in low tones.

"I don't think this was an accident." Alex made eye contact, the better to gauge his reaction to her theory. "And I don't think we should stay out here."

Phillip toyed with arguing about her analysis, but he realized they didn't have time. She was probably right, which meant the saboteur could be lurking in the alley or behind the house. "I think returning inside wouldn't be the brightest idea."

Nodding her agreement, Alex offered, "Then let's go to my house."

"How far away is it?" Phillip queried as he tried to sit up.

Alex furrowed her brow in confusion. "Phillip, you do realize that I live next door? I used to own this property."

With a muttered imprecation, Phillip scrambled to his feet and helped Alex to stand. "Of course you did. And, of course, you of all people happen to live next door. Why wouldn't you?" he grumbled.

Vainly, Alex tried to decipher the string of expletives Phillip uttered as they crossed the lawn to her row house. However, it was patently obvious he had no idea of their neighborly connection. Her trustees had purchased the entire row as an investment property before she came of age. The two homes adjoined on the opposite side stored her artwork and were rented periodically to college students or interns. Phillip's new house had remained vacant for years, but she'd authorized the trustees to put it on the market. When she returned yesterday, after spending the rest of the week with her parents, she found the paperwork from the realtor, with Phillip listed as the new owner.

Alex unlocked the door and invited Phillip inside.

Despite their identical exteriors, the interiors of their homes differed dramatically. Bold colors greeted visitors, from the vibrant green walls to the blocks of yellow and blue disguised as furniture. Where the balustrade curved down from the upper floors, a Kandinsky abstract splashed color on the parallel wall. In the living room, he recognized works by various artists. A Catlett stood on a pedestal in the corner and a vase swirled with red and purple glass graced an antique end table. But it was the portrait hanging over the mantle that arrested his attention.

The artist had captured a teenaged Alex en pointe, in a sapphire tutu. Defiant chin lifted, sultry mouth daring the painter, she appeared prepared to do nothing less than leap off the canvas. Yet, it was the eyes that made him pause. Soulful, coffee brown, trying to seem brave and wise. They dominated the portrait, drawing the viewer in, asking for answers to a million unspoken questions. Robert Walton's signature in the corner told him who the artist had been. But who was the woman in the painting? he wondered. Was the Alex he couldn't stay away from the same mass of contradiction and mystery?

Phillip turned toward Alex, to encounter an identical pose. The elfin chin dared him to comment, the great brown eyes searched his own with an emotion he could have sworn was fear. He relished the trepidation and the bravado, in equal measure. With her, he realized abruptly, each was vital. One to balance the other, to make her the woman he was fast falling in love with.

The idea staggered him, as much for its meaning as for its truth. He'd known the bewildering woman for less than a month. In fact, they'd actually only spent a full week in each other's company. Yet, he knew she'd fill the red vase with calla lilies. That the small suitcase she carried would likely contain a sketch pad and a notebook.

She'd have decorated the last pages of the pad with sketches of the festival-goers who passed by their street on the way. In the notebook, he'd find hastily scrawled descriptions, prose depicting the mood of the crowd, the smells of the afternoon.

Because he knew these details, he had no choice but to ignore the possibility of love. The second hit attempt had come too close to killing her. A third try would likely prove fatal. It hadn't escaped his attention that Alex had been present during both attempts. Until he was assured of Scimitar's target, he'd keep silent.

Although he was loath to leave her, he had to contact Atlas immediately. Perhaps coincidence explained her presence each time, and if so, his presence served to increase her danger. If she were the target or they both were, Phillip needed to allay her fears and shake loose some answers. Fearing listening devices, contact from here was out of the question. He had counter-listening devices in his home, but they'd likely been compromised.

Headquarters was the only option, and he'd have to trust that she'd be safe here for a couple of hours. He couldn't afford to bring her with him, but he'd call a friend on the force to keep an eye on her while he was gone. Satisfied with his plan, he turned to make his excuses.

Alex read the intent to leave in his narrowed eyes.

But he wasn't going anywhere until she had an explanation. "What's going on, Phillip?" she asked bluntly.

He shrugged and lied without compunction, "The scaffolding must have been jarred. Probably some kids from the neighborhood."

"No way, Phillip. Those timbers didn't collapse. They broke. And it was deliberate," she argued. Alex dropped onto the yellow chaise and crossed her legs. "Tell me what's going on," she demanded.

"Alex, I just told you. The scaffolding fell. End of story," Phillip returned in a condescending tone. He had no idea who might be listening, and he wasn't prepared to tell Alex the truth anyway.

At his continued denial, Alex reminded herself there could be bugs planted in her home. She had been out of the country when Phillip's house sold. There was no telling what the enemy could have done.

"Alright," she acquiesced. "So where are you taking me to dinner?"

Perplexed by the swift compliance, Phillip stared at her. "I'm not taking you to dinner, Alex. First of all, it's barely afternoon and secondly, I've got errands to run."

"Fine, you can feed me tonight." Alex stood, hooked an arm companionably in his, and led him to the door. "I'll be ready by eight."

CHAPTER NINE

S he knows?" Phillip repeated with disgust. "What kind of top secret organization tells everyone they exist?"

Atlas shifted in the solid leather chair and propped his elbows on the antique desk, the teak gleaming under the fluorescent lights. A discarded breakfast pastry leaned drunkenly against a late lunch of corn chips and roast beef. Phillip had stormed into his office, interrupting the makeshift meal.

According to Phillip's story, the intelligence supplied by Minnear was dead-on. Zeben had ordered a hit on Phillip, and somehow, Alex was involved. The reports on Toca were coming in, and the news wasn't good.

How the hell Alex got mixed up in all of this was beyond him. But the girl had always been a bit wild, Atlas considered. He adored that about her. Though he hadn't spent much time with her since he'd taken the helm of the ISA, Atlas made it a policy to keep close tabs on his godchild. On occasion, if the young man warranted such treatment, he'd run background checks on her beaus. And maybe once or twice, he and Robert conspired to ease an overly aggressive suitor out the door.

The labyrinthine universe of espionage offered precious little room for intimacy and affection. He'd found close friends in the Waltons, and Alex proved a trustworthy roommate for Raleigh. All in all, friendship and occupation coincided nicely in their cases.

To Phillip, however, he barked, "I can tell whomever I want to do whatever I please. I'm in charge here, son. She needed to know and Raleigh told her. End of discussion."

"It's just the beginning," Phillip countered with a sneer. "If I may be so bold, can you at least tell me why she knows?"

"Robert and Liz used to do a bit of courier work for the agency back in the seventies. Liz interned on the Hill for a senator who kept us fully funded. And Robert's international shows gave him a perfect cover."

Dumbfounded, Phillip asked in disbelief, "The Waltons are spies?"

"No, not spies. Couriers. They ferried microfiche and microchips for the organization. It's amazing what you can hide in a painting," admired Atlas.

"And where does Alex fit in?"

"Raleigh joined the team when she was barely in her twenties. Normally, she'd have lived alone or in a barracks on a government base. But Alex needed a roommate and Raleigh required a friendly face. They moved in together and the rest, as they say, is history."

Secrecy had always been the first rule of engagement.

Few field agents had the opportunity to identify their comrades, unless the situation demanded revelation. In rare instances, the ISA recruited simultaneously, as they had with Phillip and Adam.

But the rules firmly held that non-ISA spouses weren't allowed to know. Friendships existed under the veil of subterfuge. Lorei's impatience with his life stemmed, to an extent he never plumbed, from the wall of concealment forced between them. He didn't delude himself by thinking silence was the only culprit, but it forced him to hide decisions that could have explained his choices. Like refusing the Atlanta job to remain in DC. Like taking the congressional seat in part because Atlas thought it would provide deeper cover.

Rage simmered, tempered by apprehension. Lorei shouldn't have known, he agreed in hindsight, though it didn't ease the sting of betrayal. But Alex could be in danger now because of her knowledge. Saving her was paramount.

"What does she know, Atlas?"

"Minnear reported that Zeben's hired someone to kill you," Atlas noted. "Scimitar prisoners are only kept alive for information. Zeben believes passing false information among his troops will reveal traitors. We can't be confident Minnear's source is in the loop. Particularly now that Zeben is out."

Atlas tapped blunt, thick-tipped fingers together thoughtfully. "Given your accidents, I believe we can trust his source."

"And Alex? Where does she fit?" Phillip prowled across the polished hardwood floors, unable to remain still.

Atlas noted the uncharacteristic restlessness.

Coupled with the outrage at learning about Alex's clearance, he could suspect one of two options. Either Phillip's affront stemmed from his preternatural addiction to the regulations, or more existed between Alex and him than Atlas realized.

"We aren't sure." When Phillip glared at Atlas, he held his hands up in mock defense. "As I told you when I asked you to watch over her, I got strange reports from South Africa. The ISA returned the Kholari to the government and it was on display at their national museum. Until it was stolen three nights ago. And questions have been floated about the Sahalia. It's a ruby, forty carats. Disappeared almost twenty-five years ago. The Kholari and Sahalia are rumored to be part of a set. The sapphire and the emerald haven't been seen in centuries."

"What happened?"

"The ruby belonged to the royal family of Jafir. During that time, Zeben was first coming to power and had made threats on the lives of the king and queen. One afternoon, while out on a sail, the motor exploded and the boat capsized. The king and queen drowned."

"Zeben."

"Probably. Well, the Sahalia vanished as did the heirloom that proves right of succession to the throne."

"The obelisk."

"Exactly. Under Jafirian law, the royal family is hereditary, and should it cease to exist, the fortunes of the family revert to the government. Probate lasts twenty-five years. And expires in two weeks."

"Toca had Alex make a replica of an obelisk, but then he gave her the original. That doesn't make sense. If he can pretend to be the heir, why the ruse? Why Alex?"

Atlas did not meet Phillip's questioning look, instead focusing on a file on his desk. "I don't know. But you need to bring her in as soon as possible. She's probably not safe at home if someone believes she's got the obelisk or the ruby."

"We've got to bring Toca in," Phillip demanded.

Because Phillip's agitation appeared genuine, Atlas didn't correct his violation of protocol. Instead, he opened a file from his desk and slid it over the slick surface to Phillip.

Phillip studied the black-and-white photograph, reading the lines of text, hoping for insight. A connection tickled the back of his mind. "Toca," he exclaimed suddenly. "Toca is Jubalani."

"Of the Toca Galleries?" Atlas questioned. "No, he's not."

Smugly, Phillip dropped into a chair opposite Atlas's desk. "It fits his MO. Jubalani is a ladies' man who uses women to courier his goods. And Toca claims to have fallen in love with Alex after three weeks. Even more absurd, he proposed and then followed her to Atlanta. If that isn't a cover for something, I don't know what is." He crossed his arms in satisfaction, ignoring his own confused feelings for the woman.

"Damon Toca is a highly respected businessman. The Toca Galleries are the South African equivalent of Sotheby's," he contradicted. "Besides, Alex is an amazing woman. It's not hard to imagine a man falling in love with her so quickly. In fact, it's her specialty." Atlas chuckled.

"You think an international tycoon can't be a spy? Uh, Adam?"

"Adam is the exception, not the norm. But, for the sake of argument, assume you're right. What would Jubalani need Alex for? He's got carte blanche to travel anywhere he pleases. There's no reason for him to smuggle the obelisk out. And Alex paints and sculpts. She doesn't do jewelry."

Phillip shook his head in disagreement. "Toca's our guy, Atlas. I thought I recognized him and I did."

Atlas left his seat to come around to Phillip. "You saw him once, Phillip, for minutes. You couldn't reproduce him for our forensic artists, even with your skills." He laid a massive paw on the younger man's shoulder. "Alex Walton is a lovely woman, Phillip. You two have spent a great deal of time together, not to mention your near-death experiences. Don't let jealousy cloud your judgment, son."

Phillip recoiled as though struck. "Jealousy? Don't be ridiculous. I'm merely examining all the possibilities. If Toca could be our link, we need to consider it. Jealousy is absurd."

"And you have no other feelings for Alex?" Atlas struggled to keep his mouth from twitching with laughter. "None at all?"

The lie came easily, without hesitation. "She's an assignment. Nothing more."

―――――――

At eight o'clock sharp, Phillip pressed Alex's doorbell.

The end of summer flirted with autumn, resulting in warm breezes and air heavy with the promise of showers. Patchy clouds refused to cede their bounty. Across the street, the plainclothes officer parked in a nondescript sedan waved to him and pulled away from the curb. Debris from the scaffolding breakdown had been whisked away by an ISA investigative detail. They would test for fingerprints, chemical residue, any clue to the cause of the collapse.

Atlas agreed to notify Raleigh and Adam about the potential threat to Alex. The couple was due to return from the Seychelles in three days. In the interim, he'd shadow Alex and monitor her interactions.

He believed, with a bone-deep conviction, in a connection between Alex and Toca and Jubalani. Whether Atlas took his concerns seriously or not, Phillip planned to protect her from him. Through the door, he heard Alex call out that she was on her way.

Phillip snorted as he propped a foot on the Victorian blue porch rail. Jealousy. Maybe he'd thought about the possibility himself. Still, he reminded himself, even if he was jealous—which he didn't necessarily admit to be true—it didn't render his suspicions illegitimate. Toca wanted something. His conscience cackled, "You want something too."

Unbidden, he remembered how close he'd come to making love to her in the garden. How her silken flesh slid against his own, how the scent of flowers clung to every fragrant inch. Ripe, sensual lips urging him to devour, to delight. The press of angle to curve, of hard to soft, of man to woman. He nearly groaned aloud at the memory.

Because the situation demanded focus, he thrust the images aside, but they skittered again into his brain.

Phillip worked best when the rules were clear, the goal certain. Alex clouded his brain, blurred his mission. Desire, he understood. She was gorgeous, flamboyant, self-assured. Not his usual type, but nevertheless a woman who appealed to every sense. No, desire he could handle.

Instead, need and want drew him to her, made him vulnerable. He longed to understand her fully, to learn what he innately recognized. The fearlessness, and the angst, gave Alex a depth that surprised him. Caprice warred with an enviable talent, producing a sharp mind capable of glorious art and incisive questions.

Complex and complicated, Phillip realized he would possess Alex, body and soul. Soon. At the same time, however, regardless of his feelings, they would not interfere with protecting Alex. From Scimitar, from Toca, and, if need be, from himself. Contented by his decision, he pressed the bell again impatiently. Suddenly, he had to see her.

The heavy door swung open and Alex bounded out to greet him. "Oh dear, you're punctual," she chided, locking the door.

"I didn't realize courtesy offended you," came the dry response.

Alex laughed. "Only when it makes me look bad." Phillip closed her hand in his and led her to his car.

The sleek, classic lines of the Roadster suited him perfectly. Quiet elegance concealed a core of power. She noted with delight the open top and eagerly slid inside.

He leaned inside the car to fasten the seat belt, his hand sliding across her shoulders, brushing the thin straps of her sundress. Warmth simmered on her shoulders, a companion to the ball of fire in her stomach, a kindling of flame that occurred whenever he touched her. She'd resigned herself to her fate.

While Phillip raced off to consult Atlas, as she knew he had, she'd reached a number of conclusions of her own. Settling into the butter-soft seat, as the Temptations crooned about imaginings, Alex closed her eyes. Her first decision had been about the obvious physical connection she shared with Phillip. In the weeks she'd known him, she'd grown accustomed to the heat, to the shortness of breath and the skittish pulse. Phillip moved her, aroused her, as no one had. But feeling did not inevitably lead to action, and her moratorium loomed more important than ever.

Alex gave a small smile as she thought about the call she'd received after Phillip left. During her week in Atlanta, Alex had drafted the first three chapters. Evil hunted Phillip's character, a man of great daring-do. Her hero captured her imagination as little had in a while.

She'd faxed the pages to an editor friend in New York, who wanted to see the entire novel. As a muse, Phillip proved spectacular. Therefore, if she stuck close, she'd surely produce a blockbuster. She wasn't oblivious to the fact that whoever wanted Phillip dead didn't care if she went with him. Initially, the realization incensed her, then frightened her, until she realized the potential.

Phillip obviously believed she too was in danger, otherwise, he wouldn't have summoned the poorly disguised cop to sit outside her house all afternoon. Given his chivalrous manners, he'd be glued to her side until they solved the mystery. Thus, she'd have unfettered access to his life story, brilliant inspiration for her story. More importantly, she could help him figure out what was going on, a second set of eyes and ears. Like her heroine Allegra, she'd save the day.

And in the end, she'd have an incredible novel and he'd have a closed case. However, her entire plan hinged on remaining aloof. If she succumbed to the desire that flooded through her each time his mustache brushed her lips or his strong hands molded her to him, they'd drive each other to distraction. Since she seemed to be irresistible to him, it would be up to her to keep them focused.

Occupied with his own thoughts, Phillip didn't notice Alex's smug expression. "Alex, we need to talk," he said.

Alex turned to watch his profile. The high, intelligent forehead wrinkled in concentration. "About this afternoon. And the accident at the airport."

"Yes. As I assume you've guessed, neither event was an accident."

"Do we know who's behind it?"

"Not yet. But, before we get to that, there's something else," he admitted. "I'm not who I told you I was," he began.

Alex forestalled the confession. "Oh, I figured out that you're an agent with the ISA, if that's your big secret." She tried without success to hide the note of self-congratulations.

Phillip heard it and grimaced. "How did you know?"

"Raleigh's my best friend. Adam has a secretive past. And you're more furtive about your history than either of them. You were either an agent or their therapist. Nothing else made sense."

Phillip strangled back an unwanted laugh. "What else do you know?"

Alex twisted in her seat to face him. "Someone very angry, with horrible aim, is trying to kill you. I don't know if my involvement is bad luck or poor timing or what. I mean, my days as an international art thief are long behind me."

At Phillip's sharp look, she smiled. "I'm joking, Phillip."

"Adam and Raleigh are meeting with us in three days. Until we know how you're implicated in this, I need you to stick with me."

"Do you have any suspects?" Alex queried.

"None identified," he answered at length.

THE ART OF DESIRE

Alex narrowed her eyes. "I hope you lie to the bad guys better than that."

For a second, Phillip met her eyes. "I do," he responded quietly as he turned into a French restaurant's lot in Alexandria. A khaki-suited valet rushed up to take the car, whistling at the Roadster, lengthening it in appreciation of Alex. Alex rolled her eyes. The bespectacled lad bumped into the door and fumbled with the keys.

"Does every man fall for you?" Phillip grumbled as he draped an arm around her waist.

"Only the ones with pulses," she returned saucily.

Soon, they were seated at a small table, tucked into a dimly lit corner. Candlelight flickered from slim, peach tapers. A single, fragile rose rested in a crystal bud vase. Wistful piano poured from muted speakers, low enough to allow for the muffled rumble of conversation. An efficient sommelier filled their glasses with a rich cabernet.

"Phillip, you haven't forgotten about my book, have you?" Alex inquired as the steward left their table.

"It's not as though you'd let me. I must have given you at least twenty hours of interview time in Atlanta."

"Background. Now that you've revealed another facet of your life, I'll have to ask more questions."

"You can," Phillip nodded solemnly. "But then I'd have to kill you."

Alex gave a half-laugh, uncertain if he joked or not. "You're kidding, right?"

Before Phillip answered, the waiter arrived to take their orders. Alone once more, Alex tilted her head to study him. Her research on him revealed slightly more than she knew from the news. The hero's motivation called for a backstory. Of particular interest to her, on a professional and, if she admitted it, personal level, was his romantic history. She thought to maneuver her way by throwing out a softball. "You've led a very private life. Nary a scandal or political intrigue in your past."

"My father raised me well," he demurred.

"No bribes? Stamp fiascos?"

Phillip chuckled. "Hopefully, your story will be a bit more exciting than a franking debacle."

Deciding a clean thrust was better, she took the opening and said, "Tell me about Lorei. Unless it's too painful."

The typical pang of remorse was notably absent.

Instead of balking, Phillip shrugged and lifted his glass for a sip of wine. "We met while I was at law school. Adam introduced us. She was smart, pretty, charming. She was at Yale finishing up her degree in social work, so I'd drive down to see her every weekend. We fell in love."

"You were engaged to be married. What happened?"

"Our lives diverged. I no longer wanted what she did. We postponed the wedding until after my stint in the Justice Department. Then I had the chance to run for Simpkins's congressional seat. It wasn't the life she'd planned. She called the engagement off. Adam's wedding is the first time I've seen her in almost ten years." Regret darkened his eyes.

Alex reached across the table and covered his hand. "I'm sorry," she murmured. "I didn't mean to pry."

"Of course you did, Alex," Phillip corrected with a half-smile to soften the comment. "But I'm okay. Lorei was a long time ago."

"It seemed quite close at the wedding," Alex muttered.

Phillip remembered their conversation. "You denounced our relationship as over, if I recall."

"I was fishing. You didn't bite."

"I'm an open book. What else do you want to know?"

"Have you been in love since her?"

Phillip turned his hand beneath hers, pressing palm to palm, to test her, to test himself. With calm, thoughtful eyes, he said, "I don't know."

The words hung between them, as potent as the touch of hand to hand. Phillip's thumb stroked ribbons of fire across her softer flesh. Amazing how her hand never seemed erotic before him.

Alex took a deep, settling breath and concentrated on her resolution. Yes, he made her yearn with a look, ache with a simple touch. But surrendering wasn't an option. "Why did you choose to run for Congress?" she asked instead.

"The subtlety of power. And yet, politics itself is like the first time you make love with a new partner. There are equal parts desire and frustration. Like a bad lover, if you do not take care, you may achieve satisfaction, but you'll lose your companion. Ah, but if you're good at it, every action is a delicious courtship, an agony of pleasure. Each partner receives the right touch, the right caress. It's delicate and rough and a thousand shades in between. The culmination is an act of satiation greater than either of you imagined."

"Oh," Alex whispered.

Pleased with her reaction, Phillip lifted her hand to whisper soft kisses across her knuckles. "I want to own a sculpture of yours," he murmured. "I'd like to see what you'd select for me."

"A hawk," she replied instantly, tugging her hand free. He

had a habit of not letting go. Alex described the piece as she made a show of rearranging her napkin. "A bronze cast of a peregrine falcon, wings folded close as he dives."

"A falcon," he repeated.

"Peregrine. One of the fastest birds on the planet. Sleek, fast, cunning. Intelligent creatures, they stalk their prey from overhead, then dive to capture the unsuspecting."

"And I remind you of one." Phillip topped off her glass.

"Absolutely. They're gorgeous animals, like yourself. Possessing the same quiet arrogance," Alex explained as she broke open a steaming roll. "And a lethal grace."

Phillip mused aloud, "I think I should be insulted."

"Quiet arrogance can be appealing. And I did say you were gorgeous."

Phillip sipped from his glass. "Thank you," he said.

Alex laughed delightedly. "Phillip, you know you're beautiful. Lean, well-built. Solid but not bulky. Your face is a sculptor's dream. The firm, sensual mouth, framed by a silky black mustache, a painter's wish. I'd cast you in bronze or paint you in oils. But, as I'm a writer now, I'll describe you in exquisite detail, from the narrowed bedroom eyes, to the cute little butt."

"Alex," he warned, "stop it." Looking around to see if anyone overheard, he continued, "Thank you. Now, can we talk about something else?"

She propped her elbows on the table and rested her chin on her folded hands. "Why is it men can wax poetic about a woman's beauty, but are mortified when complimented? I wouldn't take you for a chauvinist, Phillip."

"I'm not a chauvinist," he replied, "I'm modest. An unfamiliar term for you, I know."

Charmed by the light derision, Alex beamed, "Ask me something else."

"Have you ever been in love?"

While the waiter delivered their meals, Alex formulated a suitably innocuous response. When they were alone again, she tossed off, "Several times."

"Don't be glib, Alex. It's unworthy of you."

Chastened, she took a fortifying swallow of wine. "No, I've never been in love. For me, it's not simply a matter of slaking a thirst. Each time, I truly believe he could be the one. The man who makes my heart race and my pulse pound. The one who gets me." Alex toyed with her fork and gave serious attention to her meal, knowing if she looked at him while she spoke, she'd see too much. "I'm impulsive and lazy. I forget commitments and jet off on a whim. My art is erratic. I'm intrusive. He never got that."

"Did he tell you this?" Phillip asked.

"He?" Alex met his eyes, somber and concerned. "No, there is no one he. It's every man I've let myself believe I could love. Gregg was too disciplined. He tried to put me on a schedule. After a week, I flew to Santiago and left him a beautiful missive and tickets to the Kennedy Center. He's engaged to the opera singer who performed that night. With Adrian, it was my clothes."

"Adrian Stillfield? The judge?" Stillfield headed the short list for the next Supreme Court opening.

She twirled her cutlery with restive hands. "One and the same. Oh, he never complained, but I heard the comments. Flashy. Overly exuberant. Never unseemly, but a bit too bright."

Stilling the fidgety motions by cupping her hands, Phillip

waited until her eyes met his. "How will you know the one, Alex?"

The fire started, and Alex tried desperately to ignore it, to ignore him. She didn't want to give voice to her wants, the secret desires she'd abandoned as hopeless.

"Alex, talk to me," he whispered.

Candlelight twinkled. Outside the window, jagged streaks of light flashed a warning. For the briefest moment, the world contracted to only their table. Perhaps, if she told him, a wish on candlelight and roses, perhaps it would come true. "I want him to be excited about waking up next to me. I want to be the reason he welcomes the morning, because he knows that gives him one more day with me," she said passionately. "I've been in *like* before, Phillip, with men who said I made them content. Who said I made them comfortable. I don't want him to feel comfortable with me. I want the man I love to be edgy and excited and more alive with me than anywhere else, at any time. I don't just want him to love me. I want him to be in love with me. If I can't have that, I can't be with him."

"Why not?"

"Because I believe in soulmates," she answered simply, her eyes brilliant and sad. "I couldn't stand anything less. I don't want to be the friend you, he, sleeps with. I want to be the woman he makes love to."

"So you push them away before they prove to be less than you require," Phillip summed up. "It's a self-fulfilling prophecy, Alex. You find a flaw, in you or in him, and it becomes fatal. You pretend to fall in love so you'll never have to love anyone."

"Whereas you don't try at all," countered Alex, dropping her fork with a noisy clatter. "Once Lorei hurt you, you stopped trying to find someone. Threw yourself into your career, your night job."

Angry, Phillip pushed his plate aside and retorted, "You know nothing about my love life, Alex."

"Washington is a small town, Phillip. You dated, but not for very long. A string of proper women who admired your brilliance and appreciated your power," she guessed. "No one to ruffle your veneer. No one to disappoint you with her expectations."

"And you date like a kamikaze pilot. I doubt the poor bastards ever know what hit them," he flung back.

Alex leaned forward to trail a fingertip across the angry line of his mouth. In throaty, passionate tones, she whispered, "I may discard men, Phillip, but they never complain about the ride."

With that, she rose, certain next she'd say something she'd regret. "I'll meet you outside. I've suddenly lost my appetite."

Phillip watched in grudging admiration as she strode out of the restaurant on lithe, slender legs. The flirty sundress, a riot of pinks and blues, drew looks; however, it was Alex who held their attention.

As he signaled the waiter, he reflected on their last skirmish. She'd scored a direct hit with her assessment of his romantic life. After Lorei, he'd turned his interests to domestic affairs and global espionage. With wry amusement, Phillip recalled his last dates before Jafir. A satisfying three-month run with a lobbyist and a six-week liaison with an accountant. His trysts ended with no recriminations, no messy goodbyes. Polite endings, punctuated by politer silences.

A relationship with Alex would be messy. And loud.

And more exciting than any mission. He wanted her for

himself—where he could experience the wonder of waking up beside her. He would watch her in dappled sunlight, the slow awakening. Of course, she would ease into morning, with a sleepy smile and a languid stretch. She'd roll over, covering her head with the pillow until he coaxed her into his arms with soft, teasing kisses.

Softly, dreamily, they would make love in a pool of light. Her scent would surround him, envelope him. He would taste only her, feel only her. She would rise to meet him, welcome him inside. Silken fire would devour him, a heat only she could create.

After a decade or so, surely the edge of need would smooth, the constant ache would dull. It would take at least that long to peel away the first layer of Alex Walton. She was marvelously complex. What she saw as frivolity, he understood as a yen to experience the world. The quirky changes in medium or subject, rather than a flaw, were a testament to a nuanced insight to art. Blessed with the ability to fit form to substance, she decried perfectionism as an attention deficit.

As for the men who tried to change her, and then let her relegate them to friend and companion, for them Phillip had no sympathy. Here was a woman who tackled the world head-on, chin thrust out for battle. How easily she could slip between universes, from politics to art to commerce. At the reception desk, he stood beside her as she charmed, debated, and held her own against formidable minds. Why would a man want anything less? he thought. Bright, strong, unafraid of being different. He could spend a lifetime getting to know her. Starting now.

Phillip paid the bill and waited for the waiter to return with his card. Taking his time, he pushed back from the table. Set on his course, he had all the time in the world. Tonight, after he and

Alex made love, the sharpness of need might subside. He hoped not.

As he stood, the valet from the lot rushed inside.

His frightened eyes skimmed over the patrons and settled on Phillip. The teenager sprinted toward him and Phillip met him half way.

"What's wrong?" Phillip demanded, his gut tightening with foreboding.

"The woman! Some men just grabbed her and threw her into a car. She screamed and I tried to help, but I was too late. I tried to help, I swear."

Phillip shoved the boy out of his way and raced out into the night air. Rain, heavy and fat, dropped from the blackened sky. Thunder sounded ominously as Phillip demanded his car. The young valet gripped his sleeve, and Phillip spun around, his eyes feral with rage.

The boy stumbled backward, holding up his hands to ward off a blow.

Calming himself with effort, Phillip questioned, "Did you see which way they headed?"

"Toward Highway One, I think. I didn't see the license plate good, but I think it was one of those diplomat plates."

A second valet handed him the keys to his car and moved away, under the protection of the shed.

"What's your name?" Phillip asked the boy.

"Jeremy. Jeremy Fowler," the boy stuttered, water running rivulets down his glasses.

Phillip extended his hand and captured the boy's wet, sweaty palm. "Thank you, Jeremy. Now, listen carefully. People will be here in a few minutes to question you. Speak only to them. Do not call the police," he instructed. He pressed a hundred-dollar bill into Jeremy's free hand. "It's imperative that you wait for my friends. No police, Jeremy."

"Yes, sir. I mean, no, sir. No police, sir," he stammered.

Phillip climbed into the Roadster and sped off into the night. He opened his glove compartment and removed a burner phone, engaged the scrambler, and punched in a series of numbers. After interminable seconds, Atlas appeared on the view screen.

"Report," Phillip barked.

"Alex. They've got Alex."

CHAPTER TEN

Phillip barely restrained an urge to punch the brick façade. Impotent fury swept through him, followed swiftly by bitter shame. To allow her to storm away, letting pique rule rather than reason, it was an unpardonable offense.

Alex's abduction rested squarely on his shoulders. Rendezvous with Atlas and the team was in two hours. He had until then to sweep her home for clues.

With an efficiency born of years of practice, Phillip opened the locks and disengaged the alarm system. Once inside, he halted at the base of the stairs. To his left, books lay strewn across the hardwood, the red and purple vase upended on the sofa. The portrait of Alex leaned drunkenly against the fireplace, likely removed in a search for a safe.

He took the stairs two at a time, careful not to touch the banister. While he doubted the intruders had been incautious

enough to forgo gloves, he didn't want to risk losing an identifying print. Unerringly, he aimed for Alex's bedroom, which was
separated from his own by a thin wall. Lace, silk, and cotton
spotted the maize carpet, torn from the suitcases spread across
the queen-sized bed. The bureau's drawers had been flung
against the opposite wall. A shattered mirror caught the room at
odd angles, reflecting back the shambles of the bed, the destruction of a desk.

Whatever they'd been searching for had eluded them, Phillip
surmised, noting the wanton damage to the mirror. Where haste
explained the broken furniture, only an untamed rage accounted
for the shards of glass.

After a thorough check of the other rooms on the second
floor, Phillip climbed up to her studio. Gentle rain pattered
against the bay windows. Storm clouds drifted across the indigo
sky, revealing a harvest moon. Phillip nudged the light switch
and brightness illumined the wide, cluttered space.

The interior walls had been demolished to create an airy
room stretching the length of the house. Canvases stacked in a
far corner braced against a table crammed with tubes and bottles
of liquid color. A small stove, with a steam pipe rising through
the roof, occupied the other wall.

He turned to survey the whole of her space. Palette knives
mingled with chisel and hammer on a worktable beneath a suspended lamp. Beside them, on a raised surface, an unfamiliar
stone had been transformed into a fairy-tale castle, complete
with turrets and moat. Dreams carved into reality, uniquely
Alex.

Phillip noted with interest that in this space, items had been
moved with care. A fine sheen of dust hung in the air, a sign of

disuse. Recent movement had lifted the particles, leaving motes dancing on ribbons of light. Near the unfinished canvases, a closet door stood ajar. Boxes filled the gap in the doorjamb, some crushed beneath an angry heel.

Standing again in the Washington office, Phillip reported his findings to Atlas.

"Toca's got her," Phillip grated out.

Atlas bent over the sweeper team's report. "Your valet reported diplomatic plates. Toca's not in the corps, nor is he related to the ambassador or her staff. He's South African." He flipped the crisp pages, delivered minutes before Phillip's arrival. Atlas scanned the analysis and passed the file to Phillip.

Phillip knocked the report aside, frustration and fear churning in his gut. "He's got her, Atlas. Have the FBI stop any outbound planes. The CIA can cancel international flights out of National and BWI. Close the regional airports. Do something, damn it!"

In silence, Atlas shuffled together the fallen papers and slid the packet across the desk's surface to bump against Phillip's clenched fist. "Read the report, Sphinx," Atlas ordered.

As he accepted the slim folder, Phillip dragged in a deep breath. Cold, desolate eyes fixed on Atlas and fell to peruse the report. Suddenly, Phillip inhaled sharply and raised his head to meet Atlas's calm countenance. "The car belonged to the Jafirian delegate?"

"The boy mentioned a coat of arms on the sleeve of the kidnapper. When they showed him the flag of Jafir, he recognized it instantly," Atlas explained.

"Zeben," Phillip spat out.

Atlas closed the file and placed it on the desk. He pressed an intercom button and James, his assistant of ten years, appeared instantly at the door.

"Yes, sir?" inquired James. He'd been summoned from his bed in Georgetown and came without question. A CIA transfer, James understood his round-the-clock duty.

Atlas quickly scribbled numbers onto a thin, wispy slip of paper James would incinerate after the message was sent. "Contact Chimera on this frequency. Transmit message: Art acquired, retrieval in progress. Rendezvous Beta Point."

S he'd become far too intimate with death, Alex thought morbidly. In a month, she'd become too familiar with its smell, its shape. She avoided bungee jumps and rock climbing and skydiving, the preferred extreme sports of her peers, all because of a healthy sense of self-preservation. Twenty-seven years of careful evasion of even a car accident, for naught.

Panic lodged in her throat, the need to scream barely repressed by her greater fear of the unknown. Men had dragged her from the front of the restaurant, bundled her into a dark car. Frantic kicks and punches landed indiscriminately, pleasing her with the sound of pain.

Her own muffled shouts for help transformed into a ferocious bite at the hand that restrained her. He—she knew it was a man from the tangy, sweat-logged scent—wrapped ties around her eyes and mouth, her hands, her feet. Another man, with softer hands, tossed her against the door. From the violent treatment, Alex assumed he was the man she'd kicked. The door slammed and one of the men scrambled over the seat into the front.

Orders hissed out in a language she recognized as Arabic, the sibilant words indecipherable. She cursed her mother for insisting on Spanish and her father's firm instruction in Italian. If Raleigh were here, she'd comprehend their conversation and save the day. All Alex could do was wait and hope someone spilled a secret in English.

In the next instant, the car lurched out of the parking lot. The distant sound of other cars gave no clue to their direction. Perhaps Phillip knew the destination. Phillip. Alex cursed herself for stalking out of the restaurant, forgetting the danger that lurked. But Phillip never should have allowed her to leave, she thought petulantly. She'd expected him to chase after her, profuse with apology. Now, she wondered if he survived at all. A sob rose in her chest at the image.

If he died, she would go mad. To finally find love and lose it so quickly, she wouldn't survive. To finally find love, the thought reverberated with the force of an earthquake. She wasn't in love with him. Absolutely not. Behind the blindfold, Alex's eyes flew open in shock.

Because she dreamed of him, sleep or awake, didn't mean she loved. Because she'd missed him, no, pined for him during the last two days, only showed that he was important.

The pressure on her heart threatened to crush her, and her breath quickened precipitously. She loved him. She loved his aloofness, his dry humor, his loyalty.

Who'd of thought a moratorium would be her undoing, she thought hysterically. Now she was in the middle of a nightmare, due in large part to her own tantrum.

Leave it to her to screw up the finest day in her life. She'd finally found her soulmate and he was probably dead.

Alex struggled for control. Phillip wasn't dead. He'd been inside the restaurant, and she hadn't heard gunfire. Not that she knew what gunfire sounded like, beyond the proverbial car backfire. Still, she had to believe he was safe. And looking for her. So she could tell him the truth. That she loved him. In her head, in her heart, the words were sure and solid. Like Phillip.

No matter what the goons in the car had in mind, she'd make it out of here alive. The cute boy who'd leered at her when parking Phillip's Roadster had seen the abduction. Surely, he'd reported her missing to Phillip by now.

She forced herself to settle down, to think. You're a writer, she reminded herself. What would Allegra do in this situation? Quickly, she began to list her options. With her eyes blindfolded, assessing escape routes was impossible. Besides, she had no idea where they were taking her. *Think, Alex, think.*

A soft, cultured voice interrupted her frenzied thoughts. "Ms. Walton, I will remove your gag in a moment. Do not attempt to scream. No one will hear you, and it will anger my employer. The blindfold and the bonds will remain. Do you understand?"

Alex nodded and deliberately relaxed her posture. Smooth palms brushed her face as the tie loosened. The cool touch lingered against her skin, and Alex repressed a shudder of revulsion.

"Where is the sculpture, Ms. Walton?" the voice demanded.

Alex stifled a panic-stricken giggle. "I'm a sculptor. I'll need you to be more specific," she replied, her voice even and faintly scornful.

Cold metal slid up her slender neck and pressed below her ear. Alex shivered, unable to stop the trembling.

Happy with her reaction, he repeated the question, the words hard and clipped. "Where is the sculpture? The one you stole."

Stolen sculpture? Her mind raced. Alex created sculptures, rarely buying for personal pleasure. When she did make a purchase, she verified the provenance thoroughly, wary of the black market in trafficked art. "I don't understand," she replied.

"The sculpture from South Africa. Where is it?"

Forty pieces returned from Durban. Which one was so important? Stalling for time, Alex searched for a lie to appease him. "In my studio. If you'll take me there, I'll give it to you."

The flat of his hand cracked across her cheek, and she whimpered in pain as her head hit the car window. "Do not lie to me, Ms. Walton," he warned mildly. "We have searched your home. It is not there. Where is it?"

Alex stiffened her spine and straightened in her seat. She angled her chin in defiance. He had to take her home, where Phillip could find her. Forcing a sneer, she retorted, "I don't know what you're talking about. However, if you're looking for a particular piece and didn't find it, I assume you searched only the primary studio."

"Primary studio?" The voice faltered, then hardened. "Your home was searched thoroughly. There are only three floors."

"I also maintain a kiln in the basement," she scoffed. "And storage spaces in the attached homes."

"Turman occupies the home next to yours," he corrected, pressing the gun's barrel more firmly to the vulnerable flesh.

"I own the entire block," Alex explained with patronizing tones. "I maintain the adjoining homes as investment properties and for storage."

The voice switched quickly from English into Arabic then into muttered Italian. The second man on their seat responded angrily and called the man Civelli. The gun at her head shifted for an instant, when Civelli responded. Alex concentrated on him, on the accent, the intonation, but the words were too low to be distinct. A third voice, faint but somehow familiar, issued a short command from the front of the car.

Alex tumbled to the floor as the car suddenly jerked and sped up. Her face brushed the carpet, and she used the opportunity to dislodge the blindfold a scant inch on the right. Near her left elbow, her satchel bounced as the car hit an object in the road. Before long, soft hands hauled her up onto the bench and strapped her into the seat. With slow, furtive movements, she angled her head to observe the occupants through the reflections off the car window. Dim overhead lighting cast poor illumination, but Alex identified her captor as Eritrean or Ethiopian. Civelli, she decided.

Her tone insolent, Alex offered, "If I knew why the sculpture was so important to you, or even what it looks like, I could be of greater assistance." Stomach roiling with nerves, she added, "I can help."

Civelli surveyed Alex critically and weighed his options. He had been hired to retrieve the statue and the ruby and to kill Turman. He tried this afternoon to find the confounded obelisk, but they returned to her home before he made his search. The collapsed scaffolding, a clumsy attempt on Turman's life, had failed as well. And he had no clue where the ruby was hidden. Zeben grew impatient, and Civelli longed for the safety of his native soil. Or Aruba, whichever.

However, he was nothing if not adaptable. Indeed, he'd accepted a second contract and would deliver the ruby to him instead of Zeben. If Zeben had the obelisk, he could claim the power, which his rival did not want. With such a hefty paycheck, Civelli could disappear forever. Lovely Alex Walton would make a feisty companion, and she seemed to be a woman willing to bend rules. According to his new employer, she had the temerity to steal from the Toca Galleries, using her own exhibition as a cover. Now, she offered to lead him to the sculpture, he assumed, for a price. Indeed, with her help, he'd locate the statue, sell it to Zeben at twice the price, and deliver the ruby for even more and keep the girl for himself.

Intrigued by the thought, he stroked the pad of his thumb along the bruise blooming on her left cheek. He did not often strike women, preferring to seduce rather than throttle. But his tolerance was dissipating rapidly.

"If you cannot identify the sculpture, this means you took more than one piece from Toca's gallery?" Civelli asked.

Playing along, her heartbeat accelerating, she responded, "Why not? I did not believe I would be a suspect." So, she was accused of stealing from Toca. If he thought her guilty, why not confront her in Atlanta? "Does Toca himself accuse me?" she demanded, her words annoyed.

Civelli smiled, scenting a fellow conspirator. "Should he?" The gun fell to his side as he threaded his fingers deeply in her black hair. They tightened, turning her to face him. And he saw the raised blindfold.

Alex flinched, expecting another blow. Instead, he reached behind her to untie the knot securing the length of fabric.

"Do not be frightened, *signorina*. My apologies for the earlier punishment. I grow exasperated with the delays in locating the statue." Civelli cupped her neck, his thumb resting lightly on the spot where her pulse beat madly. "I terrify you so, Alexandra?"

Alex looked up into soulless eyes. She shook her head and answered huskily, "My pulse does not race in fear." In revulsion and irritation, she thought crossly.

Civelli read her response as an invitation, and softly nuzzled her neck.

Nausea rose in her throat, and Alex cautioned herself not to resist. But when his tongue traced a damp line across her throat, she instinctively jerked away.

Eyes dark and angry, Civelli bristled at the rebuff.

He reached for the gun positioned on the seat between them. "If I repulse you," he began.

Alex tilted her head to meet his stare. "Before we progress to such friendliness, I require some assurances."

Civelli's short laugh did not bode well.

"Assurances? I have the gun. I have the power. You have nothing."

Ignoring the block of ice lodged in the pit of her stomach, Alex said haughtily, "I know where the sculptures are. You do not. Therefore, we must share power." Bravely, she maintained her level gaze. She tossed her hair and smiled.

Civelli watched her. The smile, the lack of concern for the gun aimed at her head, served to convince him. "And if we come to terms?" he ventured silkily.

"Then we'll both get everything we want." Alex slowly licked lips parched from fear.

Civelli grew hard and ready at the sight. The image of her writhing on black silk sheets, covered only by him, flashed vividly in his mind's eye. They would make an excellent team. For a moment, terror at Zeben's wrath suffused him. *Cos' e caduto?* No, Zeben's fury would not deter him. He'd double-crossed employers before. Some complained, others died with their tales sealed forever. Either way, Brooks Civelli always survived.

Soon, the car pulled up to the curb across the street from Alex's house. Civelli cut the bonds from her wrists and ankles and permitted her to reclaim her bag. The pistol's hard metal barrel poked into her ribs as Civelli pushed her from the car. She stumbled out and caught her balance when Civelli grabbed her arm to steady her. She cast a baleful glance at the weapon. "This really isn't necessary," she complained.

A larger man emerged from the other side, his hand wrapped in a strip of stained cloth. Cruel green eyes promised retribution. Civelli watched the interchange and whispered, "He will feel better with it along."

Alex tried to glance at the man in the front seat, but the tinted glass obscured his face. Civelli nudged her across the street, deserted by the evening showers. Hope perished when she saw the empty alley beside Phillip's house. She was on her own here. Inside her studio, tools of the trade waited as promising weapons. Alex pretended to fumble in her bag for keys to the next house. "I think they're upstairs," she explained with an apologetic smile. Near the bottom of the cavernous bag, her hand brushed against Toca's parting gift, the obelisk. It would do in a pinch.

After a brief argument with Green Eyes, Civelli instructed her to enter the house. He followed Alex closely up the stairs to the third floor.

"I keep the keys in my desk in the studio," she said.

"Be quick about it," he muttered. He was eager to find the

statue and head to the airport. Their employer didn't trust Civelli, hence the extra assistance from his contacts in the Jafirian government. But only he knew what to look for, so his musclebound partner relied on him for information. However, if he didn't locate the statue himself, he'd describe the piece to Alex. Should she prove trustworthy, she'd come to the airport with him.

From downstairs, Alex heard a crack, then a shout of pain. Civelli swung the gun wildly, and Alex seized the confusion to strike him with the bag. The sound of heavy stone crunching into his skull sickened her, but she didn't hesitate. As he crumpled to the ground, she lifted a half-finished urn from the glazing table. It too crashed onto his head and Civelli gave a final moan.

Alex slung the strap across her chest and sprinted down the stairs, grateful for the low-heeled sandals she'd chosen that evening. At the second floor landing, she heard feet pounding up the steps. She ducked inside the hall bathroom and searched for another weapon. Good thing I'm not just writer, she thought wildly, as her trembling hand closed around a vase in the bathroom. Books made poor weapons compared to pottery and stone. The vase was one of her earliest glass-blowing attempts, but she'd make the sacrifice. The steps grew louder and she lifted the vase.

"Alex?" Phillip whispered harshly.

Alex set the vase down, rushed from the room and into his arms. "Oh, Phillip, I knew you'd come. I could have taken care of myself, of course, but I appreciate the help. The rescue," she babbled giddily.

Phillip hugged her close. "The gorilla at the bottom of the

stairs won't be out for long," he whispered into her ear. "We have to go." Quietly, they made their way downstairs, moving swiftly.

Outside, they raced to Phillip's car, where the top lay open. Alex tossed her bag into the back and dropped into the passenger seat. Phillip vaulted over the closed door and twisted the ignition key. The motor started with a purr, and he peeled away from the curb. Across the street, the driver slumped over his steering wheel.

"Civelli won't be waking up for a while," Alex shared. "I think I cracked his skull."

Phillip shot her a look. "Civelli? Brooks Civelli?"

Alex shrugged. "I didn't get first names, but Green Eyes called him Civelli."

"Green Eyes?"

"The gorilla. He has very evil green eyes," she explained. "And Civelli has a hard head. I think he broke my statue." Alex yelped with excitement. "Statue! My obelisk from South Africa! He kept calling it a statue, but that's not accurate. An obelisk is more of an architectural structure than a statue."

"Alex," Phillip warned impatiently, "get to the point!"

Affronted, Alex closed her lips tightly. "Never mind." She sulked in silence, waiting for an apology.

The silence between them lengthened until Phillip relented. "I'm sorry. Please continue." When she still refused to speak, he added, "I was very rude. I really am sorry. Please tell me about the obelisk."

Mollified, she reached into the rear of the car for her bag. "When Civelli kidnapped me, he demanded I tell him where the statue was hidden. I said I didn't know what he was talking about. But he's after the obelisk I told you about. By the way, a good spy would have asked to see it by now." Ignoring Phillip's scowl at her commentary, she turned around and opened the satchel.

Aware the bottom was littered with shards of stone, she removed the broken pieces gingerly. A sign of excellent craftsmanship, the obelisk had shattered along clean lines and could be repaired. "He had the nerve to claim I stole it from Toca's gallery while I was in Durban. Which is absurd. Did I mention that he slapped me?" Remembering the brief flash of pain, Alex rubbed the dull ache on her cheek.

Phillip's knuckles tightened on the steering wheel. "He touched you?" he asked with deadly menace.

Alarmed by the cold fury, Alex explained, "Once."

"Anything else?" he demanded.

"Why?" Alex asked warily.

Phillip answered matter-of-factly, "So I can decide how painful his death should be."

Instantly, Alex decided to keep his disgusting attempt at a kiss to herself. To distract him, she continued her story. "I convinced him to take me to the house, to find the sculpture. Then, when I tricked them into taking me inside, I felt the obelisk in the bottom of my bag."

She held up a jagged stone triumphantly. It was the tower, almost six inches long and half as wide at its base. "When you caused the commotion downstairs, I hit him with my bag. Then I dropped an urn on his head." In her mind, she heard the thud of stone against bone, saw Civelli's eyes widen in surprise. Shudders skated along her spine, shortened her breath. She may have killed him, she realized.

As adrenaline surged through her veins, Alex began to shake in reaction. To settle her nerves, and keep the crying at bay until she was alone, Alex fished the remnants of the obelisk from her bag.

For his part, Phillip said nothing, either in congratulations or reassurance. He couldn't. The tremors she tried to cloak in rambling speech were obvious, but he had no right to comfort. Bitter shame coursed within him, stilling his tongue. Like a rookie, he'd left her alone. She'd been taken from him, while he nursed hurt feelings.

Civelli struck her and likely more, as her agonizingly poor lie suggested. Fury, ripe and vicious, bubbled inside him. Still, she'd managed to keep her wits about her and free herself. Pride at her ingenuity humbled him, making his rescue less daring and more a lucky twist of fate.

There had never been anyone like her in his life.

He owed her an apology, a promise.

"Oh my God, Phillip. Pull over."

Phillip glanced at her and saw the object in her hand. Suddenly, the past few weeks made perfect sense. The key to the puzzle sparkled its fire-bright answer. In her elegant, trembling hand, Alex was holding the Sahalia ruby.

After he checked the road for nearby vehicles, he steered the car onto the shoulder of the highway. They idled along a curve, in case an enemy pursued. From their vantage point, he'd see an oncoming vehicle before it spotted him, and they'd be unable to stop quickly. The sharp curve didn't bode well in the event of an off-balance semi or drunken teenagers, but he'd chance it.

Phillip watched Alex for endless seconds as she fondled the ruby, which filled her shaking palm. Reaction shuddered through her in waves she tried valiantly to fight. Wholly improper, desire for her swept over him.

Strong and sweet, it sank delicious claws into him, clouding his mind, heightening his senses. Relief edged the sharpest points, spurred him to hold her.

Deliberately, he lifted the ruby from beneath her adoring gaze. With care, he stroked his open mouth along her bruised cheek. Patient hands released her seat belt, turning her to face him. Kisses like benediction rained across her darkly golden skin, anointing her neck, her forehead, the pointed chin designed to challenge.

Sweetly, he returned to her mouth and begged for entrance.

Her lips parted on a soundless gasp, eager for the rough reality of his tongue filling her mouth, filling her senses. Instead, he coaxed her into a liquid dance, a delicate, sensual waltz. He left no corner of her mouth untouched, every surface was gently ravaged. She slipped under, reality fragile and insubstantial. In her, for her, there was only the subtle magic of smooth against hard, steel cased in velvet. His fingers streaked banked fire over her ears, tracing whorls of sensation. She arched into him, frantic and tranquil, buffeted by peaceful, brutal need.

When she would have urged speed, he meandered, his touch refusing to stray beyond her shoulders. There, he daubed feather-light kisses in the hollow of her collarbone, in the cleft where her pulse strained against its skin.

Phillip felt Alex urge him to hurry, heard the whispered pleas for more. But he could not rush, could not take. He owed her softness, gentleness, contrition. Where words failed him, his tongue traced *I'm sorry* along the slim, graceful throat, *Please forgive me,* in the damp recesses of her mouth. As though she heard him, she stilled her frenzied motions and accepted.

He lifted his mouth and touched his forehead to hers. "I'm so sorry," he whispered.

Alex raised a tender hand to his stubbled cheek. "You saved me."

"No, you saved yourself. I just gave you a ride." He gave her a hard, brief kiss. Picking up the ruby, he sighed. "Alex, we've got a problem."

Alex shifted gears, her attention once again on the huge ruby she'd found in her purse. "I take it from your tone, I can't keep it," she grumbled.

Phillip chuckled. "Only if you want to cause an international incident. This, my dear, is the fabled Sahalia ruby."

"I've heard the stories. The possessor receives the power of the gods. I was never sure which gods, though." Alex traced the legendary gemstone with a reverent finger. "The story is that it disappeared when the royal family of Jafir died." Realization dawned. "Oh, crap."

"Inelegant, but apt. Someone used you to smuggle the ruby out of Durban. My money's on Toca." The smarmy bastard had been using her all along. Now she'd see the truth.

To his amazement, Alex vehemently disagreed. "Damon wouldn't do that. Whoever hid the ruby in the obelisk intended to kidnap me to get it back. That explains the driver at the airport. I told you, Damon flew to Atlanta to propose to me, not to kill me."

Jealousy, a constant companion since he met Alex, spurred him on. "Unless his attempted murder failed and he thought flirting with you would get him inside your house," Phillip argued. "You don't really believe he fell in love with you in three weeks."

With gritted teeth, Alex said, "It usually doesn't take that long."

"To fall or the entire cycle?" At her quizzical look, he explained nastily, "The Fall and Dump. You know, when you tell him you love him as a friend."

Her fist plowed into his solar plexus, and Phillip doubled over. Alex shook her fist, pain reverberating up her arm. "Don't be a jackass," she admonished, in awe at the stomach muscles that nearly crunched her fist. If she hadn't caught him off guard, she'd be nursing a broken hand.

"When did you become violent?" he gasped, more in surprise than pain.

"When I met you." Alex reached into her bag for a rubber band to tie her hair into a ponytail. Rising up, she glanced in the rearview mirror. A dark car drove along the highway, and she thought nothing of it. On impulse, she turned to look. Less than two hundred feet away, the car picked up speed and hurtled toward them. "Phillip, behind us," she warned.

Phillip saw the car and shifted the Roadster into gear. With only seconds to spare, he whipped the Corvette onto the asphalt, gravel spraying beneath the tires. Slicked by the earlier rain, the tires spun for a moment, then caught. He revved the engine and shouted instructions to Alex. "In the glove compartment, there's a phone, a nine millimeter, and an ammunition clip. Get them."

Alex removed the items, handling the gun with care. She'd fired one before, once when dating a Naval officer. The other time had been on a camping trip with Uncle James. From memory, she inserted the clip into the base of the gun. "What next?"

A loud ping struck the side rails, and Alex saw a man lean out of the window. Green Eyes, she thought.

"Extend the antenna on the phone and open the screen. Press the blue button on the corner. When the screen lights up, let me know."

Phillip checked the mirror and saw Green Eyes take aim again. He jerked the car into the opposite lane at the last minute and another bullet struck the side rail. He'd have to disable their vehicle, he decided. They couldn't risk leading Zeben's men to ISA headquarters.

"Alex, honey," Phillip said, "I need you to crouch low in your seat and when I give the signal, fire at their front tires."

She nodded her understanding. Once in position, she said, "Okay."

Phillip watched as the car closed the distance between them. One hundred and fifty feet. One hundred. Seventy-five. "Now," he commanded.

As though she'd been trained for the life, Alex took careful aim and blasted the left front tire. The driver struggled to control the car. Green Eyes fired another round. Alex ducked and waited the space of a heartbeat. Then she popped up and shot out the right front tire. The vehicle whipped in distress.

"Brace yourself," Phillip yelled as he gunned the engine, streaking to 100 mph in under thirteen seconds.

The distance between the two cars lengthened, and the disabled car disappeared from sight. Alex fastened her seat belt. She lifted the communicator and held it out to Phillip. "Blue screen is active."

When Phillip shot her a glance, she shrugged. "I lived with an agent. I've seen a communicator before. Do your thing."

He shook his head in disbelief and depressed his thumb on a metal panel. After a verifying beep, he told Alex to enter a series of numbers. "You don't have a photographic memory like Raleigh's, do you?" he wondered.

"No. That's why I'm always late for appointments."

"Darling, you do that for the attention."

Alex laughed, not at all offended. "Touché." Suddenly, Atlas appeared on the miniature screen.

"Alex!" he exclaimed. "Phillip got you out! I knew he would! You weren't scared, were you, honey? They didn't hurt you did they?"

"Well, actually," Alex began, "I wasn't completely helpless, Uncle James. I'll have you know—"

Phillip heard the rising annoyance and intervened. "Alex handled herself just fine before I got there. I didn't think they'd be stupid enough to take her back to the house, but you'll never guess who kidnapped her."

Atlas wrinkled his brow. "It wasn't one of Zeben's men?"

"Nope. Try Brooks Civelli. The rat for hire."

"Why would anyone put a contract out on Alex?" Atlas demanded.

"Not a contract to kill. Alex, will you get it, please?" Phillip asked.

Alex balanced the communicator in one hand and retrieved the ruby from the glove compartment, where she'd stored it during the attack.

"The damned Sahalia," Atlas said. "Where'd you get it?"

"It was hidden in an obelisk a friend gave me," Alex explained.

Phillip added angrily, "Damon Toca gave it to her, Atlas."

"Don't start that again," Alex said warningly. To Atlas, she said, "Civelli tried to steal the sculpture. I'm not sure if he knows what's inside."

Phillip added his agreement. "We're coming in, Atlas. ETA twenty minutes."

"Check for tails, Sphinx," Atlas reminded him.

Duly admonished, Phillip reported, "Alex already shot their tires out. I'll ditch the car at Gamma Point and we'll come in by alternate transportation. Sphinx out."

CHAPTER ELEVEN

"What the hell is he doing here?" Phillip demanded angrily.

Damon Toca stood by Atlas's office window, staring down at DuPont Circle. Bright stars arrayed against the night competed with lamplight from the park. He'd been to Washington several times before, but he saw it now for the first time. Carefree young men his age lingered over coffee in trendy shops, or flirted with young women in raucous clubs. At twenty-eight, he'd taken pleasure in his ability to attract women, to come and go as he pleased. In the blink of an eye, his entire world had changed.

He turned from the window to confront Phillip, to explain to Alex. To accept his destiny.

Before he could speak, Atlas intervened. "Phillip, Alex, have a seat."

Phillip ignored the edict, standing stiffly by the door. Alex, exhausted from their transfer from car, to bus, to a mile hike by foot, collapsed gratefully into the proffered chair.

"Alex, what I'm about to tell you cannot leave this room. Do you understand?" Atlas moved behind his desk and waited for her response. He'd made good and bad decisions from this base. Choices he'd lived to regret with a heaviness that weighed on his heart. Judgments he applauded when justice was served. Tonight, a decision made almost thirty years ago hung in the balance, awaiting resolution.

"Uncle James, you can trust me," Alex answered quietly.

"Good." He turned to Phillip, who glared malevolently at Damon. "Phillip, please. Sit. Damon, you too."

Where Alex and Damon heard only command, Phillip perceived the sound of weariness. Atlas, as indomitable as his namesake, for the first time resembled a man. A tired old man with too many secrets. He sat.

"Thirty years ago, our world was a very different place. The Cold War raged and enemies became friends, friends, betrayers. We developed a strategy to employ the excellent geographic positioning of Jafir. It was an independent monarchy with a democratically elected government. While the president ran the country, the royal family offered stability, heritage. The family name altered over time because the eldest child, male or female, ascended to the throne. Thirty years ago, King Nelson and Queen Jaya were the last surviving direct descendants to the monarchy. Shrewd politicians deduced that if they could control the couple, they'd gain access to the monarchy's wealth and power over the people. Had either switched allegiance, the nation would likely have abandoned their government."

"After centuries of democracy?" Alex questioned incredulously.

Atlas nodded. "Jafir has always been a haven, an idyll. The social programs not run by the government were administered by the monarchy. It sounds ridiculous in our current time, but then, the world was in chaos. Jaya and Nelson were stability. Democracies crumbled almost daily. So, various attempts were made on their lives, but neither swayed in their beliefs."

"And then there was Zeben," Phillip said.

"Yes, Khadifir el Zeben, the son of a distant relative to Jaya, the direct descendant. He conspired with the Soviets to establish a stronghold on Jafir."

"Cuba in the Mediterranean."

"Exactly. The assassination attempts increased, people died. Then, Jaya discovered she was pregnant."

Comprehension dawned as Phillip watched Damon stiffen. "Damon is the heir?"

"Stop jumping ahead, Phillip," Alex chastised.

Atlas smiled approvingly. "Jaya and Nelson contacted the ISA for assistance. I was assigned as their contact. Jaya gave birth in secret in Senegal."

"Why there? Why not America?" Damon demanded, speaking for the first time.

"Your father had friends in the United States, but your mother wanted you nearby. Senegal was relatively stable and accessible. We all hoped Zeben would be neutralized and you'd be returned before too long. When apartheid fell, Bill wanted to return home, to South Africa. By then, it was out of our control. If they chose not to tell you about your legacy, I couldn't interfere."

Phillip noticed the wince of pain and felt a moment's

sympathy. To lose his parents and his trust in one night. "Zeben killed the king and queen. But he couldn't find the obelisk," he surmised. He lifted the Scimitar file from Zeben's desk, and thumbed quickly through the pages.

"No. The obelisk was given to Bill and Tucker for safekeeping."

"And the Sahalia was hidden in the base," Alex added. "Why give it to me? I don't understand."

Atlas rose and stood before a map of the region. "Three weeks ago, Zeben escaped from prison. At the same time, we received word of a theft. The autopsy and medical records of the royal family had been sealed by the government to protect the children. Only the president, the head of the ISA, myself, and the Tocas knew the truth."

Phillip explained, "The medical records would reveal that Jaya had given birth. Zeben would know there was a son."

"Not a son. Two sons. Damon and his brother, Nelson," corrected Alex. "You're fraternal twins."

"Yes. Nelson is younger by an hour or so, but we are twins." Damon lifted a paperweight from Atlas's desk, passing the sphere from hand to hand. He picked up the story. "Atlas contacted my parents. They told me the truth, that I was the heir to the Jafirian throne. If I didn't complete the Rites of Ascension by the first, the monarchy would cease. Then they showed me the secret of the obelisk."

Alex scooted forward in her seat to meet Damon's eyes. "You had me construct a replica. I don't understand."

Clear hazel eyes met suspicious brown. "Phillip does."

"Nelson Toca is Jubalani. A miserable coward who helps Zeben finance his wars by fencing stolen art and gems. I've met him once."

Damon rose, setting the sphere on the desk. "My brother and I are not close. When I took over the gallery, he began traveling. Almost monthly, he would send me a painting or an artifact to sell quickly. At first, I did so blindly, never doubting the provenance of the art. One day, while on a buyer's trip to Dakar, I met a lady who claimed that I'd stolen her emerald pendant. I protested, but she insisted. I accompanied her to the local police and eventually met with a representative from the federal police. My brother was wanted on charges of larceny and fraud. International warrants had been issued for his arrest."

Alex quickly caught on to the thread of the story. "Jubalani was a South African artist, one of the first contemporary painters to depict life for the Zulu nation. He used the name to disguise himself."

Staring out of the window, Damon agreed. "I couldn't bring myself to tell our parents, but I refused to help him any longer. We've been estranged since then."

"Did your parents tell him about the obelisk?"

"Yes, and as soon as I knew, I explained about Jubalani." He gestured to Atlas. "They put me in contact with Atlas, and he told me what to do."

Atlas circled the desk to squat in front of Alex.

Gray eyes wreathed in sorrow, he explained, "I knew from Liz and Robert that you had a show at the gallery. I instructed Damon to have you replicate the obelisk, then bring the original back to the U.S. Jubalani, Nelson, would try to take the fake and be none the wiser. Until someone who knew Shilha tried to read it. They'd open it and realize the ruby wasn't inside." Atlas patted her hand, but Alex recoiled in betrayed anger.

"You're not forgiven yet." Taking a deep breath, she turned

to Damon. "When you came to the wedding—" She paused, forcing him to answer.

"It was to retrieve the obelisk. But you were otherwise occupied. I tried again at the brunch, but to no avail. Atlas suggested I wait until Phillip brought you in and we'd get it back then."

Alex gasped in horror. "Oh my goodness, I broke it. On Civelli's head! Oh, no!"

"The pieces are shattered?" exclaimed Damon.

"No, I can repair it, but the inscriptions are finely etched. Where it cracked, you may not be able to decipher the words."

"Merlin and Chimera can," Phillip told them.

Atlas stood and rested a hip on the desk. He lifted the sphere Damon had toyed with earlier. A miniature globe, the blue of the Mediterranean winked at him. On the miniscule map, Jafir had no place. How little cartographers understood the realities of the world. "They'll be meeting you in Jafir in two days. The Rites of Ascension must be completed before the Tribunal by that midnight."

"Uh, guys, one more thing." When three pairs of male eyes focused on her, Alex announced, "I think Nelson is here. In DC. I think Civelli is working for him and Zeben."

Damon spoke first. "How do you know?"

"There was a third man in the car that kidnapped me. His voice sounded vaguely familiar, but I couldn't place it. He sounds like you. And I didn't see him when we left my house. I don't think he was in the car that chased us either." Alex saw the veil of shame fall over his eyes, and, putting aside her resentment for the moment, she reached out to take his cold hands. "You are nothing like your brother, Damon."

Damon shook off her comforting touch. "I used you, just as he would have. To claim a throne in a land I don't even know."

"You're trying to ensure that your parents' sacrifice wasn't in vain," Phillip told him quietly. "Jafir has survived the threat of colonialism, the ravages of war, and the menace of the Cold War. It may not survive Zeben's dominion. If you can help, you must."

Before Damon could protest, Atlas interjected, "This is what's going to happen. Phillip will take you and Alex to a safe house. Use the one in Bethesda," he said to Phillip. "Report to the airport at Annapolis at three o'clock tomorrow. I'll arrange for a flight to Crete. Phillip, you'll fly the company plane out to Jafir. Alex, you keep the ruby with you."

Knowing they'd been dismissed, the three rose and headed for the door. Phillip paused and motioned for them to wait outside. He turned and reentered and shut the door firmly behind him.

"You set me up."

Atlas tossed the sphere casually, his reflexes still honed by years in the field. He heard, as did Phillip, the pain of betrayal beneath the accusation. Atlas regretted the first, and acknowledged the second. "You may have been compromised. I didn't know for sure."

"I live in a hellhole for three years. I lose my family, my friends. I kill people to save lives and you doubt me. How dare you?"

"Because that's my job. Cavanaugh saved more lives than you ever will and he turned. The Sahalia is worth millions. And the life of the prince is priceless."

Phillip snatched the file from the desk. The pale sheet described Alex as "the art." "And Alex? What is she to you?"

"A terrible means to a necessary end. I trusted you to protect her, as long as you didn't know what from. Greed destroys. I had to believe you'd keep her safe until I could tell you the rest."

Phillip crushed the paper in an impotent fist. In his gut, he knew Atlas had done what he had to do. Their work did not allow for sentiment or care. Or love. In the final analysis, the only objective was spinning the earth on its axis for another day. And Atlas, like his namesake, did. "Damn you, Atlas," Phillip whispered with understanding.

"I am, Phillip. I am." Wearily, Atlas returned to sit behind the protective block of teak, lines and wrinkles creasing his face. "Now go save the world."

"Absolutely not," Phillip declared as Alex scribbled in her notebook. "Too much that you don't understand is at stake. You are not coming with me." Frustrated brown eyes bored into the top of her bent head. "Are you listening to me?"

"I can hardly ignore the bellowing," she said mildly. "And the infernal repetition. You've told me this at least ten times since we tucked Damon in for the night."

Alex sat, legs tucked beneath her, on an ottoman in the safe house's living room. Actually a duplex near the naval base, Damon occupied a separate section guarded by ISA agents. When Phillip offered to have him take the second bedroom, while he slept downstairs, Damon declined. Though he cited fatigue, Phillip realized Damon needed solitude to process all he'd learned that night. In twenty-four hours, he'd become king of a nation he barely knew.

As for Alex, she felt wonderful. She'd survived an abduction, a car chase, and the revelation that her godfather used her as a homing pigeon. It was dawn and she'd fallen crazily, madly in love. All in all, a thoroughly exciting day.

Phillip, on the other hand, was tense and angry. He'd been ranting since midnight, and she didn't expect respite any time soon. Patiently, she repeated her argument.

"I found the Sahalia. And, it seems, I smuggled it too. I also took out one of the villains, disabled the bad guys' car, and have I mentioned finding the ruby? I'm coming with you." She flipped the page. Absently, she gnawed on the eraser of her pencil. "What's a synonym for *querulous*?" she asked.

"*Querulous. Argumentative. Cantankerous. Fractious.*" Seated behind a walnut desk, Phillip gave her a pointed look. "Need more?"

"No, I think that covers it. Kevin, my protagonist, is quite cantankerous. Argumentative. Fractious." She ducked when he tossed a paperclip near her head.

"Very funny, Alex." Phillip typed commands into the computer in front of him, trying to find the words that would make her stay in DC. While the processor searched for the ISA database for files on Jubalani, he stared at glossy black waves. She had to comprehend why he must return alone, regardless of Zeben's orders. He had to make her stay. Without telling her that he loved her.

As though she'd read his mind, Alex lifted calm brown eyes to meet worried ones. "Phillip, I understand why you need to return to Jafir alone. You have demons to put to rest."

"Atlas told you about my time there?" Phillip asked incredulously.

"No, but I can read upside down. And backwards. One of the

reports on the desk was a psych profile of an agent named Sphinx. Would seem appropriate for you. You guys should really use thicker paper. You're a bit sloppy for spies." Alex nibbled the eraser for another moment. "What kind of car would a sullen, burdened antihero drive?"

Phillip sighed in exasperation. "Rich or poor?"

Alex scoffed, her smoky laugh searing his lungs. "Rich, Phillip. Poor antiheroes are the devil to accessorize."

Used to the rapid shifts in topic, Phillip played along. "An Aston-Martin V12 Vanquish. Now, stop trying to change the subject." In the hours since they'd been in the house, she'd interrogated him about his college years, his favorite foods, the music he danced to at his high school prom.

"I'm not changing the subject," Alex protested. "It's important. He's about to outrun Canadian operatives chasing him across the border."

"We're not enemies of Canada, Alex."

"Canada can produce villains. They don't all have to be Russian or American." She wagged her chewed pencil at him in reproof. "Our neighbors to the north can be just as dastardly as the English."

"I'm sure they appreciate the characterization," he said laconically.

Alex set her notebook aside and crossed the wide room.

She perched on the edge of his desk, and one leg beat a soft tattoo against his chair. "Phillip, I'm safer with you than with anyone else," she said quietly. "Yesterday, when my mouth was gagged and my hands were tied, I thought about you. Not Raleigh or Adam or Uncle James. You were the one who would rescue me. And you did." Emotions, fierce and bewildering, swamped her. She traced the silk of his mustache, the high sweep of cheekbone. Those, she'd learned, were inherited from his Choctaw great-grandmother. "I won't be without you," she whispered softly.

"You're not talking about the mission, Alex."

"No," she agreed instantly. "I'm not." On impulse, she slipped from the desk into his lap. Solid thighs flexed beneath legs. Beneath her hand, his heartbeat pounded fiercely.

"Alex, you said you didn't want this." Comfortless dark eyes tested her, challenged her. "If this begins, I won't stop. I don't know that I can."

Alex leaned closer, her soft curves melting into the long, hard lines of his body. "I want this. I want you."

In invitation, Alex covered the firm, unyielding mouth with her own. With unhurried, languorous strokes, she persuaded the lips to part. Softly, she mated their tongues, the indolent dance a mirror of the kiss they'd shared in the car.

For a moment, Phillip surrendered to the light seduction, to the questing, teasing kiss. In the next instant, he shifted his hands, binding her to him from breast to thigh. Suddenly, gloriously impatient, he kicked the chair away and strode with Alex to the staircase.

"I will have you now," he promised.

In response, she molded her mouth to his, seeking the strong, heady taste of him. Her hands caressed his neck, his shoulders, digging into hard flesh as they mounted the stairs.

In the bedroom, moonlight poured in, aided by starlight. He stood her in the shaft of brightness. Bringing his hand to the simple top, he stroked the gentle swell once, then pulled the garment from her body.

Desperate now, he skimmed the dress down her thighs, punctuating their descent with hot, sweet kisses. He knelt before her, his tonguing laving her navel, her hands clenched in his hair.

Hungrily, she sank to her knees, seeking and finding his mouth. Torrid, wet kisses, a primitive mating of lips and teeth and tongue. Her hands tore free buttons from his shirt, ripped the belt from his waist. Unwilling to lose even a touch, they rolled across the carpet, tugging at fabric until flesh met flesh.

Driven to pleasure, Phillip suckled a taut, brown peak. The scent of flowers, of spring, surrounded him. Hands filled with ripe warm flesh kneaded and stroked until she gasped beneath him.

Consumed by desire, Alex arched into his touch, twisting to taste the salty flavor of his shoulder, the piquant tang of his hip.

The icy shield surrounding the heart that he believed inviolate splintered under her ragged cries of pleasure.

Love, hot and molten, submerged the last barrier.

Inundated by emotion, he found he could not take in haste what demanded to be savored. He needed to give, to cajole, to seduce.

Rising to his feet, he carried her to the bed, kneeling above to study for an infinite moment. Long, smooth limbs. Soft, brown skin. Gentle, subtle curves. The endless legs that had fascinated him from the beginning were the first to suffer his ministrations. Wet, slow glides traced the rounded calf, the length of thigh.

Alex arched in stunned pleasure as he sampled the indentation of her waist, the undercurves of her breasts, the line of the throat. Teeth scraped delicately, soothed by velvet. Hands stroked roughly, eased by silk.

Unwilling to remain supine and pliant, Alex pressed fevered kisses to his chest, pleased by the ragged pulse. Quick, agile fingers stroked hard, determined flesh.

Across the sleekly muscled back, down the planes and angles of chest and thighs, her artist's hands discovered the beauty of form, the vibrancy of function. Exultantly, her mouth traced the whorls of his ear, the flavors of his stomach. She delighted in his frayed breathing. She reveled in his dark whispers of satisfaction.

She flowed into him, desperate for a taste. He surged over her, desperate for a touch. Shivers spread between clasped hands, streaked and redoubled where soft met hard, where heat met heat. She loved, and with her body, promised him forever. He loved, and with his body, vowed to protect.

"I love you," she whispered softly, sheathing him with trembling hands.

"Alex," he moaned, her soft touch undoing him even as he entered her.

Hot, wet, his. Phillip steeled himself against the urge to plunge deeper, to rush to pleasure. Instead, he readied her, with strokes and sighs.

Hard, strong, hers. Alex strained to take him inside, to feel every sensation. Limbs entangled, she opened and drew him deeper.

Hips danced in exquisite delight, hard buried in soft, mouths fused in heat. Together, they wrenched ecstasy from the joining. Together, they sought rapture in the holding. Together, they shattered eternity in the having.

Dawn shone through the curtains. Phillip turned onto his back, gathered Alex to his side, and drew a tangled sheet up to cover their cooling bodies. Between them, inside them both, her declaration hung unanswered.

Alex snuggled into the warmth of Phillip's side. Her pronouncement of love had been met by a fevered whisper of her name. Before, armed with a quip and an excuse, she'd cast off the offending male and lick her wounds. But she'd never said I love you before and meant it. And she had no intention of letting him use Scimitar to push her away.

In the stillness of morning, she could hear that cunning brain churning out excuses to leave her behind.

And every reason, be it for her protection or his concentration, meant nothing. He'd try not to love her and he'd fail miserably. Satisfied with her decision, she slept.

Phillip listened as Alex breathed slow and deep. Love flowed through him, generous and terrifying. Now, more than ever, he had to guard her, even from himself. When she awoke, he'd explain to her that she had to remain behind, in safety. She'd argue, like always, convinced she could handle herself. But knowing she could be in danger, either from Zeben or from Jubalani, would fracture his concentration.

Afterward, when he returned, he'd find a new home.

He'd accept Bundy's offer and move to Annapolis. Anything to put distance between them. Until Zeben was dead and every enemy captured, Phillip would remain a target, endangering the lives of those he loved. At least, with his father, he'd make clandestine visits, carefully spaced.

Yet, how could he build a life with Alex? The ISA was a part of him, and he would not do to her what Atlas had.

Whether she admitted it or not, his duplicity wounded her. Phillip saw the disappointment when Atlas explained his actions, her stoic acceptance. The weight of guilt, the sting of betrayal, the look of pained forgiveness would conspire to destroy him.

He'd found his soul in her arms and would gladly trade it to keep her safe. In mere hours, she'd be gone. So now, in the reckless light of dawn, he'd have as much as she would give him, to sate him through the darkness that waited.

He reached for his wallet and covered himself. He'd have preferred her questing fingers, but heavy with arousal, he wanted her now.

Phillip bent over her sleeping form, twining a lock of hair around his finger. He gently kissed her forehead, then the slashing cheekbones. Alex moaned softly in her sleep, stretching languidly beneath his touch.

When her eyes opened, dazed and aroused, he rolled until she straddled him. Alex knelt over him, welcoming his mouth in a duel of teeth and lips and tongue. Rough hands stroked her pliant skin, melting her in glorious strokes. She arched above him, triumphant and ready. He sheathed himself in her, desperate and hungry.

Touches turned to strokes turned to groans. Deeper, faster, she rode the waves of pleasure until their cries of fulfillment filled the room, the universe with the sound.

———————

Civelli boarded the plane, a gun to his side.

Jubalani held the weapon, his face an impenetrable mask. Behind Jubalani, his henchman carried their bags. Jubalani poked Civelli in the ribs, forcing him inside the cabin.

After strapping themselves in, the plane taxied and lifted from the earth. Flying made Civelli queasy, but he refrained from complaint. Neither of his employers was happy with him right now, and one had a gun.

"Explain to me again how you lost them?" Jubalani asked in

a deceptively pleasant manner. The hazel eyes, a mirror of his brother's, bored into Civelli's.

"I was driving the car. Bosca over there had only to shoot the tires. Turman shot ours out instead," Civelli whined.

"By now, they've located my brother and they have the obelisk." The plane leveled off and Jubalani released his belt and stood. "My aunt and uncle finally admitted where the ruby is, Civelli. Would you like to guess?"

"In Jafir," hazarded Civelli. By reputation, the admission from his relatives had probably come from extensive torture. Keen to avoid the same fate, he raised his hands in supplication when the man's eyes darkened. "I'm sorry. I didn't realize you were being rhetorical."

Twirling the gun between his fingers, Jubalani announced, "The Sahalia is inside the obelisk. That is why big brother made a duplicate. To throw me off the scent of the obelisk and the ruby."

Zeben would kill him, Civelli realized, if Jubalani didn't. Either way, he'd failed at all three missions, and had two lunatics hungry for his head. Quickly, Civelli calculated his odds. Jubalani did not yet know of his deal with Zeben, and Zeben certainly had no clue that his favorite psychopath was second in line to the fabled Jafirian throne. If he brokered the deal to unify them in common pursuit, perhaps they'd be willing to spare his life. Maybe even pay him his fee.

Aloud, he said, "I have some information that may be of use to you."

Jubalani glared at him. "Of use? You have proven to be of little use at all!"

"I know how Toca and the obelisk will get into Jafir."

"More than likely, by plane," Jubalani scoffed.

"No, by ISA-chartered jet." Showing his trump card, he revealed, "Turman is an agent for the ISA."

"The esteemed congressman is a spy?" Jubalani rubbed his chin thoughtfully. "Have I met him before?"

"Yes, when he was undercover as Stephen Frame."

"Money laundering and wire transfers. Ah, nicely done, worm. And, how, may I ask, did you come to have such information?" He tapped the side of Civelli's head with the gun's cold barrel. "And what other secrets are you hiding from me?"

Civelli flinched from the blow, but continued speaking. "Zeben first hired me to kill Turman and recover the obelisk. He also seeks the ruby. I believe, between the two of you, you may be able to each leave the table with something."

"Thanks to your clumsiness, neither of us have anything right now!"

Hurriedly, Civelli corrected him. "We know that Damon has the obelisk and the ruby. We know the ISA is bringing him to Jafir to complete the ceremony."

"Go on."

"Zeben has resources inside the Jafirian government. That's how I secured the car for the abduction. They can also get us inside the Tribunal to stop the ceremony. If you and Zeben work together, you can have the ruby and he can have the obelisk. Or vice versa."

"You know where Zeben is in hiding?"

Civelli nodded quickly. "I can take you to him."

Jubalani caressed the gun gently, examining the black casing. "An alliance with Zeben. Civelli, you may survive the day after all."

CHAPTER TWELVE

Alex slowly opened her eyes and stretched gingerly as the noonday sun streamed through the windows. Careful of the agreeable aches borne after a night of loving, she eased onto her back and blinked sleepily.

Phillip stood dressed and shaved, rifling through her satchel.

Drowsily, she yawned and sat up. "The ruby is in the zippered compartment," she offered helpfully.

"Thanks," he replied politely as he fished the stone from the bag. A black metal case outfitted with a digital lock sat open on the dresser. Phillip placed the stone in a velvet sack and set it inside the case beside the broken shards of the obelisk. After closing the lid, he entered a combination and the box beeped.

"What's the combination?" Alex inquired, anchoring a sheet around her as she climbed out of bed. Modesty had her securing the knot high above her breasts. There was still enough newness to their relationship that sauntering around the room naked was not yet an option.

"You don't need to know." The passion and tenderness she'd heard in his voice throughout the long night had faded into a stern tone of disapproval. "It's of no concern to you."

Though she'd prepared herself for the battle, Alex had imagined the night would sort matters out. But Phillip stood stiffly, spoke cautiously. Here we go, she thought, exasperated, the champion shielding his damsel. Well, she wasn't a damsel and she had no need of a champion. "It's of the utmost concern," she countered smartly. "I'll need to know the combination if something happens and you can't open the box."

"Since you won't be coming with me, knowing the combination wouldn't help." Phillip dropped the case into a gray travel bag.

It was packed with his uniform of khakis and oxfords. Until Phillip, she hadn't realized how sexy they could be. Of course, until Phillip, she hadn't been aware of quite a few things, she remembered with irritated satisfaction.

No, she thought determinedly, he wouldn't get rid of her without a fight.

Alex leaned against the newel post and watched him as he closed the bag. Strange, how she'd learned to read his moods. From the set of his jaw, she discerned worry. The thin line of his lips was a tell-tale sign of displeasure. She couldn't read his eyes with his head down, but they'd likely be cool with determination.

Loving him wouldn't be a simple matter, she accepted. He'd be irascible and distant at times. Probably continue to pretend he wasn't leaving on missions even after decades together. He wouldn't share his emotions without her nagging, and he'd still try to push her away and shut her out. She'd invade his space, lay siege to his feelings.

No, loving him wouldn't be a peaceful affair, but she welcomed the challenge.

If she'd had any doubts that he loved her, he'd dispelled them a thousand times with his gentle assault on her body, her senses. Phillip hadn't simply made love with her, he'd *cherished* her. When they lay spent, a knot of arms and legs, he'd pulled her closer rather than shifting away. No, he hadn't said he loved her, but he'd whispered endearments into her ear, brushed them into her skin.

She headed toward the bathroom to brush her teeth and take a quick shower. They needed to be in Annapolis soon. "Phillip, we discussed this. I'm coming to Jafir," she reminded him. When she brushed past him, Phillip grabbed her arm to halt her. As though singed, he quickly removed his hand and tucked it into his pocket.

Arms akimbo, he stared at a point beyond her shoulder, his face devoid of expression. "No, you're not coming with us. Atlas agrees that you'll be too much of an obstruction. I won't have time to babysit you and protect Damon. Only one of you is expendable." The words were terse, cold.

"You've never been cruel before, Phillip," Alex murmured as the barb hit its mark.

For the first time, he looked at her. The sun hung high in the clouds, bathing the room in a golden glow. She stood in front of him, wrapped in utilitarian white cotton, bare toes curled into the spare carpet in defense against the chill.

A wave of love swept over him, so strong it nearly rocked

him on his heels. The sight of her, rumpled and sexy, exhausted from a night in his arms, was almost enough to make him cave in, to beg her to stay with him. But her slender body, vulnerable and exposed, reminded him of his duty.

"Go back to sleep, Alex. The guards will let you know when it's safe to return to DC." He draped the strap of the bag over his shoulder. "Take care of yourself."

"That sounds dangerously close to goodbye, Phillip." Alex brushed tendrils of hair from her face, her movements tense. "Don't you plan to come back?"

Phillip braced himself and aimed the second shot carefully. "Not to you." Her shoulders jerked, as though she'd been struck. He wasn't cruel by nature, but fear outweighed guilt. If Zeben caught her or if Jubalani found her first, he'd never forgive himself.

"What's going on, Phillip?" she demanded. She fought the prick of tears. Of course, he'd believe he needed to be merciless to be kind.

"I wanted to leave before you woke up, to avoid all of this." Honor demanded sacrifice, didn't it? His heart, her life. His soul, her safety. Scoffing at the sheen in her eyes, he sneered, "I should have counted on you for a scene. Melodrama *is* your forte, isn't it?"

Alex blinked the moisture away, her eyes dry and direct. "Cheap shot, Phillip. Try again."

He heard the determination and realized she would not make leaving her painless. Hungry eyes roamed over a face wreathed in impatience, her sullen lips still swollen from his kisses.

He steeled himself to destroy her, to save her. "Alex, there's nothing important between us." When she opened her mouth to speak, he stopped her. "Don't misunderstand. I heard you last night. I didn't respond because I didn't want to hurt you. But I can't be with you."

"Why not? You love me," she retorted. "Don't deny it."

"I won't. It's not my fault if you've confused sex with love. And, I will admit, it was great sex." Phillip advanced to her then, to touch the bronzed skin, to feel the silken warmth. He clasped her shoulders between hard, unyielding hands. "Sex isn't enough. I don't intend to be one of the men you discard when I manage to disappoint your immature notions of love, Alex. I need a partner, not a woman who dabbles in the art of love."

Alex watched him steadily. Pain, sharp and fierce, threatened to buckle her knees. "You don't mean that," she whispered. "You're just trying to protect me. I can take care of myself, Phillip. I proved that yesterday."

"You always take care of yourself first, darling. So no, I'm not trying to protect you. I'm protecting Damon from the moment you decide you've played hero long enough, and you're ready to go home. I'm protecting the other ISA agents from you storming off in a fit of temper when you're supposed to help. I'm protecting myself from the second you see a man in the airport who may make a better plotline or portrait. None of us can afford you, honey, least of all, me."

"Is that what you think of me? After everything you've said." She flung a trembling hand at the crumpled bed. "After everything we've shared."

Phillip lifted his shoulders in ruthless dismissal. "I told you, it was great sex. But I've had you and now I'm done."

Anger, furious and ripe, snapped her head back, tilted her chin. "You liar! You want me so badly right now, you can taste me. Even now, you can't keep your hands off me. And you love me." Alex pressed a hand to the heart thudding against his chest. "You love me," she repeated in a desperate whisper. "Don't do this."

Shoving her away, Phillip held his hands up, palms out. His eyes met hers, clear and unswerving. "I don't love you, Alex. I can't." He turned on his heel and walked to the door. "I've instructed the guards to keep you under lock and key. Don't try to leave. This is a naval base; you can't escape."

The click of the lock echoed in the narrow room. Alex slid to the floor, shivering arms wrapped around quaking knees. In her mind, she struggled to remember he'd been brutal out of concern. The cold words, the pitiless assessment, all designed to make her run. In her mind, she almost believed her explanations.

It was her heart that broke when he called her useless. It was her soul that ached at how he reduced their lovemaking to a forgettable coupling. He'd thrown every secret, every niggling doubt back in her face. She'd felt his heart drum against his chest and rejected his lies.

At the last moment, in the final seconds, she'd watched his eyes. And saw nothing. No pity, no regret. Ice, cold and remorseless, stared back at her. He was gone. She closed her eyes, the orbs dry and burning, and began to accept. Once again, she'd failed.

Who was she to expect love? A dabbler in the art of love, he'd called her. A master, though, in the art of desire. He wanted her body, despised her soul.

As she recalled the time since she'd first met Phillip, the pieces tumbled into place, a picture of duty. Agreeing to be interviewed, the dinners, the walks, all designed to keep her near. With the mystery solved, he didn't need her anymore. He hadn't pretended otherwise, she could give him that. Even in passion, he made no promises of love, of affection. He sought and gave pleasure.

And Phillip left her another gift. Proof of her ability to accept, to share. To love. She wouldn't do it again, by God, but at least she had proof that she could. Why else would she feel so empty, so hollow?

After a while, Alex rose from the floor, limbs heavy. Beside the bed, her sundress lay bunched, where Phillip had pushed it from her body in passionate abandon. Woodenly, she entered the bathroom, showered, and dressed.

A knock sounded at the door. Alex forced herself to answer. "Yes?" she managed faintly. A man's voice muttered a response. She turned the knob and hope, beaten and battered, fluttered for an instant then died.

Alex stepped back to allow Damon into the room, his tawny eyes filled with concern. "Phillip told me that we are to leave for Annapolis earlier than scheduled. He says you're not coming with us."

"No. I've been cut from the strike force," Alex explained curtly. "Now that I've serviced you and Atlas and Phillip, I can go home."

Wincing at her bitter turn of phrase, Damon reached for her hands. "Alexandra—"

Alex snatched them away from him, livid. "Don't you dare touch me! You're no better than he is."

Shame washed over his face, a dull red tinting the skin. "I wanted to apologize last night." He reached for her again, accepting the recoil a second time. Rebuffed, he compressed his mouth, then spoke. "My affection for you was quite real. Our time together was as magical as I expressed that night. Even at the wedding, I wanted to see you, to be with you. But when I spotted you with Phillip, I knew there was no chance. The rest, the sub-terfuge, they were necessary. I didn't mean to hurt you."

"Apology accepted. Get out." Alex threaded her hands together.

"It's not that simple, Alexandra. I need you to understand."

When she remained silent, Damon continued. "To learn, in such a short span of time, that I was heir to a legacy older than most nations, was astounding. I was told by the people who'd raised me that I was not the son I understood myself to be. My parents, my natural parents, had perished so that I could fulfill my destiny. Such a large, meaningless word for some, *destiny*. For me, it meant everything."

In frustration, he fisted long, narrow hands. "My brother had betrayed what they died for and the restoration of their faith, the justification of their sacrifice, fell to me. I knew Nelson would stop at nothing to take, as he'd always taken from others. Atlas offered me a solution, in you."

"And you used me," she whispered.

"I did not intend to love." Alex winced, and he smiled ten-derly in understanding. "I do not love you as I'd hoped, as a man should love his bride. But I do believe we became friends."

"As did I."

"It tore at me to damage such a precious gift. Yet, there it was again, that word. That destiny. I had a choice, yes. And I may not have chosen wisely."

In golden eyes, anguish warred with determination. "I have a calling, Alexandra. A mission. One twenty-five years in the creation. Please, forgive me for my deceit. If you cannot, know at least that it will haunt me." He took her hands then, and drew her closer, cheek to cheek. "Because of my act, my brother may have hurt you. For that, I do not seek forgiveness, for I do not deserve it."

Tears she'd refused to shed earlier pressed against her eyes. "Damon, please. Leave me." Before she forgave him and found herself with no one left to hate.

"The way he did? No, my beautiful Alexandra, I will not." Ignoring her protests, he folded her into his arms. Suddenly, violently, the dam broke, and Damon rocked her gently as she wept. He rubbed her back, murmuring soothing, incoherent words.

"He said he didn't love me," she sobbed.

Damon snorted in disbelief. "Obviously, *ma belle*, he lied."

Alex sniffled. "I thought so at first. Then he looked me in the eyes and said he didn't love me."

Drawing her away, Damon lifted her chin with a gentle knuckle. "He is a master of subterfuge, Alexandra. Lies told without flinching are his stock in trade. Now, tell me, do you believe him?"

Alex hiccupped softly, considering the question. If he hadn't seemed so sincere, the eyes so direct, would she have listened? "No," she told Damon. "His heart was pounding, like mine. And his hands, where they held me, were so tight."

"He would not love a woman like you easily," Damon offered. He pressed a handkerchief into her hands. "You would challenge him, nettle him. Phillip Turman does not seem to be a man who'd bend, but for you, he'd try. This scares him, as much as the threat that awaits the three of us in Jafir."

Alex dried her face. "I told you. I'm not going. He's given guards an order not to let me leave the room," she pouted, her spirit returning. "As if I were his to command."

"It would seem you are, at least in this."

Alex's eyes lit with purpose. "Not if you help me."

"What can I do?" Damon asked warily.

"Contact Atlas. Have him come here."

"Meet me here? What is your plan?"

"I'm not sure Phillip actually told Atlas he was deserting me, but I can't say Atlas wouldn't agree if I called and whined. But he can't deny me face-to-face," she stated arrogantly. "He owes me. Can you get a message to him? Tell him I'm ill and need to see him. Maybe Civelli poisoned me. Or the ruby's supernatural powers are real. Whatever. Just get him here. Can you do that?"

"I am the prince of Jafir. He will do as I ask," he reminded her with a chuckle. "I believe I will enjoy my status, *mon cheri*. I do look the part, do I not?" He preened comically and Alex laughed huskily.

Damon nodded in approval. "Our car leaves in a few minutes. Shall I delay it?"

"No, thank you," Alex said. "When Atlas arrives, I'll make him send me. Don't tell Phillip," she insisted. "He'll find out when it's too late to do anything but accept his fate." She smiled at Damon, hope awakening.

The smile was watery and wobbled a bit, but it held.

Damon caressed her cheek. "I envy Turman. He does not seem to me a stupid man, but looks can deceive. Good luck, Alexandra. I will see you at my coronation."

———

He needed time, Phillip thought despondently. Time to unravel her from his heart, from his mind. He'd only known her a month, surely not long enough for permanent damage.

He'd install the prince, defeat the enemy, and build a new life. Without Alex.

It was the last part that tripped him up, made his heart stumble. He could no longer imagine his world without Alex. And all he could see was her stunned humiliation when he'd savaged her.

Beyond the windows of the plane, Crete waited below. Morning had already come to the island, since their flight had been delayed. The storm system that deluged them the night before in DC had grounded the naval plane for hours at the base. Hours for him to contemplate how to create a new life from the one he'd just ruined.

Damon, no surprise, hadn't been of any help. Regal condemnation masked by banal conversation had been the order of the day as they drove to Annapolis. Seated in the next row, he'd kept up a steady stream of conversation as they waited inside the stranded aircraft. Thinly veiled comments about casting pearls before swine twisted the knife deeper. When Phillip had finally barked out a demand for quiet, Damon smiled smugly.

What did he know of it? Of wanting a woman so badly it ached to breathe? Of loving so fiercely it flamed your soul? Of being so afraid to have that you'd run away?

Phillip froze. Fear? He wasn't afraid of Alex. He was afraid for her, he reminded himself. Walking away had nothing to do with fear. He'd dealt with Lorei's desertion years ago. Hadn't he proven it at the reception?

He had no reason to question himself, to doubt his motives. Alex was reckless and mercurial and headstrong. She'd pay no attention to his advice, would do whatever she pleased. In his line of work, her brand of stubbornness was fatal. He owed it to her to defend her not just against the threat of Scimitar, but the daily life of being with him. He'd chosen the ISA twice, and he wouldn't abandon it for anyone.

She didn't ask you to give it up. The thought popped into his head, unbidden. *She didn't ask you for anything. Not even love.* In the throes of passion, she'd taken a chance and declared her feelings, but expected nothing in return. When they'd taken each other, again and again, as dawn approached, she whispered it in passion and in the tranquil aftermath.

Love given unconditionally, without reservation. It terrified him. She terrified him. Because with love came commitment. He hadn't been enough for Lorei. He wouldn't survive Alex turning away.

"We are beginning our descent," the pilot announced over the loudspeaker.

Phillip checked his harness, instructed Damon to do the same. As the plane circled over the landing strip near Suda Bay, Phillip clicked off the part of his mind occupied with Alex. For the next hours, deciphering the obelisk and safely instating Damon as the next king were all that could matter.

Phillip turned to Damon. "When we get on the ground, we'll take transport to the contact point. Tomorrow, we'll fly into Jafir. Atlas explained that we'd bring in help reconstructing and deciphering the obelisk?"

"I thought Alexandra was going to repair it. Who will do so now?" he asked innocently.

Phillip flinched at the mention of her name. "It's broken stone. I can mend it," he snapped. In the race to escape her, he hadn't considered that part of the plan.

Even now, miles away, she fogged up his judgment. "We'll take a look at it when we land."

"You're in charge," Damon agreed, not bothering to disguise a note of doubt. "I do hope your failed relationship will not divert your attention from the matters at hand."

"I won't be distracted, Your Highness," Phillip grated out, bristling at the condescension. "And my relationship with Alex is none of your business."

"According to her, you no longer have one. Which appears to leave the field clear for others, *n'est-ce pas?*"

"Stay away from her," Phillip ordered harshly, glaring at Damon, all attempts at civility forgotten. "She wouldn't be tangled up in this debacle if you hadn't been so willing to use her as a pawn!"

Damon shot back, "And she wouldn't be stranded in America miserable and alone, if you weren't a bloody coward."

"Coward? I didn't use a helpless woman to do my dirty work!"

Suddenly, Damon laughed, a deep-throated chuckle. "Alexandra? Helpless? You obviously do not know her at all. I have not known a more capable woman."

"Nor have I," Phillip conceded ruefully. In crisis, she'd remained steady, her wits fully about her. Indeed, when they were chased by thugs, Alex had handled his gun like a professional. He'd once professed not to underestimate her, yet he did, time and time again. But he'd still made the right choice. She wasn't the woman for him.

Damon interrupted his dark thoughts. "We have landed, Phillip. It is time to deplane."

Phillip gathered his duffel bag and waited at the base of the steps for Damon to join him on the ground. At the end of the landing strip, manufactured for the sandy, flat upland basin, Atlas had arranged for a utility vehicle.

Phillip stored their gear and waited for the plane to refuel and lift off. The ISA had several camps set up throughout the region, and Crete's bevy of large caves made exceptional hiding places for equipment and operatives.

Today, however, they'd be camping at a hotel in Khaniá, the second largest city on the island.

In the glove compartment, Phillip found a plastic hotel key and a map. He knew the Hotel Levka Ori well.

The rear of the building faced the sea, making it difficult to approach from that direction. Excellent choice, he thought approvingly. If Jubalani or Zeben happened to track them to the island, attack would be tricky, but not impossible. With the possibility of ambush very real, along their route, Phillip checked for close-following vehicles, and he altered direction often. For his part, Damon said little, his thoughts firmly on the coming events.

When they reached the hotel, Phillip drove to the service entrance. Before they went inside, he taped a wireless digital camera to the four faces of the hotel. In a matter of minutes, they were escorted to a suite of rooms on the second floor. From any room in the suite, Phillip remembered, he'd be able to see an enemy approach. The floor's height was such that if necessary, he and Damon could jump.

He inserted the key into the lock and motioned silently for Damon to step behind him. The door swung open slowly, and Phillip detected the muted sound of voices.

Drawing his weapon, he crouched on his haunches, scanning the room. Footsteps sounded to his left, and he swerved to aim the gun at his assailant.

He dropped the gun.

"For goodness' sake, Phillip. You could at least knock first," Alex said testily when breath again filled her lungs.

Dumbfounded, Phillip stared at what he knew to be a figment of his own longing. It was virtually impossible for Alex to be standing in the living room, eating a pomegranate, and lecturing him on etiquette. He'd left strict instructions for her to be locked inside her quarters, no exceptions.

"How in the hell did you get here?" Phillip demanded.

Behind him, Damon shut the door.

"Plane, train, and automobile." Alex briskly pushed past him to reach Damon, her hands extended in enthusiastic welcome. "Thanks for your help, Damon."

"*De rien*, Alexandra." He pressed a warm kiss to her mouth in greeting. "I trust your trip was uneventful?"

Alex grinned. "The storm system that delayed your flight bypassed my departure spot. I caught a ride from Langley."

"With the Air Force?" asked Phillip incredulously.

"I have friends," she admonished sarcastically. "And not everyone finds me so useless."

"I never said you were useless," corrected Phillip.

She speared him with a baleful glare. "No. I believe you said 'expendable.'" Hooking her arm into Damon's, she led him to the sitting room. She plopped down onto the sofa and patted the cushion by her side. Lifting the remote control, she gestured at the flickering images on the screen, the source of the voices Phillip had detected.

"I think I've been watching Greek soap operas. I don't understand a word of the language, but they're all so beautiful and riddled with angst."

Damon tucked her against his side, too close for Phillip's taste. He started to protest, then realized he had no right. Still, she seemed rather familiar with Damon, despite his own admitted perfidy. He let her smuggle in dangerous objects, like a pack animal, and there she was curled against him. Laughing at a story neither could possibly comprehend.

Jealousy, now as familiar as the ache of desire, coursed through him. How he longed to snatch her from his arms, to carry her into the bedroom that lay beyond the doors. Instead, he fortified his resolve. If she could so easily switch allegiances, didn't that prove him right?

But the accusation sounded false even to his own ears.

Angry with himself, furious with her, Phillip plucked the duffel bag from the hallway. While Alex and Damon giggled like teenagers over the television, he installed security devices. Miniature motion detectors, linked to a handheld unit, lined the perimeter of the room and the stairwells leading to their floor. He would activate them when they retired for the night. Above the doorway, he installed a digital camera that he networked to one in each bedroom. The two rooms, connected by the sitting room, faced perpendicular views of the sea.

While in the second bedroom, it occurred to him that there were indeed only two rooms. Alex, of course, would take one and Damon the other. He glanced at the sofa, its length slightly shorter than his tall frame.

Alex's throaty laugh drifted into the bedroom where he checked for bugs. To torment him, his mind flashed images of Alex rising above him, sinking onto him. He hardened in damning response. It didn't matter, he thought sourly. He wouldn't be getting much sleep tonight anyway.

After a thorough check of the suite, he returned to the sitting room. Alex nestled into Damon's shoulder, his arm draped around her shoulder. She murmured something Phillip couldn't hear, and Damon stroked her arm in response.

"We need to think about dinner," he announced loudly.

Alex lifted her head slowly and gave him a measuring glance. "I assume we're confined to quarters. Will we be dining on field rations or salt and tack?" she asked sardonically.

"We'll order in," Phillip replied pithily, his jaw set and heavy.

Out of spite, Alex trailed a finger along Damon's shoulder. "What are you in the mood for?"

Playing along, Damon nipped at her jaw. "What are you offering?"

The tether on Phillip's temper snapped. He stalked over to the sofa and pulled her up to face him. Damon, realizing disappearing would be the better part of valor, slipped away and quietly closed the door to the bedroom.

"What in the hell do you think you're doing?" Alex demanded.

"I was about to ask you the same thing! I distinctly recall giving orders for you to stay in Bethesda."

"You, Phillip, are not the boss of me!" She tried to jerk her arm away, but his grip didn't loosen. Refusing to dignify his actions with a struggle, she skewered him with a look. "And the next time you lie to me, I'll deck you. Uncle James had no idea you planned to leave me behind!"

"I did what was best," he hissed, conscious of Damon behind the next door. Furious, he dragged her into the second bedroom and slammed the door.

Alex rounded on him, eyes livid with hurt. "What was best?

Breaking my heart? That's what's best?" She yanked her arm away. "To hell with you, Phillip," she said softly.

"I wanted to protect you," he began.

"I didn't ask for your protection. I didn't even ask for your love. And now, I don't want either one." Alex crossed her arms, to hold in the words straining for voice. The plea to be folded against him, into him, until dawn came.

On the flight to Greece, she'd replayed their scene in her head over and over. In every scenario, with every possible excuse, only one conclusion was possible. He loved her. He didn't trust her to love him back.

The realization almost made her beg to be returned to Washington, but she too knew about honor. Raleigh and Adam were leaving their honeymoon early to assist a man they'd barely met. She'd given her word to help Damon. Repairing the obelisk required more than a layman's touch. Her expertise would bring him one step closer to his destiny.

So she'd closed her mind to the motion of the plane. Somewhere over England, she found the courage to forgo his touch. In the air above Italy, she accepted he didn't trust her to love him well. By the time they'd reached the hotel, she'd rid herself of the thought, the essence of Phillip.

Then he'd burst into the room, weapon at the ready, the avenging angel he could be. And she'd wanted. Needed.

Her skin burned where he'd held her, not in pain but in yearning. She'd loved him last night with tenderness. Now, watching, craving, she made her choice.

She would seduce him, take him into her bed. But she would hold her heart separate, not forgetting her purpose or his distrust. With a final act of love, she'd purge him from her body, from her soul.

"I don't want your love," Alex declared as she reached for the buttons on his shirt. "I want you. Now."

Confusion, desire, washed over him. Fighting the urge to take, he stilled her hands with his own. "Alex, nothing has changed," he warned.

"No, Phillip, everything has." Pulling her hands free, she drew the shirt away from his body, down the sinewy arms, and tossed it to the floor.

"I won't change my mind," he panted as she traced a damp line down the center of his chest. Hard hands fisted in her hair.

"I won't change mine," she retorted, reveling in the banquet of flavors on his skin. Turning, she pushed him to the bed and crawled over him. "Tonight, there will be no declarations of love. Just you and me and this." Her mouth closed over his, ravenous and agile.

Heat met heat, will battled will. Where he touched, she burned. Where she kissed, he ached. Desire twisted with want, tangled with need. Gasps, moans, desperate sighs filled the air, filled the night.

Frantic tremors shook them both, neither willing to cede even the smallest touch. Every kiss, every taste, a battle for more, for supremacy. Even the act of protection, a struggle of wills.

He rose above her, triumphant. She clenched around him, victorious. In union, in combat, they rode the night into exhaustion, into completion. In satiation, they turned into each other's arms, in denial, in revelation.

And slept.

CHAPTER THIRTEEN

Adam, can you hand me the fitch? It's the brush with the rounded ferrule and the long handle." Hunched over a makeshift worktable in the kitchenette, Alex used an outliner to swab the epoxy residue from the joint where the pyramidion met the tower. Having left her tools behind in Washington, she'd sent a pensive Phillip out to purchase a set of painter's brushes and art knives, the adhesive epoxy and turpentine.

"Need more light?" Adam inquired, pressing the brush into her outstretched palm. "I can request another lamp from housekeeping."

Alex shook her head. "No, I think we're almost there. Lucky Civelli's head is as hard as it is. The stone essentially broke at the cap and near the base, where the inscription circles the tower." With the fitch, she applied a thin coat of the common solvent to remove the excess adhesive.

She carefully matched the cap of the obelisk to each of the four faces, where lines of deeply incised text ran vertically up to the obelisk's apex. Before finally adhering the pieces, Adam had reviewed the Shilha syntax, to be certain the inscriptions matched. Soon, the obelisk would be ready, and the next phase could begin.

By tomorrow, if they succeeded, she'd board a plane for home. Home, where a barely begun manuscript mocked her attempt at transformation. Self-destruction was, by far, more accurate, she decided grimly. Whatever rationale she'd formed to explain her behavior last night seemed rash and, frankly, stupid in the cold light of dawn. Rather than reinforce her decision to move on, she'd found herself more deeply enthralled. Making love with Phillip seemed to burrow him deeper, not discharge him from her heart. He, however, seemed to have endured the night, distrust intact.

The proximity detector, tripped by Adam and Raleigh, had dragged her from uneasy slumber. She'd stumbled into the living room to find Phillip standing by the door, his bleak countenance an impenetrable mask. By tacit agreement, neither returned to bed. Instead, Phillip demonstrated his security precautions to the newcomers and left to gather supplies. Damon, awakened by their arrival, joined Alex in the sitting room. They'd explained the weeks' events, leaving nothing out.

Adam had bridled at the revelation that Alex had been an unwitting player, memories of his last trip to Jafir fresh in his mind. In empathy, in apology, Raleigh twined slender fingers with broad, strong ones, her wedding ring flashing in the light. Anger settled, dissipated.

He'd learned from Raleigh the inexorable pull of obligation, the hold a strong sense of duty cast over reason. Without speaking, Adam shifted until he could wrap his arms around her, Raleigh's short curls tucked beneath his chin.

With shadowed eyes, Alex had observed the unspoken communication, felt the bonds of love and trust stretch between them and hold fast. Phillip would never, could never feel the same for her, share so much of himself with her. He'd been brutally honest in that at least, she acknowledged. No words of love, no declarations of trust. Only the communion of body to body, flesh to flesh. And because she loved, it would never be enough.

"Alex, are you okay?" Adam ran a hand down her hair to tug at the braided end, snapping her pained reverie. "You've been abnormally focused today."

"We have a mission, don't we?" She lifted her head to aim a glare in Phillip's general direction. "I don't want to be accused of not pulling my weight or distracting anyone." Mouth set into a mutinous line, she continued to wash the epoxy away with the turpentine.

Adam followed the line of her disgusted, covetous gaze. In the sitting room, Raleigh, Damon, and Phillip discussed the possibility of ambush at the capitol, where the Tribunal had been assembled.

"According to President Robertsi, the Tribunal is constitutionally bound to meet today. Until midnight, any citizen can come forward and attempt to claim the throne," Raleigh explained.

Damon interjected, "I have no proof of citizenship. I am officially of South Africa."

"You'll have the obelisk. That will be your ticket for admission," guaranteed Raleigh.

"Zeben will certainly be there, waiting to attack." Phillip drew an X near the palace entrance. "I'd expect a sniper here, behind the columns. And another here," he told them as he marked a spot on the palace's turrets.

"I can rig a device to detonate noxious fumes. If we time it properly, we can hit the snipers on either side, without raising an alarm." Raleigh turned to Damon. "While I set off the charges, Adam will take you inside. Phillip, you're a better shot than Adam, so you should be responsible for the snipers."

"I heard that," Adam growled, entering the sitting room, Alex by his side. He laid a hand on her shoulder and squeezed playfully. "Say it. Phillip does not shoot better than I do."

Raleigh patted his hand. "Of course, he doesn't, dear. He just hits his targets better." She wrinkled an impudent nose at him, which Adam bussed playfully. Smiling, she indicated that he and Alex should sit. Adam crowded onto the sofa beside Raleigh, and Damon and Phillip occupied the two chairs. Both stood up to offer their seats, but she refused.

"I'll sit on the floor." Then she realized the only free space with a clear view of the table was beside Phillip. Careful to avoid even accidental contact, she walked past him to take up her position. Wordlessly, Phillip handed her a cushion from the sofa.

"Thank you," she murmured, eyes firmly fixed on the map.

"You're welcome," Phillip answered stiffly. He waited for her to look at him. Despite their protestations to the contrary, something *had* changed between them. She had changed.

He didn't recognize the dark siren who'd seduced him with bravado, for she possessed a confidence Alex had not. Even this morning, she'd focused on the task at hand, issuing orders like a veteran. Yet this woman, as much as her predecessor, confounded him. How could he want what he could not trust, take what he knew he'd lose?

He needed to see her eyes, to read what lay behind the metamorphosis. Phillip stared at her, willing her to look at him. When she didn't, he returned his attention to the battlement. "We've got to expect that Jubalani has his own men or that he's coordinating the attack with Zeben."

Damon spoke again, with antipathy. "Nelson is a coward. He will almost certainly be conspiring with Zeben. And he has several contacts in the government who assist with his smuggling. You should anticipate they will have men inside the palace."

Nodding, Phillip gestured to the floorplan of the palace. "The Tribunal meets in this room. All applicants must pass through metal detectors along this corridor. If Zeben and Jubalani have men on the palace guard, they'll have firepower we won't." Phillip looked longingly at the cache of weapons resting near the closet. "Those will be of little use to us if we can't get them inside."

"No problem." Adam poked Raleigh in the ribs. "Show them what you've made, darling."

Raleigh reached into the case she carried with her at all times. She lifted an innocuous octagonal disk of thick putty with a hole in its center. Elongating the putty into a tube, she explained, "It's made from a polymer blend." With rapid motions, she snapped the tubing into three parts—a barrel, a base, and a lever. In less than thirty seconds, she'd constructed a handgun the size of a Derringer.

Phillip said as much. "Pretty nifty, Raleigh, but Derringers are no match for automatic rifles."

"Still, you doubt me, Phillip? I'm crushed." She inserted a

slim magazine into a slot in the base where the tubing was hollow. She aimed the weapon at an urn sitting near the entryway. Levering a vertical trigger, the vase shattered instantly, the bullet lodged in the wall. "The polymer creates a vacuum when reconnected and instantly adheres. I cooked it up last summer and finally made these prototypes."

"Amazing," Phillip admitted, reaching for the weapon. "I thought you were antigun."

"I am. But when the techs and I discovered this chemical, I had to experiment. Don't worry, I have my own weapons with me too. This is for you guys."

Grinning, he turned it, and asked, "What's the capacity?"

"With a full clip, it has a fifty-round magazine and fires like a MAC-10. The slide lever is designed to release the bullets in continuous succession, based on the kinetic theory of gas. You know, particles moving in straight lines with high average velocity. The bullets continually encounter one another and change their individual velocities accordingly. This causes pressure from their impact to build against the walls of the chamber, forcing even more speed. So it's faster than your average submachine gun and more accurate. Cool, huh?"

Damon stared around the assembled group in disbelief. "Is anyone else frightened?"

Alex raised her hand in commiseration. "I think I preferred you as the mad scientist," she said faintly.

"How do we get it inside?" queried Phillip. "They'll frisk us."

"It's lightweight and undetectable by conventional scanners. You could carry it in your pocket. Once we're inside, I recommend immediate assembly. Before we bring in the prince."

"So, Raleigh will take out the guards on the ground. Adam will guard the prince. I'll eliminate any snipers on the roof."

Alex chimed in, spearing Phillip with a defiant stare. "And where will I be?"

Raleigh and Adam exchanged eloquent glances. Damon twisted in his seat to catch their eyes and share their amusement. The three interlopers braced for the inevitable explosion. The nervous, annoyed tension between Alex and Phillip had been palpable all day. No one expected this confrontation to be any less edgy.

"You'll be here." Phillip set the gun on the table. "Now that the obelisk is assembled, you've done your part. It's better for everyone if you wait here. And by *wait*, I mean stay put," he added with a glower.

Alex curled her lip in a sneer. "I don't plan to pay any more attention to that this time than I did before. Give me an assignment, Phillip."

"Stay out of our way! We've got to get inside, get Damon before the Tribunal and not get killed. What possible help could you be?" he raged, oblivious to the shocked looks of those around him. Adam, who'd known him the longest, had never seen Phillip this furious. He could count on one hand the number of times Phillip's famed patience had been tested so sorely. None of his opponents had fared well in those contests.

But he'd misjudged Alex. She scrambled to her feet, then leaned forward to poke Phillip in the chest. "I am sick and tired of being told how useless I am to you. I found the ruby, not you. I escaped from Civelli without you. I disabled their car, and I repaired the damn obelisk. You don't have to love me and you don't have to trust me, but you will not ignore me. Now, figure out what you want me to do. I've got to use the bathroom." With that, she stalked away, chin jutting, head held high.

Phillip remained in his chair, his expression flummoxed. Three pairs of interested eyes gauged his reaction. Damon saw the pride warring with irritation. In Phillip's stunned gaze, Raleigh witnessed mortification at the audience, to their confrontation and unwelcome desire. Adam saw love.

He stood, walked over to Phillip, and tapped him on the shoulder. "Come on," he told him. Adam entered the bedroom Damon had occupied. After Phillip followed him inside, he firmly shut the door.

"You did this for me, so I guess I'll have to do this for you." Adam shoved him roughly onto the bed. Phillip fell and barely caught his balance.

"What are you doing?" Phillip said angrily.

"In lieu of actually striking you, I'm trying to knock some sense into that hard head of yours." Leaning an elbow on the armoire, he added, "You're an idiot, Phillip."

Phillip sprang off the bed and stormed to the door. "This is none of your business, Adam," he ground out between clenched teeth. "It's between Alex and me."

Adam kicked the barely opened door shut with a booted foot. "Since I'm partly responsible for the reason I assume you're being such a fool, it is my business." When Phillip yanked on the knob, Adam slammed the door again.

"Stay out of this, Adam," Phillip rasped.

"You're spending a lot of time telling people to stay away from you. Eventually, you'll end up alone," Adam shot back.

"That's better than the alternative," grumbled Phillip. Releasing the doorknob, he moved to the window where the sea crashed mightily into the rocky shore. "I know what I'm doing, Adam."

"Pushing Alex away just in case she turns out to be like Lorei?" Adam guessed.

Phillip raised tortured brown eyes to sympathetic black. "She's nothing like her, I know. But in fundamental ways, they are the same. I can't make that kind of investment twice in one lifetime." He dragged an unsteady hand through his hair. "What I felt for Lorei is nothing compared to this. Lorei was a fantasy, ethereal and romantic. Alex is real, solid."

"Then what's the problem?"

"If—no—when she decides I'm not enough, I won't be able to let her go, Adam. And she will do it. Even though she thinks she loves me now, I won't always be enough for her. She's brilliant, strong, so full of ideas, she can't sit still." Phillip laughed without humor. "She calls herself flaky. But it's not that simple. Alex sees the world through a prism, a billion shades of chance. And she has the talent and the drive to make everything she dreams come true. If I let myself have her, she'll want me for a while, then she'll want more than I can be, can give her. And she'll move on."

"You don't trust her," Adam summarized. "So, on the off chance that she finds some shinier toy, you're willing to throw away the love of a lifetime."

"Yes," Phillip stated without conviction. "I don't have a choice."

"No, it's Alex who doesn't have a choice. Too bad she fell in love with a coward." Adam turned toward the door. "Suit yourself, Phillip."

"Now, wait just a minute! I am not a coward! I'm honest enough to see the writing on the wall."

"Bull. You're too scared to try in case it works. I expected more, Phillip. Much more. You both deserve it." Adam left the room, the door ajar.

Alex sat on the sofa in the seat he'd vacated. Her eyes were red-rimmed but dry. Good for you, he thought. Don't let him get away with this. He started to speak, but Raleigh beat him to it.

"Alex, I think I know what we need you to do."

"I'm up for it," she replied gamely.

Though it disturbed Raleigh to involve her in danger, she understood why Alex needed to be included. She was intimately acquainted with the compulsion to prove oneself, particularly to yourself. She wouldn't deny her. "I confirmed Adam's reading of the inscription. It says that the rightful heir must bear the obelisk and its secret. Our best chance is to divide and conquer. If you can get the ruby into the palace, and Damon reaches the Tribunal with the sculpture, Zeben won't be able to use the fake."

Phillip spoke from the edge of the sitting room. "I'll take her in. If Adam covers Damon and you monitor the grounds, we can make it inside." He saw Alex start with surprise.

Taken aback by the capitulation, Raleigh hesitated. "I re-examined the diagrams of the palace interior and compared them to the reconnaissance information we received from a pal of Atlas's." She pointed to a series of underground pathways. "Look, here, these tunnels lead into the palace from a spot near Eagle Point."

Phillip knew Eagle Point well. It was the base camp where Raleigh had taken him after she'd kidnapped him, prepared to kill him. "Makes sense. If they needed a quick escape, the royal family would be able to exit near the plateau or near the shore, depending on which route they selected."

Adam leaned over the map and the diagram. "If I take Damon in through this tunnel and Phillip brings Alex in through here," he pointed to a winding corridor beneath ground, "we should emerge on either side of the Tribunal chambers." He laid a hand over Raleigh's on the table. "You'd be on your own."

"I can handle it. Of course, it means we won't have to sneak our guns past the metal detectors. And I've been working on some more new toys," she pouted.

"The guns will still come in handy. They're lighter than anything I brought with us, and in case one of us is captured, no one will take them in a search."

"Then we're agreed." With a kiss in his palm, Raleigh assured her husband, "I have every intention of finishing our honeymoon." Oblivious to their audience, Adam drew her into a scorching kiss.

They reviewed their plans for a while longer, until Phillip was confident each member knew her or his role. He studiously avoided eye contact with Alex, unwilling to face what he'd agreed to allow her to do. When he asked, finally, if anyone had any questions, Damon cleared his throat.

"How do I begin to thank you for everything? Phillip, you risk your life for a country that is not your own. You two jeopardize a new marriage, a new family, for a man you do not know." He smiled solemnly at Alex. "And Alexandra. I can't begin to express how—" His voice, low and subdued, broke over the words.

Alex reached out to him then, eyes overflowing with friendship and affection. "In Durban, on the beach, you asked me what I wanted. I couldn't answer you then. But I have it now. Purpose.

And, despite your less than chivalrous delivery, you did give me my heart's desire." She inclined her head imperiously, her smile mischievous. "Although I am partial to jewelry."

"Will crown jewels do?" he teased in return, gratified by her forgiveness.

"We need to get ready," Phillip interrupted the light banter curtly. "We'll depart at eight p.m. That'll limit the amount of time Zeben or Jubalani have to stop us."

"Aye, aye, sir," Adam responded with a mock salute.

The wound from Adam's denunciation still raw, Phillip did not respond. Instead, he looked at the women seated on the sofa. "Raleigh, do you have clothes for Alex?"

Raleigh nodded. "Sure. Come on in the back, Alex. We have a lovely selection of basic black and camouflage. Your choice."

Inside the room, Raleigh rummaged through the suitcase she'd stored there earlier. She removed a pair of black pants, boots, and a black tee, twin to the outfit she wore. "These should fit," she told Alex.

Too used to one another for modesty, Alex quickly stripped and dressed in her borrowed clothes. She nimbly braided her errant hair, then anchored the mass with a band at her nape. She laced the boots, a size too large, but the thick socks absorbed much of the excess.

"Are you sure you want to do this?" Raleigh asked, sitting on the bed beside her.

Alex became rigid, the laces on one boot dangling. "I told you, I'm a part of this. Did Phillip ask you to talk to me?"

"No. He hasn't said a word since you told him you loved him." Raleigh leaned forward to catch her eyes. "When did that happen?"

"I don't know. The first time he saved my life, maybe. Or when I saw how much he loved his dad. I don't know. And I can't seem to get rid of it."

"Phillip is stubborn, Alex. I warned you. But I've never met anyone as obstinate as you are."

"Well, I'm tired of trying to convince him that I'm worthy of his love."

Raleigh's amber eyes darkened. "He said that?"

Alex's bottom lip trembled. "And he said that I'd desert you because I'd be distracted," she added.

"How dare he? You're the most loyal, trustworthy person I know, and that includes Mr. Self-righteous. I ought to take my gun back! How dare he?"

Bolstered by the instant support, Alex continued her complaints. "He said I'd leave him for another man. That I wouldn't be able to stay with him."

"Alex, you do have a habit of discarding men," Raleigh offered cautiously.

"I didn't love them."

"You're sure you love Phillip?"

"I said I did."

"You've thought so before," Raleigh reminded her.

Suspiciously, Alex considered her words. "Whose side are you on?"

She raised her hands in self-defense. "Yours, of course. But you can't blame the guy for wondering."

"I thought best friends gave unqualified support?" groused Alex.

"You're included in the mission, aren't you?"

"Yes. Now, how do I not prove him right?"

With rapt attention, she learned how to assemble Raleigh's newest weapon and marveled at her friend's deadly ingenuity. When Raleigh left to distribute the disks and clips to the rest of the team, Alex sat on the edge of the bed. Slowly, the reality of what she'd committed to do sank in. In the pouch at her waist was a jewel worth millions. She was in a hotel room in Greece about to infiltrate a palace to coronate a king.

No matter what she wrote in the future, her imagination would by no means equal the reality of this moment, she admitted. As she'd told Damon, if her life had lacked purpose before, she'd undoubtedly found it.

The passion, the meaning, lay not in what she did with her life, but why.

She'd agreed to help Damon because the region deserved peace. Zeben, or any threat like Jubalani, must be stopped. And she loved Phillip, not because romance was her hobby or even because he made her wanton and alive. She loved him because it was right.

She might fail at the first as miserably as she had at the second, but at least she'd tried, Alex thought glumly. Perhaps she could write self-help books about it, though.

Living without Love. Mission Impossible: Conquering Caprice. A Flake's Guide to—

In the sitting room, a siren blared, the noise familiar. The proximity detector, Alex realized. She slid off the bed, checked the pouch for the ruby and her putty-gun, as she'd inelegantly termed it, and reached for the door. It swung open before she could turn the knob, and Phillip grabbed her by the arm.

"Zeben's men are in the stairwell. We've got to go. Now!" At the hotel window, Adam busily pushed the sliding panels open. Raleigh jumped first, her backpack secured. Damon followed, then Adam. Phillip helped her climb up on the ledge. "Go," he whispered harshly. She leapt to the ground, the bushes below breaking her fall.

Phillip leaned out of the window. "Meet at Rendezvous Point Theta. I'll hold them off as long as I can."

"Phillip, no!" Alex yelled. "Come with us!"

Raleigh twisted her bag to retrieve a canister. "Heads up!" she shouted. She tossed the canister and Phillip snatched it out of the air. "When the door opens, pull the tab and jump. The fumes should incapacitate them for at least fifteen minutes."

Phillip nodded. "Go!" he barked again. "I'll meet you at Theta."

Adam took Alex's arm and urged her into a run. "He'll be right behind us."

In the suite, Phillip ducked behind the sofa arm, watching the monitors he'd installed. The siren's blare ricocheted incessantly, the noise deafening. A stream of men, at least six of them, he counted, emerged from the stairwell and approached the door.

When one of them used a key in the lock, Phillip knew an insider had informed on them. The door burst open, and the men rushed in, weapons at the ready. He jumped out, pulled the tab, and flung it into the center of the room.

Fumes poured out of the canister, choking the soldiers. Wild shots fired, one cracking the plaster above his head. To exacerbate the commotion, he threw a lamp into the fray, the crashing of glass disconcerting the already nauseous guards.

The vapors wafted toward him, and as he saw the first man

succumb, he dove out of the window. Coughing, he secured his pack and headed for Theta Point where the plane waited to take them to Jafir. They'd be arriving a bit ahead of schedule.

At the plane, the four of them were already inside. Phillip climbed into the cockpit and accepted the pilot's headset from Adam.

"You feel up to flying this thing?" Adam asked stiffly, adjusting the headset.

"Adam, you shoot better than you pilot," was the laconic response.

Satisfied that the anger had passed, Adam replied deadpan, "It doesn't help that I'm afraid of heights too." The sharp look from Phillip was met with Adam's deep laughter.

"Boys, I'm glad you made up, but while I'm good, I'm not that good," Raleigh said from the floor of the cargo hold. "We don't have that much lead time, so if you would like to get this show on the road, we'd appreciate it."

Damon whispered, sotto voce, "Can't you fly a plane?"

"I can, but I don't like to show off." Raleigh laughed.

Once airborne, Phillip reported what he'd seen. "Six men. All with the Scimitar insignia. They looked like his personal guard."

"If he's got six over here, there's probably an army waiting for us in Jafir," Adam deduced.

"How'd they know where to find us?" Alex asked.

"Either a tail on Adam and me, or a tip from the hotelier. Atlas secured the first three floors. It was a risk, but it bought us the time we needed."

The plane landed after a short flight, and they swiftly made their way to Eagle Point. The cavern was accessible only by a rope ladder suspended from the face of the plateau.

Alex dropped to her knees at the bottom of the rope. The hike had been strenuous enough to have her swearing to return to the gym if she made it home alive. From behind her, Phillip shoved his canteen into her chafed hands. The hilly terrain had cut at her skin when she'd fallen.

Phillip stayed with her, helping her stand, not touching her any longer than necessary. She gratefully gulped the cool water, trying to ignore the brief tingle from the feel of his hand over hers.

"Thank you," she murmured as she returned the canteen.

"Do you need a break?" he asked quietly.

Alex's spine straightened and she glared at him. "I can keep up. Don't worry about me." She turned away, prepared to follow the group. They passed the entrance to the cavern, slowly making their way along the narrow ledge. At four feet across, it was wide enough to give a person a false sense of safety. Unless she looked down.

Alex made the rookie mistake and was immediately overcome by vertigo. Behind her, Phillip pressed a gentle hand to her nape, angling her head forward. "Just walk, I've got you." With his free hand, he guided them along the cliffside.

"It should be up here," Adam announced from the lead.

Where he stood, the ledge widened into an expanse of at least fifteen feet. The path was overgrown with vines, after two decades of disuse. "It should be a couple of yards ahead on the right."

At the spot Adam had indicated, brush and wild vines grew over the cliff. Below the ledge they stood on, the ground gently sloped to the shore below. Damon and Adam pulled at vines while Raleigh and Alex cleared brush.

Phillip remained on the ledge, watching for Scimitar. Once

the entrance was visible, Adam felt around the edges. Near the top, he depressed a mechanism and the cavern opened.

"We're in," Raleigh said, removing a flashlight from her pack. In a single file line, they entered the dank, webbed space. Tiny feet skittered across stone, frightened by the flashlight's glare.

Adam handed Alex a light and gave one to Damon as well. "Check the wall for a switch," he instructed Phillip.

The wall closed with a grind, plunging the cavern into a more hostile darkness. Tepid light streamed from their hands, but the endless black promptly swallowed the beams. Phillip joined them as they headed deeper into the cave. Flashlight crossed and bounced as they searched for the tunnels.

"Up here," Damon called, his voice echoing eerily in the chamber. The cavern forked into two tunnels, lined with torches. Musty air hung heavy in the space, the scent of kerosene long since distilled by time.

From memory, Phillip issued their orders. "Raleigh, Adam, Damon, you head up the left tunnel. Raleigh, when you reach the second fork, take the right tunnel. It leads to the gardens. You can circle from behind and take out the guards. Adam and Damon, continue to the end of the left tunnel. According to the map, you should emerge in the antechamber where the Tribunal will be seated. Alex and I should come out on the opposite side, in what appears to be a closet of sorts. We'll wait for you if we arrive first, otherwise, begin the rites."

Phillip looked at them each in turn. "Synchronize watches," he said. The veterans laughed, Alex and Damon exchanged uneasy glances.

"Lighten up, guys," Adam said. "We're professionals. This will work."

"See you inside." Phillip tapped Alex's shoulder and they made their way into the gloom. As they walked, he assembled the weapon Raleigh produced. Silence, deeper than the pitch-black channel, spread between them.

He hated it. The way her eyes cooled when she looked at him, the way her voice chilled when she spoke to him, the way she moved away whenever he touched her. He missed the husky laugh, the unremitting chatter, and the satin skin. He hated the distance and knew he'd created it with thoughtless, well-planned words. He despised the pain and understood the only panacea was forever beyond his reach. Too late, he realized what had changed between them when she'd taken him in the tumult of the night. There, when he'd found release in her silken warmth, she'd exorcised him from her heart.

At the end of the tunnel, he searched for the mechanism to open the door. The entrance led to a smaller compartment, what he'd identified as the closet. An ornate handle made of brass glinted in the sunlight streaming in from the tall, gilded window. Phillip crossed to the window to see if he could locate Raleigh.

Alex pressed her ear to the doorway, listening for the sound of Damon's voice. When she heard nothing, she slowly turned the knob to crack the door slightly. Still nothing. She nudged the heavy door a bit more, holding on to the handle to prevent it from swinging open.

Finally, she heard a voice. The muffled baritone undulated in what sounded to her like an incantation. She gestured to Phillip, who had managed to pry open the window.

In the gardens, he saw Raleigh detonate the first charge as smoke rose from the lush grounds. He turned to check on Alex, who had her ear pressed to the door. She motioned for him to join her, but just then, in the garden, a palace guard approached Raleigh from behind.

Phillip hissed to Alex, "Raleigh!"

She nodded her comprehension. "Go, help," she whispered.

Beyond the door, in the Tribunal Council, the voice continued the recitation. It was Damon, she was almost sure. The tones were low, but familiar. She eased the door open another inch, to catch a glimpse of the speaker.

Suddenly, the handle was snatched from her grip and she tumbled into the chamber. Ruthless, violent hands like manacles jerked her to her feet. She kicked out, connecting with a shin. The bony hands merely tightened their grip.

"Damon," she called to the man reciting the Rites.

The speaker turned to face her, the face familiar and foreign.

Nelson gave a short bow. "My apologies to the Tribunal. Ah, Ms. Walton. You have something for my associate, I believe."

She turned to look at her captor and, with knowledge born of fear, knew she looked upon the face of Zeben.

CHAPTER FOURTEEN

Weaponless, trapped, Alex considered her options. If she screamed for help, it would alert Zeben and Jubalani to Phillip's presence. If she gave up the ruby, Nelson would become king in his brother's place, and he'd surely execute them all as his first official act. Of course, if she'd just stayed in the closet, she wouldn't be in this predicament right now. She looked around for a possible route of escape, but armed men blocked every door. Even the Tribunal faced the threat of weapons. Out of options, Alex relied on the one weapon she did have.

"Mr. Toca, or may I call you Nelson?" Alex asked in a husky voice, still caught in Zeben's grip.

"Please, Nelson. Our families are old friends." Nelson smiled, a curve of lips similar to his brother's, but the eyes remained flat and cold.

Alex cast an aggravated glance over her shoulder. "As old friends, would you kindly have your lackey release me?"

The clawlike hands constricted even further, forcing a whimper of pain. "I am no man's lackey," the malevolent voice hissed into her ear.

"You'd do well not to antagonize him, Alexandra." Nelson turned to the Tribunal, who watched the events with bewilderment. He explained their expressions to Alex.

"More than likely, none of these ancient men and women expected a sincere contestant to the throne. For twenty-five years, they've met in this room for twenty-four uninterrupted hours, rejecting petitioners with alacrity. Then I arrive, obelisk in hand. And, once I finish my recitation, you will deliver the key."

"For what price?" Alex challenged boldly. "I will not forfeit a gem like the Sahalia for nothing."

"You have it? You have the Sahalia?" Zeben demanded, "Show it to me!"

With the little freedom of movement left to her, Alex crossed her arms. "No."

"My advice to you, my dear, would be to do as he says. Even now, his henchmen are murdering your friends." Alex blanched. Seeing her fear, Nelson approached her, stroked a lean finger along her cheek. "Deliver the Sahalia, and we can discuss your survival."

"Not until we've come to terms," she asserted, her heart beating too rapidly. She had to keep him talking, to stall him until Adam and Damon arrived. Until Phillip and Raleigh were safe.

Nelson gripped her face in his hand. "There are no terms, other than these: deliver the ruby and you may not die."

Alex met his cruel hazel eyes, and did not blink. In a low voice, she countered, "I think not. You see, you're not reading from the true obelisk."

Nelson snorted, but he too kept his voice low. "I know this is a replica you created. I know my foolish older brother thought to hide the truth of our destiny from me with his machinations. How else would I know that the ruby is not inside?"

"There is also the fact that I reproduced the inscription. Do you really think your brother would have me do them accurately?" An inspired lie, she thought. Damon had indeed suggested she not be completely accurate, but she was a sucker for authenticity. It would be her saving grace if he bought the falsehood. She saw the moment realization set in.

"The Rites of Ascension have been verified," he argued uncertainly. "Zeben, you've read them?"

Zeben's grip loosened a fraction and blood again flowed into her upper arms. "It was Civelli's job to have the text verified." Both men scanned the room, as did Alex. Civelli was nowhere to be seen. "Where has the sniveling miscreant gone?"

Pleased by the turn of events, Alex smirked. "So, you see we do have something to discuss." She relaxed in Zeben's grip, pretending a nonchalance she did not feel. "If you would be king, I will have my own recompense."

Zeben's thin hand wrapped wiry fingers around her throat. "You will give me the ruby, or you will die."

Nelson snapped, "She's not bluffing, Zeben. Let her go."

"I do not take orders from you, whelp. This arrangement is at my pleasure. Anger me and my men will murder you as I did your parents."

Caught between them, Alex prayed that neither would notice

the pouch tucked beneath her tee. The Sahalia was her only bargaining chip. As long as they fought each other, they'd ignore her.

"My parents died in a boating accident," Nelson stated rebelliously. "And this *arrangement* is a partnership. Without me, you'd have lost the girl and the ruby. I already had the obelisk."

"One that she doctored that is of no use to you." Zeben snapped his fingers and a guard detached himself from the wall. "Radio the grounds. I want Civelli located. And kill the intruders."

The order, delivered in a loud, clear voice, caught the attention of a Tribunal member. The wizened man, skin leathery from sun and age, stood stiffly at his seat. "We must continue the Rites. There are others who wait to be heard."

"Sit down, old man!" Nelson shouted irritably. "I am the crown prince. The others mean nothing."

"I am the crown prince, Nelson. Do not presume to proclaim otherwise," Damon declared from the far end of the room.

Nelson's head swung around. "Kill him," he ordered without hesitation.

In the flurry of activity, Alex jammed an elbow into Zeben's stomach, stomped on his instep, and ran. She'd made it as far as the closet door when someone grabbed her arm.

Fist at the ready, she turned.

Phillip pulled her into the antechamber, where they knelt on the carpeted floor. In the main chamber, the staccato report of gunfire reverberated. Screams of agony melded with shouts of anger.

"There were only fifteen guards. Who's making all the noise?" Alex whispered, sagging with relief.

"The cavalry. President Robertsi got word of a declarant for the throne from his older advisor and sent the state police."

Relief was soon supplanted by distress. "We have to get back out there, Phillip! Damon and Adam are in there!"

"It's okay. I saw Adam pull Damon back inside the other room. Raleigh's in there as well. Once the fighting stops, the true coronation will begin," he explained.

Alex began to shiver in reaction. Once again, she'd come face-to-face with death, she realized. And this time, she'd seen its cold, beady eyes, she thought dramatically. Phillip, feeling her shake, wrapped comforting arms around her.

Warmth surrounded her, sank into the cold recesses where fear had been. She turned in his arms, buried her face in his neck. "He wanted to kill me," she whispered roughly, tears crowding her throat.

"But you stood up to them." Phillip pulled back to meet her eyes with his own. "I heard you in there. You were magnificent. Nelson was confused and even Zeben lost his temper. I've never seen that before."

Huge, wet brown eyes stared at him. "I needed to give you time to save Raleigh. I couldn't let you all down."

Phillip closed his eyes in shame. "You've never let me down, Alex. You couldn't. I'm so sorry I doubted you. That I made you doubt yourself."

He enfolded her in his arms, an embrace of comfort. Passion, so present whenever he was near her, slid away. Now, all he wanted was the solid feel of her in his arms, the peace of her a balm to his soul. He had to tell her, he thought suddenly. He had to tell her he loved her.

"Alex," he began.

A Jafirian guard opened the antechamber door. "Mr. Tur-man? Ms. Walton?"

"Yes," he barked.

"The Tribunal has requested your presence," the woman told him politely. "The Rites of Ascension are to be read."

"And the criminals?" Phillip asked.

"They have been taken into custody." She offered Alex a hand. "If you'll follow me, please."

In the Tribunal chamber, Damon read from the soapstone. With the help of Raleigh and Adam, his inflection, his translation was perfect. Alex knew from the expressions of approval on the Tribunal's faces, they accepted him as king. When he read the text encircling the base, Alex produced the Sahalia.

The collective gasp of the Tribunal and the crowd that had gathered in the chamber ensured his recognition.

Soon, Damon was lead from the chamber to the Throne Room. In a brief ceremony, he received the totem that had once belonged to his parents. The news spread like wildfire through-out the villages and the city, and crowds cheered at the palace gates.

Impromptu celebrations sprang up all over the city, and Da-mon attempted to visit each one. President Robertsi himself met the group at the Desira Plateau, where celebrants lit fireworks in honor of their new king.

"Your Highness," the president said as he bowed.

"Please, Mr. President," Damon protested. "Do not bow to me. I am sick unto death of bows and curtsies from men and women who only this morning would have waved or ignored me altogether."

President Robertsi clasped his shoulder. "Damon, you are now king. The people will need you to honor their customs, and I will need you to stabilize our land." He gestured to the Mediterranean glistening beyond the plateau. "We have an opportunity to reclaim what Zeben has stolen with his violence. I will be the head of the people, but you, Damon, must be their heart. They remember your parents, as do I. So if they bow, accept their homage to your parents, if nothing else."

Humbled, Damon acquiesced. "You do realize I will need a tutor. I am arrogant, but I have never been royalty before."

Everyone laughed and the president turned to face them. "Once again, you have saved my country. Phillip, I would give my presidency to restore those years we've taken from you."

Phillip shook his head. "We all do what we must, President." He smiled at the president, but his gaze fixed on Alex. "And if we are wrong, we have to accept it and move on. I have."

The group traveled for hours, an informal honor guard to the new king. At last, they returned to the palace. "Indermark, head of the Tribunal, informs me that rooms have been prepared for each of you. I hope you will be my guests."

Adam cradled Raleigh in his arms. "A honeymoon in a palace. I think we can make the most of that."

From nowhere, a man appeared and bowed. "Please follow me, sir, madam." The uniformed servant led them up a wide, shallow staircase.

Another servant approached Alex and Phillip. "This way, please." She curtsied.

They followed the young woman up the stairs and she deposited them in front of an open doorway. "Goodnight," she said as she scurried away.

"Wait!" Alex called, flustered. The room had only one bed. From the doorway, she could see the enormous four-poster with its purple velvet duvet. She turned to Phillip, her cheeks hot. "I'll just go downstairs and get another room. Obviously, they've made a mistake."

Phillip gently took her arm and led her inside. "There was no mistake, Alex. Unless you count my own." He pushed the door closed.

"I won't do this again, Phillip," Alex said frostily. "Last night was an aberration. I don't intend to repeat it." With a toss of her head, Alex walked to the door.

She yanked the handle and opened it. She had to escape before she gave in again. Another night in his arms would raze the final vestiges of dignity she'd managed to salvage. If he touched her again, she'd beg. And she'd sworn she wouldn't beg.

From behind, Phillip's arm shot past her ear, slamming the wood into the frame. "Alex, please, listen to me."

"Get out of my way, Phillip," Alex pleaded, dignity forgotten. Now she fought for survival. "I've heard everything you have to tell me."

"No, you haven't." Phillip speared his hands through the tousled waves of hair that refused to remain bound. "You haven't heard it because I haven't said it."

Alex felt her knees weaken, her pulse race. Again, she thought, he'd do it to her again. Make her believe in the possible then snatch it away. "No," she cried and shoved him away. She fumbled for the handle and raced into the hall.

Phillip staggered back a step, unprepared for the force of her blow. He quickly recovered, chasing her. Near the stairwell, he caught her around the waist.

When she struck out at him, he hoisted her into a fireman's carry. "You're going to make me do this the hard way," he growled, heading back to the room. Inside the door, he kicked it shut and tried to ignore the rain of blows she pummeled into his back.

"Put me down, you jackass! You Neanderthal! When I get down, I'll geld you like the capon you are!" Alex threatened wildly.

Without ceremony, Phillip dumped her on the bed and followed her down. Anticipating her, he rolled when she rolled, arched when she aimed a knee, determined to follow through on her threat.

"Damn it, Alex, just listen to me," he insisted as she thrashed beneath him. He gathered her wrists in his hands, tangled her legs with his own. Their hips met at their most vulnerable point, and Phillip struggled to keep his mind on the task at hand.

"Alex, I'm sorry," he said softly. "For every mean remark, for every cruel lie. I am so sorry."

She stilled her movements. Staring up at him, she asked, "Why?"

"Why did I say it? I don't know. To push you away. To shield you from Scimitar." Phillip shook his head, determined to give her the whole truth. "Because I was afraid. I was afraid you'd fallen in love with me because I was different and exciting. And as soon as you met someone more different, more exciting, you'd leave me." When her eyes narrowed, he hurried on. "I know, it wasn't fair. But I'd just built a new life for myself, Alex. One without love. Then you showed up and suddenly, I could imagine us together. Forever."

He released her wrist to brush his thumb across her forehead.

"You are magnificent, Alex. You can do anything, have anyone. Who I was hadn't been enough for Lorei." Alex tensed beneath him, and he finished, "She's nothing compared to you. You're brave and loyal and beautiful. I couldn't stand losing you, so I pushed you away."

Alex studied him with calm, dark eyes. Finally, she repeated, "Why?"

Confused, Phillip said, "I just told you why."

"No, you just told me why you did it. I want to know why you're sorry." She shoved at his chest. He released her and rolled away. Sitting up, she stared at him. "I told you I love you, and you hurt me. I showed you I love you, and you dismissed it. I proved to you that I can commit to someone, to something, and still, it wasn't enough. Tell me why you're sorry. Why I should forgive you."

Phillip left the bed, his face set.

Alex read his expression, and the heart she believed shattered broke again. "Please, Phillip. Leave me alone. I—I'm begging you." With painful steps, she walked toward the door.

Watching her leave, he could see his future without her in it, and it stopped his breath. "Why?" Phillip repeated the question softly, his heart pounding in his ears. He crossed to where she stood in the center of the room. "Why am I sorry I hurt you? Because I am excited about waking up next to you. Because I want to welcome the morning now because I know that gives me one more day to be with you." He knelt before her, taking her trembling hands in his. "I've been *in like* before, Alex, with a woman who didn't know who I was. Who wanted me to make her life comfortable. I don't want you to feel comfortable with me. I want you to feel what I feel, to be edgy and excited and more alive with me than anywhere else, with anyone else, at any time. I don't just love you. I am desperately, hopelessly in love with you."

He rose then, and met her eye to eye, heart to heart. "I want to be your soulmate, if you'll have me."

"Oh, Phillip. I love you," Alex whispered as she opened her mouth for his kiss.

Breaths sighed, hearts healed.

Hours, moments, seconds later, she asked him, "You love me? After only four weeks?"

With a smile that knew forever was his, he answered, "I don't know what took me so long."